5-7-83-8W

Vera

L
Vera

A

CANDLELIGHT REGENCY SPECIAL

CANDLELIGHT ROMANCES

The
Impossible Ward

Dorothy Mack

A CANDLELIGHT REGENCY SPECIAL

Published by
Dell Publishing Co., Inc.
1 Dag Hammarskjold Plaza
New York, New York 10017

Copyright © 1978 by Dorothy McKittrick

All rights reserved.
No part of this book may be reproduced or transmitted
in any form or by any means,
electronic or mechanical, including photocopying,
recording or by any information storage and retrieval system,
without the written permission of the Publisher,
except where permitted by law.

Dell ® TM 681510, Dell Publishing Co., Inc.

ISBN: 0-440-13994-5

Printed in the United States of America
First printing—November 1978

CHAPTER ONE

The untimely death at the age of forty-eight of Peregrine Carstairs, fifth earl of Melford, from injuries sustained in a freak accident on the hunting fields of Leicestershire, achieved the rather unique distinction of surpassing in notoriety a life spent (or *mis*spent, according to one of his more acid-tongued relatives) in committing the sort of follies that give rise to scandalous conjecture amongst the members of that stratum of Polite Society, to which he belonged by right of birth, if not subsequent behavior. It was not the fact of his putting a violent period to his life that caused raised eyebrows and clacking tongues, for some such end to his daredevil career had confidently been predicted ever since his naval days when he had distinguished himself by acts of reckless bravery during the siege of Toulon. At Calvi, where Nelson lost an eye, the second son of the fourth Melford sustained the loss of two fingers on his left hand with no invalid period before returning to duty. In fact it was not until news reached him during the battle of the Nile in 1798 of the tragedy of the twin deaths of his father and elder brother in a boating accident that the new earl, with extreme reluctance, resigned his commission and returned to his homeland after an absence of over five years.

Some of his intimates ascribed the vicissitudes of his later years to disappointment at having to renounce his naval career for the duties attaching to a position he had never coveted or thought to occupy. Others, less tolerant, dismissed his actions as being those of a man bent on suicide.

Certainly the fifth earl's subsequent unheedful activities had provided fuel for scandal flames for better than fifteen years. Though his name had been coupled on numerous occasions with any number of reigning beauties, both married and single, from the most eligible heiresses to the most outrageous courtesans of Covent Garden fame, not the most enterprising female had succeeded in dragging him to the altar. Therefore his will, read before a small group of relatives and mourners scated in the sunny library at Maplegrove, the late earl's principal seat, by a senior member of the firm of Dillingham, Tillinghurst, Upton and Dillingham, Solicitors, was destined to create something of a sensation.

Mr. Dillingham, Senior, coming at last to the end of a long list of bequests to servitors and family retainers, paused momentarily to clear his throat, glancing briefly at the assembled listeners. The predominant expression adorning the faces of his audience was polite boredom, but his next words changed that.

". . . and all the remainder of my personal property and fortune I bequeath to my daughter, the Lady Marianne Carstairs, to be held in trust until . . ."

It was extremely unlikely that the trust arrangements under which the Lady Marianne Carstairs would henceforth receive her income penetrated the consciousness of any but one of the astounded gentlemen staring openmouthed at the prosaic, bespectacled solicitor before the combined noise of exclamations of shock and disbelief and a subsequent buzz of speculation compelled that cavernous, soberly clad personage to pause yet again in his reading.

"And the sole reason behind *my* dim comprehension," the one exception was explaining to his maternal parent on the following day, "was undoubtedly that well-known human weakness of vanity that enables one to discern one's own name even in the Tower of Babel." A self-mocking little smile played around the corners of his well-shaped mouth.

"*Your* name? What can you mean, Justin? What possible connection can you have with this, this . . . unacknowledged daughter?"

At the sight of the suddenly squared shoulders and indignant expression turning his soft, charming mama into a bristling lioness preparing to defend her young, his smile widened to a satisfied grin. Ahh, that had caught her! Truth to tell, he had been surprised and more than a little disappointed at her unblinking reception of what he had confidently expected to prove earth-shaking news.

"No connection at all, so far," he said soothingly, "but I strongly doubt my luck shall hold in future, since Perry has been so misguided as to appoint *me* his daughter's trustee."

"What!" Her reception of this piece of information atoned for any earlier want of feeling. "He must have been all about in his head," her ladyship declared flatly, "to select an unmarried man of barely thirty years to be guardian to a child—and a female child at that."

"In the interests of accuracy, I must correct you, Mama, on one or two points. My unenviable position is that of a trustee, not a legal guardian, and the female in question is not a child, being, if I recall correctly, some two and twenty years of age."

"Two and twenty!" gasped the marchioness. "But Perry was not even in the country twenty-two years ago. At least—I cannot quite recall, but surely that was about the time his ship was sent to the Mediterranean?" A distressing thought crossed her mind and was given immediate utterance. "Justin, do you suppose this girl is the result of an entanglement with a . . . a *foreigner?* I suppose there *is* proof that a marriage did take place? Or it could all be a hoax. Yes, that would be just like Perry—I vow he would do anything to shock Society," she enunciated in bitter accents, and launched herself into a tirade, recalling some of the earl's more scandalous escapades and roundly condemning his thoughtlessness in involving her son in his affairs.

Knowing it from long experience as an exercise in futility, the young marquess did not endeavor to interrupt his parent in full spate but waited

8

patiently for her to calm down before he attempted to mollify her.

"Now, Mama," he soothed, "it is not so bad as you fear. There definitely was a marriage, all right and tight and aboveboard."

"To a foreigner?" she demanded straightly.

"No, no, I promise you." He hesitated briefly, then continued. "Actually the girl Perry married was the daughter of an Irish scholar." He ignored his mother's derisive sniff. "Her parents objected to the marriage, so he obtained a special license and they made a runaway match of it."

This time the sniff was closer to a ladylike snort.

"They objected to an alliance with one of the oldest families in the land and a title to boot? You may have been taken in by such a tale, but I assure you *I* am not such a . . . such a *flat* as to swallow whole that farradiddle!"

"Mama! Such language from a lady! I am appalled!" But the marquess' eyes twinkled as he smiled indulgently at his now guiltily blushing parent. One of her most endearing traits, in her sons' eyes, was her ability to enter wholeheartedly into their concerns from earliest childhood. They were so in the habit of discussing their affairs with her that over the years she had built up quite a vocabulary of slang and cant terms that occasionally found their way into her conversation at awkward moments, to her intense embarrassment and the everlasting delight of her loving but wickedly appreciative offspring.

His eyes grew serious again. "It is true nevertheless, Mama. Old Dillingham gave me a letter Perry

9

had dictated the day he died. The will had been made long since of course, but he wished to acquaint me with the whole story. To no one, not even Papa—and you know how close they were— had he ever disclosed the existence of a child or the story of his marriage, but he wanted me to know so I would be better prepared to help his daughter. The girl he married was very young, an only child of a late marriage, and her parents doted on her. Perry's father and brother were alive then so there was no question of a title, and he was always very wild, you know. In any case her parents forbade the match and he knew Melford would have cut up stiff if he learned what was in the wind, so he married her out of hand. They had barely a year together. Her parents knew after the elopement of course, but he did not tell the Carstairs. Hostilities broke out again in 1793 and Perry was ordered to the Mediterranean just about the time the child was due. He planned to take his wife and baby and leave them with his family when he had to report, but before he could prepare them, his wife died giving birth to the child, and he went berserk with grief. He had brought her back to her parents to await the birth and, Mama, he said he refused to look at the baby who had cost his wife's life. He left it with the stunned grandparents and went to war without telling a soul. He was gone over five years, as you must remember, and returned only at the death of Melford and Jack."

"Did he not go to see the child then? Why hide all these years? Is there something wrong with her—Justin, she is not an imbecile or something of that nature, I trust?"

"He never once set eyes on her, Mama, but he corresponded with the grandparents at infrequent intervals. The girl is perfectly normal. Since her grandmother's death ten years ago she has resided with her grandfather on a small property Perry purchased for them in Yorkshire. I gather they live quietly in the country near Leeds."

"The poor child." His mother's large blue eyes softened in commiseration. "Never to know either parent, hidden away from her rightful inheritance, with only an old man for company, and a scholar at that! She might well not exist for him if he is like some, shut away forever in a musty library, living in a world of books instead of people. What are you going to do, Justin?"

"Bring her here if you are willing. Perry wished me to see to her future, find her a husband, and establish her in Society, as well as handle her income for a time."

"Well, I must say that is the outside of enough! He does not ask much! You are to take a country-bred girl, still unmarried at two and twenty, which tells one straight away that she is either an antidote or has never stirred from her grandfather's side, and thrust her into a society for which she cannot possibly be prepared, and he expects you to find a husband to establish her. A Herculean task indeed. It might be different if the girl had a fortune, but most of Perry's property must be entailed and therefore goes to his nephew, which is indeed a sorry situation, for a bigger wastrel than

11

Aubrey Carstairs I have yet to meet. Perry can't have had much of a personal fortune, not with his being a confirmed gamester. Why if but *half* the tales of him are true he was wont to lose as much as five thousand pounds in a single night in those hells he was forever frequenting."

"Now *there* you are quite out, Mama."

"You mean the rumors were not true; Perry did not lose large sums night after night in St. James's Street?"

"Oh, the tittle-tattle was true enough, but your assumption that Perry had little in the way of a personal fortune is glaringly false. The truth is he made fantastically successful investments here and in the colonies and will probably cut up to the tune of around a quarter of a million, all safely invested in the Funds." He flicked open a gold filigree snuffbox with a graceful gesture of his left hand, took a small pinch, and inhaled it easily without taking his appreciative eyes from his mama's very expressive countenance.

"Close your mouth, love. You resemble a very startled goldfish at the moment—a delectable goldfish if I may say so, but of rather dim mentality." His teasing laugh robbed the words of any wounding intent and, in any case, the marchioness secretly rather delighted in the affectionate raillery directed at her by her sons, both of whom had tried very hard to make up to her for the loss of her firstborn three years before at Salamanca, scarcely surviving his father by a year.

Indeed, looking at her it was difficult to imagine a more pampered little creature, for she was delightfully tiny and delicately made without appearing fragile. As Lady Georgina St. Clair, she had been hailed as the most beautiful debutante of her season when the young marquess of Lunswick had crossed her horizon and straightaway set out to storm the citadel, to such success that they were married within two months of her initial appearance on the London scene. The gold in her hair had faded somewhat, and there were fine lines about her mouth that had not been there before the sudden death of her husband and the subsequent loss of his heir on the field of battle, but she was still a remarkably lovely woman, and when animated, could have denied with no fear of contradiction, ten of her forty-nine years, if such a thought had ever crossed her mind. Her intensely blue eyes had gradually lost that haunted look that had so concerned her remaining sons, but the elder was thinking now that the animation and vivacity that had been her most appealing characteristic had been in complete abeyance for the last few years.

He frowned unseeingly at the small box still in his hand as it flashed across his consciousness that this unknown ward, or more correctly, obligation of his, might just prove a blessing in disguise—if only his mother could be brought to take a real interest in her fate. She had always wished for a daughter. Perhaps she might even be induced to leave Lunswick Hall next year and begin to resume some of her former activities in Town during the season, in order to oversee his ward's initial appearance. In the past, his generous-hearted mama had always been more than happy to devote time to her various nieces during their seasons; in fact, until mourning had driven her into this uncharacteristic apathy, she had been the most gregarious creature alive. If this girl had any possibilities at all she might provide just the challenge needed to jolt his parent out of her present inertia. His frown deepened as he quelled the nagging thought that Perry's daughter might prove to be utterly impossible.

As if reading his thoughts, the marchioness echoed this one hesitantly:

"You know, Justin, she may turn out to be hopelessly ineligible despite the fortune."

"Nonsense, love," he chided bracingly. "No heiress is completely ineligible, be she ever so illfavored or underbred. I have the utmost confidence in your ability to make a silk purse out of this particular sow's ear, if so she should turn out to be. In any event I fancy I can guarantee the lady one eligible suitor at the very least."

His mother raised an inquiring eyebrow.

"Melford," he replied shortly. "He was green when it turned out that all Perry's private fortune went to this unexpected daughter, though how in the circumstances he could have anticipated benefiting by one groat more than was necessary under the entail I cannot imagine. Everyone knew Perry held him in the greatest contempt and could be expected to divert any assets he could from falling into his nephew's hands."

"Well, the estate is in fair shape, is it not?

Aubrey will not now be driven to seek an advantageous match."

This time her son's answer was slower in coming. "I have no certain information of course, but Perry seemed convinced that Aubrey's been living on the expectation for years. Seemed to think he's gotten himself deep into the clutches of the moneylenders, in which case he'll need everything he can wring from the estate to settle with them. If past performance is anything to go on, he'll be under the hatches in less than a twelve month. He had no idea how wealthy Perry's daughter is, of course, but I'd not wager a groat on our chances of keeping this news from becoming one of the choicer *on-dits* of the year."

The marchioness rose from her chair, shook out her pale lavender skirt and moved over to the fireplace where her son stared thoughtfully into space. She placed both hands around his arm and nuzzled her head gently against his chest for a moment before smiling up at him.

"Well, we shall just have to preserve her from Aubrey's designs. I wish he were not quite so handsome with that facile charm that is so deadly to inexperienced girls, but perhaps she will not prove to be at all impressionable. What did you say her name was, Justin?"

"Marianne."

"Pretty," approved his mother. "I hope the girl is attractive too." She gave a delightful gurgle of laughter. "Do you know, Justin, I am quite looking forward to meeting your ward."

"She is not my ward, Mama," he reminded her patiently. "I am merely her trustee."

"And marriage broker," she added impishly. "Shall you go north to bring her here yourself?"

"Yes, I feel Perry would expect me to meet the grandfather and assure him the girl will be well cared for."

"I shall write to her, and you will deliver my invitation personally."

"Thank you for your cooperation, Mama."

This time there was no element of teasing in the gentle smile the tall man bestowed on her, along with a brief bear hug that rocked her off her feet and brought forth an indignant protest that he had sadly disarranged her cap, not to mention her dignity.

"What dignity?" inquired her unrepentent son with a grin.

CHAPTER TWO

The sun was just beginning to dip beneath the rim of the distant foothills as the marquess drew rein before a wooden gate a sennight later. He sat almost motionless except for an absentminded gentling action on the neck of a huge bay horse while he narrowly surveyed the property called Crestview Farm that had been home to Perry's daughter for the past ten years. The lovely stone house set back no more than one hundred feet or so from the lane never started existence as a farm-house, he decided. Its charming proportions and ornamented windows proclaimed it a rather taste-ful small villa, and he thought it likely that it had replaced an earlier structure perhaps no more than fifteen or twenty years before. The pristine con-dition of the surrounding outbuildings gave mute testimony to the prosperity of the farm. The roof-ing looked new, the paths were cleared and swept, and there was no lack of fresh paint anywhere. Small, well-kept lawns in front and to the right as far as the bend in the tree-bordered lane made of it a most attractive setting for the jewel of a house. This and the scent of late blooming roses in a riot of colors, in front of a row of hedges, contributed to a mounting sense of relief mingling with the more visual pleasure in his surroundings as he opened the gate and leisurely approached the house.

The hitherto unacknowledged but pervasive miasma of discomfort that settled on him whenever he considered the deeper implications of his er-rand lifted a bit as his senses absorbed the green peacefulness of the scene, completely devoid at the moment of another human presence than his own. Useless to deny that he had rather dreaded ap-proaching this young woman whose acquaintance her own father had never once desired to make. With no company and plenty of time for reflection on the long journey, his wayward fancy had per-sisted in picturing her as existing at a subsistence level, filled with resentment at the retired life she was compelled to lead through no fault of her own;

17

but surely no brooding melancholy could perpetuate itself in this idyllic setting. Perhaps his mission could be reduced to its simplest terms after all: that of removing the girl to his mother's protection during her period of mourning and her inevitable introduction to Society, followed quickly by a provident marriage to someone who might be more than willing to divide his time between Yorkshire and Town, or even to retire to this locality permanently. Surely any young woman, no matter how contented with her existence, would experience a sense of excitement and thrill at having her provincial horizons expanded. The girl did not exist who could turn her back on such an opportunity.

Inexpressibly cheered by all he saw about him, he hitched the bay to the wrought iron rail and proceeded to bang the shining knocker. He had written to Perry's father-in-law immediately after the funeral, apprising him of his son-in-law's death and his own planned visit to discuss Lady Marianne's immediate future. The household should certainly be anticipating his arrival, but not knowing their circumstances, he had left his chaise and postilions at the Rose and Crown at the village crossroads, and ridden the short distance to Crestview Farm on Mountain, his favorite mount.

The marquess was idly admiring the remains of what must have been a lovely flowering border in summer when he finally heard a heavy, slow tread approaching. He straightened and smiled at the old woman who opened the door and stood regarding him with an unflattering lack of interest.

"Good afternoon, I am Lord Lunswick. I believe Mr. O'Doyle is expecting me."

The woman's flat-featured countenance did not lose one iota of its impassivity at this pronouncement.

"T' master's asleep in his study. Miss Marianne says Ah mun not disturb him when he drops off like that, not for nowt." She declaimed the words as though a formula learned by rote.

"No, of course not," Justin agreed hastily. "In that case may I see Lady Marianne?"

His smile had been declared an unfair weapon by more than one London miss, but his second effort had no more effect on the implacable servant than the first attempt.

"Miss be down at t'barn," she declared, shutting the door firmly on the words.

For an instant the marquess simply stood there staring at the paneled door, natural irritation struggling with a mounting sense of unreality. His first stubborn impulse was to persist in his efforts to gain admittance, but his hand was stayed in mid-air from rapping more forcefully on the door by an equally strong disinclination to tangle again with an undoubtedly half-witted old crone.

Shrugging aside his annoyance, he retreated around the right side of the house toward the cluster of farm buildings. There were no signs of human activity at the large hen house or in the dairy, but as he approached the barn he noticed a shadow from a lamp within playing over the door frame. Entering the dim interior he stood quietly for a moment adjusting his eyes after the glare of

19

late afternoon sunshine. He was immediately aware of the contented movements of several animals, but as he moved further inside he saw no one save a black-clad female farm worker bent over a milking stool, too intent on her task to realize his presence. He passed her and headed slowly down the length of the barn, glancing quickly left and right as he passed two workhorses and more cows. The only lantern was placed to aid the milker near the entrance, which convinced him that Lady Marianne could not be here. He turned to retrace his steps with the intention of interrogating the farm woman and met the incredulous stare of the latter, who had risen carrying a pail in each hand and was standing there quite motionless with a look almost of wonder on her face. His disinterested gaze flicked across her person, dismissing her as an object of interest as he continued to approach at an unhurried pace.

All expression died out of the girl's face as he diminished the distance between them. She remained silent, and he who had rarely felt ill at ease in the presence of a female, found himself resenting her silence and constrained to break it.

"Can you tell me where I may find Lady Marianne?"

Realizing he had spoken rather abruptly, he smiled at her to soften the force of the words but noted with a mental shrug that this young woman was as immune to any charm of manner he might possess as the old crone who had shut the door in his face earlier. He wondered idly if this might perhaps be her granddaughter. He could not know that to the silent girl standing in the flickering light of the lantern he had seemed for an instant to be the living embodiment of all the Norse legends, the hero of countless fairy tales. For perhaps two seconds while he had turned and come toward her she had felt irradiated with sheer joy as her eyes dwelt with pleasure on the handsomest man she had ever beheld. Then as his cool glance had flicked dismissingly over her with contemptuous indifference, she experienced a rare surge of intense dislike that swamped her initial reaction and left her slightly shaken. His curt words did nothing to lessen her dislike, but she answered politely enough.

"I am afraid there is some mistake. My name is Marianne Carstairs, but I know of no Lady Marianne in this vicinity."

Initially the deeper implications of this speech failed to penetrate the dismay induced by the girl's calm recital of her name. He closed his eyes for an agonized second. This dark gypsy of a female with skin burned brown by sun and weather, carrying two milk pails and wearing a none too clean apron over a shapeless black gown could not be Perry's daughter! It would be utterly impossible to try to foist such a creature into the *Ton*. *She* was utterly impossible. For a moment he was speechless, as he ruefully recalled his laughing assurance to his mother that no heiress was entirely ineligible. How little he had known!

The girl had stiffened at the expression of restrained disgust on his features, and dislike turned to active hatred, completely eradicating even the memory of that first fleeting approval. Swiftly she set down the milk while she extinguished the lantern. Before she could repossess herself of the pails, however, the stranger had picked them up and was standing politely aside for her to precede him from the barn. For an instant she seemed about to protest, then she shrugged and complied silently.

The girl glanced warily at him from under her lashes as she passed outside, but he was preoccupied with some thoughts of his own which obviously gave him no pleasure, judging from his frown. After a few steps, however, he stopped and faced her determinedly.

"As I explained to your grandfather I was a friend of your father's, and it was his dying wish that I come here to see you."

He could not have said quite how he expected her to react to this news, not with tears, surely, since she had had time to get used to the fact of her father's death, and since she had never even met him, could not be expected to grieve greatly. However he had *not* thought to see an expression of shocked amusement cross her face and he raised questioning brows.

"I am persuaded your devotion to your friends is most selfless and highly to be commended, but do you generally take so long to carry out deathbed wishes?"

He stared at her blankly. "The earl's funeral services were held just a sennight ago. I set out almost on the heels of my letter."

It was the girl's turn to look blank, but she recovered almost immediately. "Now I am certain

22

there has been some error," she declared lightly. "My father was not an earl, he was a sailor, and he died over twenty years ago in the Mediterranean from wounds suffered during a sea battle with the French."

The marquess carefully set down the brimming pails of foamy milk. His startled eyes never left the girl's composed face as she paused of necessity and awaited his response with somewhat obvious patience. It was some time in coming for his brain was rioting with conjecture. An initial faint hope that he might indeed be mistaken in her identity was dismissed at birth. She had given her name as Marianne Carstairs. He had been directed in the village to the farm of one Sean O'Doyle whom Perry had identified as his father-in-law. Unless the girl were lying, and there was no earthly reason for such an action, she was in total ignorance of her father's circumstances. He moved impatiently and the movement nearly upset one of the milk pails at his feet.

"Take care," the girl warned, reaching again for the milk and moving it out of accident range.

Suddenly the bizarre humor of the situation struck him forcefully. How Perry would have appreciated the irony inherent in the simple fact that the daughter he stubbornly refused to meet had never known of his existence. His guilt at his desertion of his paternal responsibility had no foundation in reality, though in combination with his grief it had colored his life to a disastrous degree. Just as suddenly, all inclination to laugh at the grim joke deserted him and he was over-

23

whelmed with mingled regret and pity for the man he had long liked but never understood. How completely alone he had always been! What a criminal waste of a life!

She had been covertly watching the play of emotions animating his handsome face but had made no attempt to interrogate him, and now moved decisively toward the back of the house, once again carrying the milk pails with an easy fluid grace.

"Wait!" he commanded urgently.

When she did not pause, he caught up with her in several long strides and seized her, none too gently, by the shoulders. Some of the milk sloshed over the tops of the pails, splattering them both liberally. The amusement visible in the girl's hitherto impassive face at his obvious annoyance increased that quality tenfold. Much later he admitted to himself with considerable regret that it was largely due to this petty sense of pique at her uncompromising attitude that he told her the truth so bluntly.

"There has indeed been some error," he drawled hatefully, staring relentlessly down into proud dark eyes, "but it is not of my making. Your father was Peregrine Carstairs, fifth earl of Melford, and although he was indeed wounded in the Mediterranean some twenty years ago, his wounds were negligible. For the last fifteen years he has been residing at his family estate in Somerset, close to my principal seat. He sent me to you."

"And you are . . . ?"

He was forced to reluctant admiration at her self-control as evidenced by the steady voice, especially since he had felt the quick tremor that had run through her at his callous words, and witnessed the draining of all color under her burned skin. When he was quite certain she had conquered the momentary dizziness, he released her shoulders and stepped back.

"I am Justin Raymond, marquess of Lunswick, completely at your service, Lady Marianne," he replied, sweeping off his high crowned beaver and making her an elegant bow.

She suspected mockery and raised her chin in proud defiance. It should have been a totally incongruous gesture, but rough clothes could not disguise the proud carriage of the tall slim girl whose strong brown hands were still grasping the milk pails. For the first time a flash of interest enlivened the man's eyes, but the girl was frowning into space, so failed to note the response that might have served to mitigate some of the humiliation she had suffered at his earlier reaction to her appearance.

"Lady Marianne?" she faltered at last.

"Of course. The title and entailed property go to a cousin of yours, but you are the sole beneficiary of all his personal fortune."

The girl was in total command of her emotions again. If anything her face appeared colder and more remote than before.

"I see," she remarked coolly. "Did my father never remarry then?"

Justin hesitated. The girl waited quietly.

He spoke with obvious reluctance. "No, in truth I must tell you that his marriage to your mother and your subsequent birth never became known."

The dark shadowed eyes widened but she remained silent, staring off into space.

Justin could not call to mind a more uncomfortable conversation nor, shifting his weight irritably, a less comfortable partner in a conversation than this girl. By now he was cursing his own inept and tactless handling of the situation. How ridiculous they must appear discussing life and death over pails of milk, a significant portion of which was spilled on both their persons! He slanted a glance at the silent girl standing within touching distance but as remote from him as though she were on another planet. After the initial shock, she had displayed no emotion whatsoever, and he still had no clue as to her reception of the news. It seemed she had no slightest intention of ending the oppressive silence engulfing them, and with a gesture of resignation, he continued his explanation.

"It was your father's wish that you make your entrance into Society under my aegis. My mother has made me the bearer of an invitation to you to pay us a prolonged visit. Naturally during your period of mourning any social life will be sharply curtailed, but you shall have plenty of informal opportunities to meet your father's friends before any official presentation."

"Never!"

The ejaculation, uttered in throbbing accents of pure rage, quivered in the still air. They had paused under the spreading branches of a large beech tree and the girl's face was partially shadowed, but he was shocked by a suggestion of glittering eye and flaring nostrils.

"My dear Lady Marianne . . ." he began in reasonable accents.

"Don't call me that!" She turned on him, her body rigid, fists clenched at her sides. Only her face was alive with fury. "My father saw fit to ignore my very existence for twenty-two years. Well, now I choose to ignore the fact of his death. How can I mourn a man of whose existence I was totally unaware? I am completely satisfied with my life as it is. I thank you and your mother for your kind invitation but I must decline to leave my grandfather. Good-bye, Lord Lunswick."

She would have left him on the words, the milk entirely forgotten, had not Justin grabbed her arm. He was angry at her rude behavior but, having glimpsed the pain underlying her fury, he controlled his own reaction with difficulty and answered quietly:

"He did not ignore your existence, you know. This charming property was purchased for you by your father. He has always provided for your comfort."

At these words the girl ceased her struggles to remove her arm from his steely grip and stood motionless, her color fading.

"Do you mean to say my grandfather does not own the farm?"

"You own the farm."

Her face had regained its earlier cold impassivity but he thought he detected a shade of relief. He guessed shrewdly that she now felt herself in a

27

stronger position to refuse his request, and knew an instant's malicious impulse to puncture her complacence by telling her just how much control his position of trustee gave him over her actions; but something of her unhappiness touched him and he decided to postpone any further discussion until she had come to grips with the fact of her father's willful desertion.

"I must see your grandfather while I am here. I intended speaking to him before seeking you, but the old woman who opened the door said he was not to be disturbed when he fell asleep in his study."

She did not miss the dryness of his tones. At mention of the servant some slight flicker of something —amusement perhaps—softened her expression fleetingly, but he was well aware of the reluctance with which she invited him to dine with them, despite her civil words. For the first time since their unpropitious meeting he found he was enjoying himself. He brushed aside her apologies for a meager meal, asserting suavely that he well understood the country custom of dining at midday and had consequently partaken very liberally at a good posting house earlier in the day. She lowered her gaze hastily and began walking toward the house, but not before he had glimpsed the disappointment therein.

"She'd enjoy seeing me go hungry," he realized with grim humor, "or seeing me discomfitted in any fashion whatever."

* * *

28

Later, alone in a charming small drawing room, dimly but cozily lit by a crackling fire and two branches of candles, Justin had ample time to reflect on the rather harrowing events of the past hour as he waited for his hosts to join him for supper. In a way, his meeting with the old gentleman had been almost as difficult as the earlier collision with the granddaughter, but at least with the grandfather there had been none of the latent animosity thinly veiled with chill politeness shown him by the girl. Indeed Mr. O'Doyle's gentle countenance had expressed pleasure as he welcomed their guest with real though absentminded cordiality when his granddaughter had tenderly roused him from his peaceful doze in his study. Justin had followed her into the room, blandly ignoring her ill-concealed annoyance. For some reason as yet dimly perceived, he had preferred not to allow them any private conversation before the introduction was performed. Their entrance had not roused Mr. O'Doyle, who had evidently fallen asleep as he sat reading in a wing chair by the fireplace. In the brief time that elapsed while Lady Marianne removed the book from the slackened grasp and gently shook her grandfather's shoulder, Justin realized that Mr. O'Doyle was quite a small man; indeed, his slight form was rendered insignificant by the noble proportions of the crimson-brocaded chair. The initial picture of great age and fragility was shattered beyond recall, however, when he opened a pair of deep blue eyes, instantly alert, and made even more vital as

29

a contrast to an abundance of silky white curls and bushy gray brows. His smile for his granddaughter was a blend of mischief and apology as he arched his neck and stiff shoulders.

"You were correct as usual, my dear. I was tired and would have done better to lie down upon my bed. Now I am paying for falling asleep in such an uncomfortable position." The blue eyes fell on the expectant young man and turned back to the girl with a question in their depths.

"This is the marquess of Lunswick, Grandpère. He was a friend of my father's."

"Oh, dear!" The amiable countenance wrinkled in thunderstruck consternation, and the old gentleman leaped so awkwardly to his feet that it was necessary for him to accept his granddaughter's supporting arm for a few seconds until he had steadied himself. The girl's utter calmness aided him in regaining his own composure, but anxiety lingered as he grasped both her hands and said urgently:

"He wrote to me and I meant to have a talk with you about your father before his arrival, my dearest child, but I put it off and put it off, and now see what has happened. Did he tell you about Perry's death?"

The marquess had been standing silent but intently observant and now ventured, "Yes, I fear I have given Lady Marianne a rude shock, and I must apologize for my ill-timed arrival, but may I offer by way of extenuation the assurance that had I the least idea how matters stood, I should not have approached her before speaking to you, sir."

The old man made a slight mechanical gesture accepting and dismissing this specious apology and, as his granddaughter had before him, echoed hesitantly, "Lady Marianne?"

Justin noted the expression of weary sorrow before it was slowly replaced by interest in himself, as the old man extended his hand in a surprisingly firm clasp and raked his unexpected guest with an estimating, and the younger man was convinced, extremely discerning eye. He said with simple courtesy:

"It is a pleasure to meet you, Lord Lunswick. May I offer sincere apologies for the nature of your welcome? I hope you will pardon an old man's lapse of memory. You will of course remain to share our repast." He glanced at his granddaughter, accepting her slight nod as confirmation, and proceeded to offer his guest some quite tolerable sherry.

If Justin had expected to hold a private conversation with Mr. O'Doyle before dining, he was foiled by Lady Marianne who had remained with them for a few minutes before drawing her grandfather away to change. Now as he stared thoughtfully into the flames in the fireplace his lip curled with amused contempt as he considered her tactics. Obviously she had no intention of allowing him to discuss his plan to remove her to Somerset before she had made her own objections known to her grandfather. Well, much good it would do her in the long run. If the old man should prove obstructive, he held the winning card in his control of her assets. Not that he desired to use coercion on a man

31

with whom he already felt an instinctive rapport. Mr. O'Doyle struck him as being a genuinely likable person. It was otherwise with his granddaughter however. He stirred and kicked a log with unacknowledged irritation. Never had he met a less prepossessing female! It was not that she was particularly ill-favored. Frowning in concentration, he attempted to bring her features before his mind's eye with minimal success. All he could recall was that she was dark skinned, which must be reckoned a serious flaw, and dark haired, what he had seen of it, for she had worn a concealing cap. In fact all her dark drab clothing had better served the purpose of concealing than enhancing any claims to good looks that she might possess. Of course she had been working when he met her. No doubt her appearance would be considerably improved when she joined them for supper. He devoutly hoped her attitude would have undergone a similar change for the better, for he found her calm impassivity singularly disaffecting.

However when Lady Marianne reappeared, Justin's optimistic prophecies were both found to have been based on wishful thinking. Certainly she had made an evening toilette, but any overall improvement in her appearance was too slight to be of any significance. She was still depressingly garbed in black, this time in a heavy, stiff silk gown, shiny from wear, which would have proclaimed its venerable age had not the outmoded style made that distinction redundant. Another cap, of yellowed lace and muslin this time, unbecomingly covered all of her hair except right in the front where the dark hair grew from a point in the center of her forehead. His eyes ran over her measuringly and he sighed silently. Scrawny as a plucked crow! As his assessing glance met hers for an instant, he would have taken his oath that her dark eyes were filled with a sort of triumphant mockery and his own narrowed thoughtfully, but he kept his expression blandly civil and offered his arm to lead her into another small but lovely apartment where a plain though beautifully prepared meal awaited them.

They were served by a very young girl who appeared nervously fascinated by the presence of a noble guest. At one point she dropped a plate of vegetables and was only prevented from going off into tears by Lady Marianne's quelling look and calm words. As she fumblingly cleared away the mess of spilled peas, Justin smiled comfortingly and the girl's comely face brightened. He missed the faint surprise that fleetingly animated his hostess' deliberately aloof features.

Though the game pie he was eating would rank among the best he had ever tasted, the evening as a social event was destined to be memorable only for the air of discomfort that his practiced ease of manner could do nothing to dispel. He maintained a determined flow of polite conversation, intermittently aided by Mr. O'Doyle, who was pleasant but inclined to go off into periodic reveries. The girl contributed as little as bare civility would permit. At first he wondered if she might be suffering from a disabling shyness which could not be wondered at, living retired as she likely did, but after a thoroughly exasperating hour of attempting to set her at her ease and draw her into the conversation, he came to the uncharitable conclusion that she suffered from nothing save an unreasonable dislike of himself and an ill-natured determination to resist all of his conversational overtures.

This conclusion received unneeded support when they removed to the drawing room for coffee and port. Justin broached the subject of his visit, addressing his conversation entirely to Mr. O'Doyle. Now the wretched girl decided to enter the discussion. In a voice in which Justin thought he detected a touch of bravado, she said:

"I have already told Grandpère of your mother's kind invitation and he agrees with me that it will not do. I am needed on the farm and Grandpère is not well enough to be left alone. Perhaps at some other . . ."

"Marianne!"

At the gentle rebuke in Mr. O'Doyle's voice the girl's hands became very still on the coffeepot. A faint hint of color appeared in her cheeks and she kept her eyes down. Justin waited.

"I shall miss you very much, my child, but I feel strongly that you should at least sample the life your father's position entitles you to lead before making any great renunciation. Clara will take good care of me and there is nothing wrong with my health except that I am no longer a young man."

Justin had leaned forward unconsciously and he caught his breath at the full impact of misery in the girl's overbright eyes as she raised them imploringly to her grandfather's face. She said nothing, merely pleading with those huge dark eyes. The old man swallowed with difficulty. His elderly, rather angelic face mirrored his deep love, but his voice was quietly insistent.

"You must go, my child. Give it a fair chance."

She rose to her feet then, clasping her hands tightly in front of her. "Very well, Grandpère. I will do as you wish. If you will excuse me, Lord Lunswick, I . . . I have a slight headache. With your permission, Grandpère, I'll retire."

Despite his basic hostility toward the girl, Justin was moved to compassion by the husky note in her voice and the memory of the naked misery he would not have credited to such an apparently cold-natured girl. Now as she bent to kiss her grandfather good-night, he strolled to the door and opened it for her. She kept her eyes averted as the silk whispered its way across the room, but he prevented her from slipping quickly out by extending his hand and wishing her good night. After an instant's hesitation she placed her hand rather reluctantly in his and said stonily, "Good night, my lord."

When her eyes met his, Justin received his second shock in as many minutes, not so much at the excess of antipathy contained therein, but at the astonishing evidence that the eyes he had assumed brown or even black in the shaded glare of the sunset and across a large dimly lit table, were, in actual fact, a deep intense blue with a hint of purple in their depths. What's more, they were set in a veritable forest of thick black lashes. If it had not been for their antagonistic expression he would have had no hesitation in declaring them supremely beautiful. He stood almost hypnotized, unaware that his grip on her hand had tightened involuntarily until she pulled hers away abruptly and disappeared up the stairs. She did not glance back at the man staring after her with a thoughtful frown causing a line to deepen between his brows.

Only when she was well out of sight did he turn to rejoin his host in the drawing room, and only then did he allow an expression of mild triumph to reign.

CHAPTER THREE

But the cold clear light of dawn brought second thoughts concerning the appropriateness of any triumphal war dances, no matter how privately observed. He must have been suffering a temporary mental aberration if the petty triumph of overriding that unlikable girl's objections could have seemed like a victory. What kind of victory saddled him with an unwilling, uncivil, unappealing houseguest for an indefinite period of time? As he let Mountain amble his sure-footed way down the shaded lane he had noticed the previous day, he was preoccupied with his troublesome thoughts to the exclusion of any real appreciation of the clean cool air and dew-bedecked plants. What had he taken upon his shoulders when he had blithely set forth to carry out Perry's last wish? Completely unlike him in appearance, she possessed her father's cool insolence in full measure. He gave a short bark of laughter at which Mountain perked up his ears. Absently he patted the big stallion. "Yes, old boy, an arresting quality to be sure, but not one to win admirers even in a more eye-catching female."

He frowned, thinking that it was his mother who would bear the greatest burden of this ill-natured girl's company. In the few days prior to his departure for Yorkshire, she had talked herself into a state of pleased anticipation and was eagerly looking forward to outfitting her "borrowed daughter," as she had gaily referred to the unknown Marianne. A sour smile routed the frown temporarily. Well, in that department at least she would have unlimited scope for her talents. He had never seen anyone in greater need of a thorough overhaul than his reluctant ward. So far he had seen his charge in nothing save unrelieved black, even before she had been made aware of her father's death. That dress last night had the appearance of having been fashioned for a much larger woman, the ugly cap was yellow with age, and she had worn no ornament of any kind—not so much as a knot of ribbon. Surely even in the country, fashions filtered down from Town after a time, and there could be no serious lack of funds, judging by the condition of the farm and the contents of the house. His frown deepened as a remembered picture of a girl's mocking face danced before his eyes. In that instant an unassailable conviction smote him that she had deliberately made herself as unattractive as possible—but why? He was examining this unsavory theory when

Mountain came over a small rise, and instinctively he reined in the bay to survey the delightful scene sloping away from him.

The lane ended at a small lake, its sparkling waters reflecting the pure blue of an almost cloudless sky. Sunlight gleamed on the waters and gilded the long grass waving gently right down to meet the water, except in one spot to the right where a shelf of rock-strewn sand formed a narrow beach. On the opposite side the land rose gently again. Hedges outlined fields already harvested. He could see to a line of low hills stretching across to the north and east, and an occasional cottage tucked in among the hills.

A movement some distance to his left brought his attention back to the near shore. The subject of his solitary musings of a moment ago was racing toward the water from a field behind the house. Even hampered by heavy skirts that she alternately kicked and lifted, he had to admire her speed. She was nearly to the water's edge now and had cast off the shawl she had been wearing. Good Lord, what was she about, ripping at the fastenings of her gown with impatient hands? Surely she did not have the intention of swimming at this time of year! Without conscious planning he swung Mountain off the lane and urged him down the sloping ground to a fallow field, then up a rise before descending near the spot where the girl had been ripping at her clothes. By the time he had topped the final rise and once again could see the water, she was already emerging from the lake, staggering a little under the weight of an inert bundle in her arms, greatly impeded by her chemise which clung to her legs, making it difficult to climb up the sloping bank. Within seconds he was off Mountain and had raced to her side, removing the bundle which he could now see was a young child. Her arms freed, she climbed unaided out of the water before he could put the child down to come to her assistance. So far neither had uttered a syllable, the only sound in the world was the coughing and choking of the now partially revived child.

"Thank God! For a moment I feared he was dead."

The girl hastily retrieved her woolen shawl and, kneeling, wrapped it around the little boy Justin had laid in the grass. As she gathered the now retching and sobbing child into her arms and rocked him, murmuring soothing phrases in what Justin dimly recognized as a broad Yorkshire dialect, he removed his riding coat and placed it around her shoulders.

"Here, let me take him now. Put this right on, you'll catch your death. Where does he live?"

She allowed him to take the child, but shrugged off the coat and rose to her feet.

"I must not deprive you of your coat, thank you, my lord. I'll get back into my gown." She picked up her discarded garment, eyeing the long rip with dismay, but attempting nonetheless to put it on.

Justin, impassively surveying the now shaking girl, did not fail to register the interesting fact that she was not, after all, the scrawny crow she had resembled last night. The dripping chemise clung to a very nicely curved figure, the sight of which seemed to increase his irritation unreasonably.

"Put it on, I said," he growled, again thrusting the coat at her, this time with no ceremony at all.

Now Marianne complied thankfully, having succeeded only in further tearing her gown by her agitated, barely controlled movements.

"Ooooh, that is heavenly warm, thank you." She approached the child again with outstretched arms, but Justin stepped back.

"I'll return the boy to his home. You must get into dry clothes immediately. Just tell me where to take him."

"He lives in the cottage just beyond that rise. You can see part of the roof and chimney from here," she said, gesturing with an outflung arm, "but I shall come with you or Margery will be terribly alarmed."

"Margery?"

"His mother. Jamie's parents are tenant farmers. They are a great help to me."

"Well, she had best take care of her son and forget the farm. She nearly lost him this morning." They were now striding quickly in the direction of the thatched roof that was becoming visible.

"Margery is a wonderful mother!" cried Marianne, stung by his criticism, "but Jamie's baby sister has been ailing recently and Margery has had to be with her constantly. Jamie is an extremely adventurous four-year-old, but he knows the lake is a forbidden playground, don't you, Jamie?"

The bedraggled little boy seemed completely cowed by his recent experience, and was unhappily aware of his helplessness in the strong arms of the grim-faced giant carrying him. At Marianne's stern tone he hung his head and refused to look at either noncomforting adult.

Marianne was finding it extremely fatiguing trying to keep up with the marquess' long strides, her wet chemise hampering each step, but fortunately they had not covered half the distance before an agitated young woman appeared on the path, breaking into a run as she spotted the ill-assorted trio approaching the cottage. The anxiety in her voice was apparent.

"What's amiss, Miss Marianne? T'lad's not bad hurt, is he? Oh, th'art wet, not t'lake again?"

"He's quite unharmed, Margery," Marianne replied soothingly, "but where he fell in this time was deeper and I fear it was a close run thing. It was fortunate that I was walking over the rise and saw him go in."

The marquess observed that the comely young woman's color faded at this intelligence, but she thanked Lady Marianne with parental fervor and turned with outstretched arms to relieve him of the now whimpering child.

"I'll take him wi' me now, sir. Miss Marianne mun get out o' those wet things. I'm reet grateful to you both." She sighed and glanced at the child in her arms with fond despair. "Happen this time he'll learn a lesson, think on?" The patent doubt behind the hopeful words caused the marquess' finely cut mouth to twitch slightly.

Marianne patted the child's damp tow-colored head. "I am persuaded he has. Be a good boy,

41

Jamie." She had half turned away, then remembering, added, "Margery, will you ask Jonathan to come and see me before he goes home tonight?"

"Of course, Miss Marianne. 'Tis true, then, th'art going away?" Her fine gray eyes flashed accusingly in the direction of the marquess for an instant, and he reflected that gossip traveled no slower in the country than in a crowded town.

"Yes, Margery, I am sorry. I shall miss you and Jonathan and Jamie and little Marianne, of course," she added with a slightly wavering attempt at a smile.

"But, th'art coming back?" the country woman persisted.

"Oh yes, it will be just a short visit with friends of my father's, but I fear I shall miss little Marianne's first steps." She had flicked a challenging glance at the marquess with this declaration of intent, but by the blandness of his polite expression, he might not have heard or seen the challenge. "This is Lord Lunswick, Margery," she added hastily. "He will escort me to his mother's home."

The Yorkshire woman gracefully managed an unsmiling curtsy despite the burden in her arms.

"We shall take very good care of Lady Marianne," he promised with his charming smile focused full strength on Margery.

The slight belligerence faded from her pleasant face and she nodded, smiling shyly.

Justin noted the slightly sardonic expression on his ward's face, surmising with inward amusement that she'd give no quarter in any contest, but he only said abruptly: "You are shivering, we must get back to the house."

He took a civil but hasty leave of the farmer's wife, barely allowing Marianne time to promise a farewell visit to her namesake on the morrow before hurrying her away with a hand under her elbow. The shivering had increased, for the air was crisp despite the sunshine. Frowning slightly, he put two fingers to his mouth and emitted a shrill whistle. Mountain, who had been leisurely cropping grass at the top of the rise, raised his handsome head and whinnied, then trotted down to the waiting pair.

Marianne was too astonished at this performance to object when the marquess mounted quickly and held down a hand to her. She was a tall girl, but slimly made, and was effortlessly lifted up before him on the saddle.

"I'll get you all wet," she protested feebly, not at all sure she liked the feel of his arm around her waist, but unable to ignore it as she would have preferred.

He deigned no reply to this bit of foolishness except a slight tightening of that constraining arm. The short ride to the house was accomplished in total silence. Marianne, rigidly denying a traitorous urge to relax back against the marquess, sat uncomfortably erect, resentment at his lack of embarrassment in a situation she found totally untenable imbuing her with the necessary persistence to maintain a precarious balance. She left him with a murmured word of thanks and hastened to her room to change.

A very few minutes later she entered the family parlor carrying the borrowed coat. Seeing a crackling fire burning in the grate in the empty room, she hesitated briefly, then assuming the marquess to be with her grandfather, decided to take advantage of the respite to dry her hair which had gotten slightly wet. She removed the cap and pins and knelt before the fire, loosening the heavy hair with her fingers in lieu of a brush.

Thus it was that the marquess discovered her ten minutes later as he quietly entered the room. He stopped at sight of the kneeling figure and his eyes widened on beholding the heavy curtain of hair falling well below her waist. "Like black velvet," he thought involuntarily, "with red lights from the fire." It was unlikely she heard his softly indrawn breath, but she paused suddenly in the middle of a graceful gesture with both hands gathering together the loose tresses, and glanced over her shoulder. As their eyes met he thought she stiffened for an instant, but her face wore its customary expressionless mask when looking at him and her voice was as cool and unruffled as ever.

"Come in, my lord. I beg pardon for my *déshabillé*. I thought you were with my grandfather and seized the opportunity to dry my hair." She had risen to her feet in one swift movement during this speech and was deftly twisting and pinning up her hair.

"Not at all, my dear Lady Marianne. Our acquaintance is progressing by leaps and bounds. What matters a little hair·drying between . . . friends?"

The oblique reference to the enforced proximity of the ride home and the slight pause before the last word grated on Marianne's nerves, but she made no comment except to indicate his coat lying on a table beside an upholstered settee. As he shrugged into the perfectly fitting coat of brown superfine, she had to admit such a beautifully cut garment was unlikely to have come from the hands of a provincial tailor.

"Come, sit down. I wish to speak to you."

If the sudden abandonment of his suave civility surprised her, she gave no sign of it as she obediently settled herself in a capacious chair with intricately carved arms and legs, and waited quietly while he prowled briefly around the room before selecting a chair opposite her.

"Who manages the farm for your grandfather? Margery's husband?"

"No, I do."

There was no elaboration even though the silence was deafening and his eyes frankly disbelieving. Marianne, preoccupied with her own thoughts, turned startled eyes to his when she found her hands seized and examined minutely. Her attempts to tug them away were unsuccessful, but after a thorough study he calmly released them.

"Small but capable hands, I agree, with nicely shaped fingers and nails, but much too brown and much less soft than those of a lady of quality."

The hands in question curled defensively in her lap.

"I am not a lady of quality!" she flashed, for

45

once allowing the irritation he provoked to appear in her face. "I am a farmer."

"You *are* a lady of quality and your farming days are over."

"Temporarily," she put in acidly.

He ignored this thrust. "When you see Margery's husband tonight, tell him to hire whatever help he may need to keep the farm operating at its present high level of efficiency."

She ignored both the implied compliment and the mocking little bow that accompanied it, and merely raised her chin a trifle, looking at him steadily with unfriendly eyes.

"Is there someone who can wait on you during the trip to Somerset?"

Her eyes widened at the abrupt change of subject but her comprehension was swift.

"No, and in any case I do not require a lady's maid to assist me into my clothes." Her chin tilted still more as one lifted eyebrow conveyed his opinion of her clothes. They had certainly taken the gloves off in this discussion, she thought suddenly with wry humor. However his next words curtained any inclination toward amusement.

"That of course is for you to decide, but you certainly must have some respectable woman to accompany you."

"Why?"

"You will of course correct me if I am wrong, but surely, my dear Lady Marianne," he drawled hatefully, "even in the West Riding a lady does not travel unaccompanied with a man who is not her husband or a close relative?"

Only the bitter knowledge that she had invited this set-down enabled Marianne to keep her countenance and preserve that expressionless mien she had instinctively realized was displeasing to him, though whether to his masculine vanity or sense of power she did not yet know. She could not prevent a slight betraying rise of color, however, and as the silence lengthened, felt constrained to break it.

"Clara cannot leave Grandpère and I do not know any other women."

"Perhaps Margery might welcome the extra money. I would pay her well."

"Unthinkable. She would never leave the children, especially with the baby ailing."

"Well then, ask one of your women friends to recommend a temporary abigail."

"I have no women friends except Margery."

His eyes narrowed and a small line appeared between his brows. "Do you mean me to comprehend that you are not upon ordinary visiting terms with the local matrons or farmer's wives?"

"Well, you see, we did not come here until after Grandmère died when I was twelve years old. There *was* no woman in the house to call upon. Grandpère, as you may have guessed, is not a particularly social being, although the dearest man alive, and consequently I do not have any female friends." There was a tender expression on her usually impassive face when speaking of her grandfather and certainly no regret or complaint in her voice, but the marquess' brisk tones softened somewhat as he murmured:

"A lonely life for a young girl."

"Oh no, pray, do not think it. I had Grandpère and the rector, who is Grandpère's greatest friend and mine also, and Jack of course. And in the last few years Margery and Jonathan and the children too. I have never been lonely except just at first after Grandmère's death."

"Who is Jack?"

"Jack is Squire Richmond's son. Grandpère tutored him until he went to Cambridge—in fact we shared lessons for years and I was forever visiting the Manor while Mrs. Richmond was alive."

"Do you have some idea of marrying this Jack?"

This time one of her delicate black brows arched, clearly conveying her opinion of such an impertinent question, and she vouchsafed no reply but continued to look at him steadily. For some reason he preferred to delay the confirmation of a strong suspicion that she was so entirely lacking in the decorum and training expected of a young female as actually to engage in a staring contest with a gentleman. He explained a trifle hastily:

"My position as your trustee gives me certain . . . er . . . rights in your life. The marriage settlement for instance will be arranged by me and it . . ."

"Well, I do not intend to marry so that need not trouble you," she interrupted coolly. "When do you wish to leave?"

"As soon as we may engage an abigail for you. Perhaps the rector will know of somone."

But in the end it was Jack Richmond to whom

48

they were indebted for the solution to this irksome problem. He came that afternoon to Crestview Farm to verify the wild rumors circulating widely in the district that a London lord had come amongst honest country folk to remove old Sean O'Doyle's granddaughter, who had turned out to be a titled lady. Upon receiving confirmation on all the essentials from Marianne herself, his honest face became troubled and vaguely unhappy. He and his tutor's granddaughter had been the best of friends for almost ten years, and during his time at Cambridge it had been her companionship that he had come to miss most. Only three and twenty himself, he had as yet given little thought to marriage and had been content to go along in the familiar pattern of many years' standing, but now he felt as though an enemy had deliberately set about to destroy the design of his future.

"Do you *wish* to go amongst the nobility, Marianne?" he asked bluntly, studying her anxiously with candid blue eyes.

"Not in the least, but Grandpère is determined that I should seize this opportunity to live the sort of life he says my birth entitles me to lead. I cannot convince him that I am completely content with the life I lead now." She sighed deeply. "He has made my consent a test of filial obligation. Never before has he demanded anything of me, so I must obey him in this; but, Jack, I do so hate to leave him. You will not neglect to call often, will you, and if he seems at all unhappy you must promise to write to me immediately."

"Of course I will, and the rector too will bear him company often. He is bound to miss you of course, but if he is so determined to have you go then you must bow to his wish. How long do you mean to stay in Somerset?"

"As brief a time as possible," she answered with tightened lips.

"And when do you go?"

"Ah, there's the rub. The marquess insists that I must have a woman to accompany me on the journey." She ignored his surprised, "Well, naturally," and continued. "But I do not know of anyone who might be available. He intends to ask the rector's advice."

"I can help you there, I believe," Jack answered unexpectedly. "The Abbingdons' former governess is traveling to Bath to take up a new position. Bella Abbingdon said she was to leave on tomorrow's stage. She was ecstatic over the prospect of getting rid of her at long last, says she's excessively henwitted and a long-winded bore into the bargain."

"Thank you so much," Marianne said dryly. "Not that it matters how uncongenial we find each other for a three-day journey. The marquess is already chafing at the thought of a prolonged stay in the wilds of Yorkshire."

"How unpardonably rude of me to have displayed such rank ingratitude for Yorkshire hospitality, if I did so," interjected a suave voice from the open doorway. As he strolled languidly into the room, he observed the familiar frozen lifeless-

50

ness slide down over the girl's features, but she betrayed neither embarrassment nor apology as she made the two men known to each other. She watched with a supercritical eye but could detect nothing of patronage in the marquess' manner toward the younger man. Once again those perfect manners were very much in evidence.

While the gentlemen indulged in a few moments' desultory conversation, Marianne noted with irrational satisfaction that, although Jack could not compete with the sartorial splendor of a London buck, his neat appearance and well set up figure were not cast into the shade by the elegant marquess. The appearance of both men gave pleasing evidence of robust health and natural athletic ability. Jack was not quite so tall as the marquess but his shoulders were every bit as broad and his carriage was graceful and erect. She told herself that although his features did not possess the classic perfection of those of the marquess, she much preferred his open expressive mien to that satirically smiling yet unrevealing mask habitually adorning the latter's handsome countenance. She grudgingly admitted that gold-streaked, dark blond hair and light brown eyes, vividly contrasting with tanned skin, rendered the marquess' coloring more spectacular than Jack's ruddy-faced, brown-haired and blue-eyed combination, but was confident that in every human quality and personality trait Jack would have the edge. Content with the results of her silent comparison, she interrupted their discussion of the fishing in the area to inform the marquess of the possibility of securing the services of the Abbingdons' former governess as a traveling companion.

The marquess expressed suitable appreciation for this information and accepted Jack's offer of an immediate introduction to Miss Twistleton.

After this, events moved with astonishing rapidity as the marquess demonstrated an organizational ability that would have been heartily welcome in the military or civil service. Somewhat bemused by the entire situation, Marianne allowed herself to be maneuvered into the niche prepared for her by her efficient trustee, scarcely demurring even when he ordered her to pack a wardrobe sufficient only for the trip, remarking carelessly that his mother would see to her outfitting immediately on her arrival in Somerset. Truth to tell, she barely absorbed any information concerning her proposed visit, being almost totally involved with the imminent pain of parting from her grandfather for the first time in her twenty-two years. She accomplished her minimal packing mechanically while she devoted her mental energies to enumerating a long list of instructions and reminders to Clara concerning the diet, comfort, and well-being of her grandfather during her absence. For the remainder of the day and evening she went about her alloted tasks as absently as a sleepwalker, only surfacing briefly when Jonathan arrived to discuss the running of the farm. Even in this sphere the marquess' suggestion prevailed and Jonathan assured her he would have no trouble hiring sufficient labor as it became necessary.

Thus it was not surprising that, as the moment for final good-byes arrived, scarcely thirty-six hours after his arrival in the district, Justin should be feeling well satisfied and in command of the situation.

Alas that these agreeable sentiments should prove no more than fond illusions, destined for extinction before even the second stop for a change of horses.

CHAPTER FOUR

Marianne's air of bemused compliance did not survive the short drive to the post road. The initial period was spent in a silent struggle to suppress the unhappy tears she was determined not to shed in the presence of the hateful marquess. Consequently she fixed a somewhat fierce scowl upon her face and stared rigidly out of the window, responding in monosyllables to Miss Twistleton's diffident conversational overtures. After a time the latter, thus rebuffed, turned to the marquess with determinedly agreeable though slightly desperate efforts to put a good face on an awkward situation.

"I daresay the poor child is feeling wretchedly unhappy leaving home for the first time. Such a pity. But one comprehends perfectly, of course. I well remember leaving to take up my first post, not that the situations were truly comparable, of course. I had no close relative living, merely an aunt who was not really an aunt at all but only a sort of cousin—but I called her aunt, you see, since I was living under her protection until I was old enough to take up a position. Naturally there was not the same degree of *attachment* as in the case of this dear child and her grandfather, but one experiences such a sense of *strangeness* at partings and even a touch of fear for the future." She emitted a deprecating little laugh and flashed an apologetic glance at the marquess, whose countenance was taking on a rigid set and hurried on.

"Not that I meant to imply that Lady Marianne need fear the future. I am persuaded your dear mama will make her most welcome, but one cannot deny that the strangeness of a new experience can give rise to doubts and put one out of countenance for a time until one can adjust to the idea. But what am I about," she cried with another little laugh, "letting my tongue run on like a fiddlestick, just as if my dearest friend, Miss Denton, had not told me times without number that many gentlemen simply cannot abide female chatter." Her hopeful glance at the marquess was met with a laconic, "Just so."

She nodded sagely, "Yes, I well remember Mr. Atwell, the husband of my first employer and a truly estimable man in most respects, but whenever the ladies were gathered together he would pick up a book and simply *hide* behind it, pretending to hear nothing of the conversation. It was often necessary to address a remark to him *several* times before he would be so obliging as to respond." She tittered again. "How upset Mrs. Atwell would become, but I always told her one cannot change a

54

gentleman's nature; one simply has to put up with their odd humors and habits as, of course, they are obliged to endure ours." She was reminded then of an odd quirk in her second employer's behavior and was immediately launched into an anecdote relating to this.

Marianne, whose struggle to keep back the demeaning tears had left her filled with black resentment toward the author of her troubles, gradually became aware of the strong current of suppressed irritation emanating from the marquess, and as the endless flow of inconsequential chatter from their traveling companion began to penetrate her self-absorption, of the reason for his somewhat glazed expression. Once he glanced her way with something suspiciously akin to appeal in the light brown eyes. Hastily she averted her face to hide her amusement, and passingly considered a pretense of sleep which should effectively abandon him to this very fitting punishment for his attitude when she had questioned the necessity of a chaperon. For a short time she did actually impose the stillness of complete relaxation on her features, but presently she decided she must intervene to prevent the marquess from giving the garrulous Miss Twistleton a stinging set-down. She was basically a kind-hearted girl and though no more content with this enforced companionship than the marquess seemed to be, she strongly suspected Miss Twistleton's mindless meanderings stemmed from a nervous awe at finding herself in his intimidating presence, and from a real dread of a prolonged silence. Clearly it behooved her to alter the pattern and quickly. It may have gone against the grain to rescue the detestable marquess, but she shuddered to contemplate the scene should an ill-considered masculine action cause Miss Twistleton's sense of inferiority to erupt in a *crise de nerfs*. The taut little woman obviously prided herself on her sensibility, and her suffering would be in proportion to the fancied delicacy of her nerves.

Consequently Marianne entered the conversation with well-feigned affability, and with the marquess' skillful connivance succeeded fairly well in keeping to impersonal topics until they reached the posting house where he planned to stop for a change of horses and some refreshments for the ladies. They found the ordinary bill of fare quite tolerable and sincerely welcomed the opportunity to stretch their legs, especially Marianne, who was not only completely unused to the rigors of traveling but also to physical confinement of any sort. She had told no more than the simple truth when informing the marquess that she ran her grandfather's farm, to which her calloused hands and sunburned skin gave mute testimony. The sight of the marquess taking advantage of a lull in the rain to have Mountain saddled gave fresh impetus to her seething resentment as she stared fixedly at the chaise with distaste before entering it. In all fairness she could not but sympathize with the marquess' desire to ride, but an uncharitable emotion she had no difficulty in recognizing as envy caused her to take a jaundiced view of his action. Not that she had so far experienced the slightest desire for his company, but now she would bear the full brunt of their companion's excessive civility for the seemingly eternal afternoon. Never had an indifferent countryside been more thoroughly discussed. Except for Jack Richmond the two women had no acquaintance in common, and here all Miss Twistleton's sly questions and hints of a closer bond than friendship between Jack and Marianne were met with a blank stare from the latter which, had Miss Twistleton been better acquainted with Marianne's upbringing and lifestyle, she would have known reflected genuine surprise. As it was she felt rebuffed and became stiffly correct and formal in her manner, but since this was not accompanied by a corresponding lessening in the volume of her chatter, Marianne could not be said to have benefitted by the change. Indeed by the time they reached the posting house where they would put up for the night, Marianne was so surfeited with a steady diet of "your ladyship" this and "your ladyship" that that she must needs clamp her teeth tightly together to prevent a scream of sheer frustration at this hateful form of address. When at long last the marquess assisted her to descend the steps of the chaise in the inn yard, she fixed him with such a fulminating eye that he looked momentarily taken aback. By the time the trio had entered the large reception hall, however, he had grasped the situation and was wearing a faintly amused expression that did nothing to mitigate Marianne's sense of ill usage.

Later, in the private dining parlor he had hired, their host exerted his not inconsiderable charm to entertain the ladies at dinner, but his efforts met with indifferent success. To be sure, Miss Twistleton was all atwitter and giggled appreciatively at his wit in a manner more appropriate to a budding debutante than a maiden lady on the shady side of forty, but Marianne remained singularly unmoved by a really creditable performance, only speaking when directly addressed. She pleaded fatigue at the earliest possible moment and fell into bed in a state bordering on blank despair. She was intensely homesick and worried about leaving her grandfather and, despite his assurances that he was looking forward to devoting most of his time to a study of Egyptian history during the next months, was convinced that he would feel the gap in his life made by her absence much more keenly than he was admitting. They were very deeply attached to one another and he had had complete charge of her education for the past ten years. Consequently she had received the same type of instruction as his former university scholars, and her mind was trained in the same manner. A day spent in the unnerving company of Miss Twistleton had served only to emphasize how sadly unfitted she was for the company of women. Her days were crammed full of practical problems concerning the running of the farm and her evenings spent in the erudite company of her grandfather and the rector. Until today she had never realized how subtly her life had changed following her grandmother's death. In the past few years she had not even once experienced the pangs of guilt that had first assailed her whenever she thought of the exquisite embroidery work that her grandmother was noted for. She had been attempting to teach Marianne the skill with conspicuously little success at the time of her death, and Marianne had not picked up a needle in the intervening years. Her grandmother, being a thrifty Frenchwoman, had stressed homemaking skills, and Marianne was well able to order a household, but, she thought with unaccustomed self-pity, how little benefit such practical arts would be in the environment of wealth to which she was heading. For the first time ever it occurred to her that she had no feminine accomplishments at all. She had not once touched a pianoforte or a needle in ten years. As a very young child her drawings and attempts at watercolor painting had caused her grandmother to go off in fits of laughter. "You will never be the artist, chérie," had been Grandmère's judgment. "We must see to your musical education." So while she lived, Marianne had been well taught and there was promise of future proficiency on the pianoforte. She had a pleasing voice too, but both skills had been abandoned when they moved to the farm following her grandmother's demise. They had taken few possessions with them; her grandfather had been desolate at the loss of his wife and quite beyond thinking about music teachers and pianofortes at the time. Later, when they had settled into a comfortable routine on the farm, Marianne had been too thrilled by the freedom of outdoor living and the workings of the farm to regret the loss of her music. As her grandfather gradually became interested in taking over her education, she found herself completely happy with his program and his companionship.

"I should have been born a male," she mourned aloud, with sudden shattering conviction. "I have been educated as a boy would be, I've had the freedom of a boy—I am no kind of female at all." It never occurred to her that, in all probability, if she had been a boy her life would have been very different, for her father would undoubtedly have taken over the upbringing of a male heir. She never thought of her father at all, for at this point in her unhappy musings she fell into a disturbed sleep in the unfamiliar, too soft bed.

In the morning things seemed no better as she looked around the impersonal room with listless eyes, absently assessing its heavy solid appointments —anything to avoid dwelling on the prospect of another long day confined in a carriage with Miss Twistleton. A hasty glance outside confirmed her gloomy mood. A driving rain beat a tattoo against the window. The reluctant daylight barely lightened the shadowed corners of the room. She pulled a wry face as she swung her legs reluctantly out of the warm bed, then a thought caused the corners of her mouth to reverse direction and tilt up in amusement. She would confidently wager her next corn crop that the marquess was even less pleased with the weather than she was. The grin grew wider. No riding for him today! Well, she thought with a determined gleam in her blue-violet eyes, he could take a turn at being the little governess' captive audience since he had arranged for her presence on this interminable journey. And to this end she began rummaging through her meager baggage, emerging triumphantly a moment later

60

carrying the book her grandfather had pressed upon her at her departure.

Thus armed she appeared at breakfast, wearing her customary cool composure as a protective cloak to cover her unhappiness. Her trustee, however, fixed a penetrating stare upon her face and thought he detected shadows beneath her eyes causing them to appear darker than ever. Marianne would have been astonished to discover that beneath his polite urbanity he was shrewdly assessing her every action, and had conceived a very fair notion of the anxiety she was experiencing as a future rushed up to meet her that she could never have contemplated in her wildest imaginings.

He permitted a hint of a smile to lighten his expression as his eyes fell on the book she had placed beside her with a faintly defiant air. However he said nothing, preferring to allow her the discovery that reading in a carriage, no matter how well sprung, traveling at speed over indifferent roads was an impossible situation.

And indeed she soon realized that a pounding head and swimming eyes represented too high a price to pay for a bit of isolation, no matter how desperately she wished for solitude. The second day was even more interminable than the first, now that any sense of novelty had worn off. The rain continued unabated throughout the long day, but the marquess seemed to have hit upon the correct approach to reduce Miss Twistleton's spate of anecdotal prattle to endurable, though admittedly tedious, proportions. He alternately teased and flattered her, pandering to her taste for tales of titled persons, describing visits to palatial estates that held the governess enthralled. When she succumbed to an anecdotal urge, he promptly capped her tale with one of his own. All of this was done in a perfectly straightforward manner, but from time to time Marianne, darting piercing glances at his serious countenance, surprised a dancing gleam in his eyes that gave birth to a potent suspicion on her part that his charming manner masked a strong and probably reprehensible sense of humor. At first she was inclined to be indignant for Miss Twistleton's sake, but closer observation of that lady revealed that she was having the time of her life, revelling in the friendly attentions of a titled gentleman. Any hints that the titled gentleman in question was amusing himself at her expense would only serve to crush her sensibilities; so except for sending him a number of scathing looks which he blandly ignored, Marianne remained silent.

On this and the following day her contributions to the conversation represented no more than the bare minimum demanded by common civility. She had been thinking deeply about her changed circumstances, but could find only one aspect that promised an agreeable situation. The marquess had told her that a cousin had inherited her father's title and entailed estate. On questioning the identity of this cousin she was agreeably surprised to discover that not only was this unknown relative the son of her father's younger brother, but that he was only a couple of years older than Marianne herself. She was even more delighted to learn that she was also possessed of a female cousin. Aubrey's younger sister, Claire, was twenty years of age. Apart from her grandparents, Marianne had never had any relatives before, and she was inordinately pleased with this sudden influx of them. She longed to question her trustee more closely about Aubrey and Claire but there was never one moment during the journey when she could be private with him and, as it was clearly ineligible to be discussing family matters in the presence of Miss Twistleton, she was compelled to contain her impatience to learn more about these newly discovered relations.

She reflected with wry humor that if she already chafed at the artificial restrictions imposed by Society on the nature of any and all contact between unmarried persons of the opposite sex, she would likely prove a severe trial to the poor marchioness who had undertaken to be responsible for the social behavior of her son's ward. A very disconcerting question in her mind was just how willingly the marchioness had complied with her strongminded son's determination to carry out his friend's dying wish. Marianne had been loved and wanted all her life by her doting grandparents. The discovery that her father had never even wished to make her acquaintance at any time during the twenty-two years of her life had been a severe blow. She had been much more deeply wounded than her pride would allow her to admit, even to her grandfather whose loving concern could always be relied upon. As for the marquess, her trustee, one glance at that handsome, confident, uncaring face had served to imbue her with a steely determination never to reveal *any* emotion or vulnerability in his presence. She had departed from this resolve only on that first occasion when his careless listing of her father's plans for his previously unacknowledged daughter had so augmented the pain of being told her true situation that it had culminated in one short burst of fury and defiance. Since then she had not permitted herself to relax her imposed control in his presence. It had not been easy to maintain this rigid composure so foreign to her warm, impulsive nature, but she had instinctively divined his displeasure at her cool treatment of him, and all her perverse latent femininity rose to bulwark her defense against his insidious charm. She did not attempt to reach any understanding of why she was so bent on preserving herself from him; in fact, she refused to dwell on this aspect of her behavior, not even admitting to herself the existence of a malicious satisfaction at witnessing his well-concealed annoyance at her emotional inaccessibility to his charming overtures. Rather she diverted her apprehensive thoughts toward the situation awaiting her at the marquess' estate, but this produced no abatement of her despondency. Would the marchioness resemble her shining son in looks or personality? Her gloom deepened as she envisioned a beautiful confident woman overwhelming her country visitor with patronizing charm. She was bound to prove a stunning disappointment to her hostess, she despaired, gloomily passing her meager wardrobe before her mind's eye.

Clothes and fashion had played no part in her life to date, since her only social outings consisted of an occasional Sunday dinner at the manse. Jack and the rector were their only regular visitors and neither would notice what she wore. Frowning in concentration, she tried to remember when she had last purchased a new gown. Of course, the green velvet length Jack had brought her from London. She had had the village seamstress fashion a dress, but somehow the results had been rather disappointing. Still it was a lovely color and ordinarily she would have worn it the night the marquess dined with them, had she not been so bent on confirming his obvious first judgment that she lacked all feminine attributes that she had startled Clara with a demand to retrieve an old black dress that had been her grandmother's from a trunk in the attic. The yellow lace cap had been unearthed during a wild rummage in an old chest of drawers, and she had stubbornly persisted in wearing it over her usually unadorned locks ever since. Her lips quirked for an instant as she recalled Jack's puzzled glance that had strayed to her unbecoming headgear on several occasions during that last meeting. That he had not twitted her about it was an indication that the news of her leaving had shocked him out of his customary bantering manner toward her. She sighed, knowing that Jack's undemanding, good-natured companionship was another thing she would miss in the immediate future. He approved of her no matter what she wore.

The occasional sight of a well-dressed feminine traveler during the last three days had convinced her that her appearance would prove a blow to any expectations the marchioness might have held of establishing her *protégée* socially. Marianne had never seriously considered her appearance but she did so now, reviewing her features individually and collectively. There was nothing particularly displeasing about any single aspect of her physiognomy she thought judiciously, but she feared the familiar collection failed to add up to an interesting whole. Also the marquess had told her her hands were not soft and white as a lady's should be and she knew sunburned skin was frowned upon. In fact, she thought with an unhappy sigh, her dark coloring was very far removed from the standards of feminine beauty long admired in England. She grew increasingly restive as apprehension overcame the determined calm habitually wrapped around her vulnerability. Her contributions to the conversation became less and less, decreasing as the miles to their destination decreased, until she was answering in monosyllables.

They were deep in rural Somerset now and the rain of the past two days had ceased. There were small patches of blue in the western sky and the lowering sun was gilding the pink edges of some fast-moving tattered clouds, as they turned off the road onto a lane that suddenly ran between stone posts past a charming wood and brick gatehouse.

Her first sight of Lunswick Hall drew an admiring gasp from Marianne. Built of mellowed brick, it was a graceful Tudor structure with large windows ornamented with terra cotta enrichments in the Italian manner. Two wings extended at right angles from the main facade and, although she could not see the back from this vantage, she hazarded a guess (later confirmed) that the house had been designed in the shape of a letter *H*. There were many twisted and ornamented chimneys so typical of buildings of this period, and it was obvious from the appearance of the lawns and drives that no care and attention were spared to maintain the sparkling condition of the property. She was so busy admiring her surroundings that it came as a surprise when the chaise swept to a halt in front of the central entrance. Immediately the doors were opened and what seemed to the bemused girl to be an army of retainers hastened down the steps to assist in their descent from the chaise.

"Welcome to Lunswick Hall, Lady Marianne," said the marquess smoothly as he handed her down.

"Thank you, my lord," she replied with equal formality.

But all formality ceased as a diminutive, blue-clad figure appeared in the entrance way and moved with swift grace down among the footmen bringing in baggage under the direction of the butler to cast herself upon the marquess as he moved forward to arrest her flight.

"Hello, dearest, you made excellent time, despite the wretched weather."

Marianne stood still with a startled expression, surely the first real emotion she had displayed during the journey, the marquess decided as he led his mother up to her guest with an arm lightly around her waist.

"May I present Lady Marianne Carstairs, Mama?"

The marchioness extended both hands smilingly

67

as Marianne rose from an awkward curtsy. "I am delighted to welcome you, my dear child. I was very fond of your father and I shall call you Marianne if you do not object?"

"No, no, of course not, Ma'am," stammered Marianne with wide eyes, "but can you really be his lordship's mother? You seem far too young."

The marchioness gave a delightful crow of laughter. "Well, I assure you I am not too young, but I thank you for the compliment, deserved or not."

A faint color rose in the young girl's cheeks as she answered, "It was most sincerely meant, I assure you, Ma'am."

"Bless you, child, I know it was. Your face gave you away," said the marchioness, squeezing her hands lightly before dropping them and turning expectantly to Miss Twistleton.

It was a lesson in the social graces to watch the marquess' vivacious mother welcome the governess and thank her for her offices on the journey, then persuade her to join the family for refreshments while the marquess had fresh horses hitched to the carriage for the remaining few miles to Bath. In no time their hostess had organized a tea party in a charming blue and gold saloon, and was easily eliciting a review of the events of the trip just completed. Marianne could only marvel at her ability to draw and keep all present in the discussion. By the time Miss Twistleton had been speeded on her way she had relaxed enough to abandon the expressionless pose she maintained in the marquess' daunting presence and was animatedly describing her first reaction to the beauty of the house when the butler announced the earl of Melford and Miss Carstairs.

There was a split second of silence before the marchioness rose from a gold brocade chair and crossed the floor, smiling a welcome to the young couple who were just entering the softly lit room.

"What a delightful surprise, my lord, and how nice to see Miss Carstairs again. Do come in and meet our guest."

Her voice held just the correct amount of warmth appropriate to greeting pleasant acquaintances, and Marianne decided she must have imagined that a fleeting flicker of annoyance had crossed her hostess' exquisite countenance, but she could not so easily dismiss the quick tightening of the marquess' mouth before he seconded his mother's welcome. However, she was too much interested in the charming picture presented by her newfound cousins to dwell on her host's reactions at the moment.

And indeed nature had been most benevolent when bestowing gifts upon this favored pair. Her cousin Aubrey, though not above medium height, was startlingly handsome with dark wavy hair worn in a fashionable Brutus, and had classically perfect features. She had not thought a man could be better looking than the marquess, but now admitted with newly discovered family pride that her cousin's long-lashed gray eyes and finely modeled lips above a well-shaped chin gave him a slight edge, though he had not the aggressively masculine aura that was so much a part of the marquess' attraction.

His sister was his feminine counterpart, a remarkably pretty girl with an enchanting smile, being
directed at the moment to the marquess. Her soft
ringlets beneath a ravishing creation of pink silk
trimmed with darker pink velvet and adorned with
a single black ostrich plume, showed the ruddy
glow of chestnut rather than the crisp brown of
her brother's hair, but they shared the same dark-
lashed gray eyes and perfect features. As far as Marianne could tell, her figure was delicately made and
quite as perfect as the rest of her. She tore her
fascinated gaze from her lovely cousin as her hostess
made her male cousin known to her. His bow was
a miracle of grace and he flashed her a winning
smile.

"What luck to find you here, Cousin. Claire and
I just dropped in for a moment on our way home
from a drive to learn if there was news of your im-
pending arrival, and here you are, whisked from
the north posthaste by your very efficient trustee."
He executed a sketchy bow in the direction of the
marquess who was watching the meeting with half
his attention while listening to a laughing remark
by Miss Carstairs.

"Do bring that graceless sister of mine over here
to make our delightful cousin's acquaintance,
Lunswick," he added, raising his voice a trifle and
catching his sister's eye.

She blushed prettily and begged pardon in a
light sweet voice before turning her dazzling smile
in Marianne's direction. "I am so happy to meet
you, Lady Marianne. Oh dear, that sounds so ab-
surdly formal when I hope we shall be the best of

70

friends. If you do not object I shall call you Marianne, and I am Claire."

"Please do call me Marianne, both of you. I am quite unaccustomed to being called anything else, and quite detest 'my lady.'"

As his reserved ward suddenly smiled widely at her two cousins, revealing stunningly perfect teeth, Justin's eyes narrowed and the corners of his mouth pulled in. It had occurred forcibly to him that in the five days of their acquaintance she had not once smiled spontaneously in his presence. An impartial observer noting his reaction could not have said that he derived any pleasure from the attractive picture his ward presented as she talked with her new relatives, her very lovely eyes made a luminous sapphire blue by excitement at the unexpected meeting. Both cousins were studying her intently and his mother was looking on approvingly, pleased that her *protégée* was receiving such a warm welcome. Justin's expression was thoughtful when a soft laugh at his side recalled his attention to Miss Carstairs, who was pouting prettily at what she termed his "going off in a trance." He returned a laughing rejoinder that caused her to look self-conscious and satisfied. To Marianne, who knew as much about the art of flirtation as about the art of glassblowing, their conversation seemed completely pointless and she concentrated her attention upon her other cousin and her hostess. They had moved back into the room, but the newcomers refused all offers to stay for tea or dinner with a flattering show of regret, asserting that they had guests coming for dinner

71

themselves and must return quickly. Before taking their leave however they accepted an invitation to dine *en famille* the following evening. Marianne noted for the first time that her cousin wore black gloves and wondered what would be expected of her. Her traveling dress was black but the only gown she possessed that would possibly be suitable for dinner in a manor house was the green velvet. However she was too exhausted to care about anything at that point and gratefully accepted her hostess' suggestion of a light meal in her room, followed immediately by a long night's rest. She bade the marquess a polite good night and followed his mother thankfully from the room.

The marchioness, having left her guest to the motherly ministrations of her own dresser, returned to the saloon a few minutes later to find her son awaiting her. He had been kicking idly at a log in the fireplace, but at the soft rustling sound of his mother's dress, turned to face her with a rueful smile.

"I feel I owe you an abject apology, Mama." At her questioning look he explained, "I believe I once declared that no heiress was completely impossible."

As the meaning of this cryptic remark penetrated, the marchioness protested with a reproving tone in her soft voice.

"Justin, how can you be so unfair? She is a delightful girl and will present a lovely appearance when we have refurbished her a bit."

It was her son's turn to look pained. "I found her utterly impossible, cold to the point of rudeness, with no looks to speak of and no conversation at all."

"Nonsense!" declared the marchioness roundly. "I had no difficulty in drawing her into a conversation, and surely you must admit her voice is beautiful, low pitched, and musical with a fascinating little lilt—due to her Irish ancestry perhaps—and with none of that horrid north country brogue I feared we should have to break her of. She certainly has breeding, and if you had the wit to see beneath the admittedly dowdy exterior, you would know that she is a handsome girl at least, perhaps even a beauty." To her son's speechless surprise his gentle mother continued in severe tones. "I have never known you to be so harsh in your judgment before, Justin. I know I am going to love having Marianne here, and you shall regret those unkind words when I have finished with her. Her complexion is very brown to be sure, but it is beautifully clear and when the effects of too much sun and wind have faded will be one of her strongest assets, I am persuaded. Her eyes are magnificent, her features good, and her smile simply lights up her face. I cannot quite tell about her figure yet, swathed as she was in that disguising dress, but the right clothes will make a difference."

Justin could have told his mother that there was nothing at all wrong with his ward's figure, but prudently remained silent. Her next words aroused him however.

"That awful cap must go of course, and we shall have to arrange for her to have a fashionable crop. I shall—"

"No!" The single syllable was short, sharp, and quite definitive.

The marchioness blinked. "But, dearest, she is too young for a cap, even a pretty one. It would set her amongst the spinsters, and long hair is unfashionable these days. Look at Caroline Lamb, not that I mean to hold *her* up as a model of feminine beauty, but you cannot deny that the shorter styles are *à la mode* at the moment."

"Her hair is her best feature. It is long and smooth and black as night. I won't have it cut. Surely she does not have to conform to fashionable dictates in every last particular?"

If her ladyship wondered how her son could so explicitly describe his ward's hair when the girl apparently kept it constantly concealed, she did not allow her curiosity any vocal expression.

"Well, perhaps we may devise some attractive style without cutting," she temporized. "She will need a complete wardrobe of course. It is most unfortunate that she is in mourning; black is so unflattering to a fading suntan, but we shall contrive something."

"Black? Must she be garbed completely in black?" Justin looked both startled and displeased.

"Well, she is in mourning, you are aware. If she wore colors it would set up people's backs, and that would never do. She will be the cynosure of all eyes anyway, thanks to Perry's ill-considered and selfish actions."

"You are correct of course, Mama. When she appears in public she must wear black for a time, but surely here in the house she may be permitted more latitude. In fact," he continued with some reluctance, "she may prove difficult on this point. She told me she could not mourn a man she never knew existed. One must concede there is some merit in her stand, and less hypocrisy than to appear wrapped in black from head to toe."

His mother heaved a deep sigh. "I can see there might be some unexpected problems ahead of us, but," she went on more optimistically, "I do believe Marianne will allow me to be her guide in matters of social custom."

Her son was staring at her with a rather enigmatic smile. "I wish you success, of course, Mama, but for my part, I have not found Lady Marianne to be at all biddable."

The marchioness permitted herself the tiniest of smiles before saying gently, "Yes, it has struck me that you two do rather rub each other the wrong way." She fought back a giggle. "Like two strange cats meeting on neutral ground."

"It is always an object with me to provide you with entertainment, of course, Mama," he said smoothly, and grinned engagingly when the giggle refused to be suppressed any longer. His mother was wearing her mischievous imp expression which had been completely absent for four years. For the first time he felt in his heart that there would be some benefit to having Perry's daughter foisted on them. He could not prevent himself from indulging the strong sense of curiosity he had been feeling since noticing the instant rapport that had sprung up between these two women who were so unlike in all respects.

"Lady Marianne seems to have made quite an impression on you." The words were idle, but his sharpened gaze was not.

"Yes," she replied, "it must have been a pure maternal urge; that poor child was so apprehensive about her reception here that my heart went out to her. I cannot conceive what she expected *me* to be like, but the relief on her very expressive face almost overset me."

Her son's *not* very expressive face was exhibiting stunned disbelief at this speech.

"Mama, can it be that we are talking about the same person? I have been acquainted with Lady Marianne for five days now and quite frankly my observations would give credence to the theory that *nothing* intimidates her. She runs her grandfather's farm, bosses the help, performs whatever physical labor is necessary, and according to her friend Jack Richmond, has assisted at the birth of lambs, calves, and one human infant—who incidentally is named for her—and has yet to encounter the horse she cannot handle. I myself have seen her rescue a child from drowning without turning a hair, and I am persuaded she is here today, not through any fear of whatever financial pressure I might bring to bear, but solely to please her grandfather, who is determined she should not turn her back on the life she is entitled to lead without first sampling it. As for what you inexplicably term "her very expressive face," in five days of enforced proximity, I had not seen one real smile or show of interest until her arrival here;

76

nothing, in fact, save cold disinterest," he finished, unaware that the mounting iritation in his voice as he catalogued his ward's traits was inducing a mood of great thoughtfulness in his mother. However, although she looked searchingly at him for a long moment, her voice was casual as she answered:

"Everything you have said is probably quite true, dearest, but do you not see, none of it prepares a girl to go into Society. Although her manners reflect good training, I should be quite astonished to find Marianne possessed of any of the usual accomplishments deemed necessary to a girl making her debut—indeed how could she be, with no woman to influence her? No doubt her understanding is quick enough to appreciate this fact, and it is making her apprehensive of her future here with us."

The arrested look that had come over her son's features during this speech suddenly dissolved into laughter.

"I fear there is yet another handicap to overcome, Mama. She is not merely quick of understanding, but intelligent too, even *blue,* if the book of Latin poetry she was reading in the carriage is any indication."

His mother laughed at the mock horror in his voice.

"In short, our Marianne is not just in the common style. We shall simply have to present her as an original." She sobered abruptly. "How very *stupid* Perry was, to be sure. This girl might have changed his life."

To this uncharacteristically severe judgment on the part of his normally charitable parent, the marquess returned no answer.

CHAPTER FIVE

A stray beam of sunlight on her face woke Marianne from her first restful sleep in almost a week. Blinking drowsily, she sat up and stared blankly around at unfamiliar surroundings before the realization dawned that she had actually arrived at her destination. This, then, was where she would be spending at least the next few weeks—she refused to consider any prospects beyond a reasonable visit.

She looked around her with considerable interest, liking what she saw of her sunny bedchamber. She had actually seen very little of the Hall on her arrival the previous day. Not only had she been much more concerned with the people she was meeting but so extremely travel weary as to have difficulty registering any save the barest impressions of her physical surroundings. She clearly remembered being escorted by her hostess first into a small sitting room and then into this pleasant chamber, but after being introduced to a smiling, capable woman with gray-streaked red hair, she had none but the haziest recollections of being assisted to undress (her meager baggage had already been unpacked, she had noted with surprise) and being helped into a nightdress and urged to bed. There she had made a pretense of drinking some soup so as not to seem disobliging in the face of such kind attentions, but sleep had overcome her almost instantly.

Now the morning sunshine glinted off highly polished furniture and emphasized the deep blue color of the sheer silk hangings at the bedposts. She stretched lazy arms over her head, enjoying the sensation of the sun's warmth on her neck like a pampered cat. Her eyes fell upon the unadorned sleeve of her severely utilitarian nightdress and she grimaced ruefully. It was decidedly out of place in this beautiful room. Her glance roamed from the high chest to a delicately shaped dressing table, appreciating the graceful curving lines of the pieces and the dark gleam of the wood, showing reddish in the sunlight. Above the chair rail the walls were white, and below they were covered with a thicker fabric in the same deep blue as the bed and window curtains. On the polished floor were two large rugs patterned in shades of blue on a white background. White velvet draperies tied back with deep blue cords enriched the effect at the two windows.

She jumped out of bed to take a closer admiring look at the gorgeous silver frame of the mirror over the dressing table, and stopped short at sight of herself in the glass. Her thick black hair, tousled from the bed, tumbled over one shoulder of the white flannel gown. As she stared at her image she recollected the shining ringlets of her lovely cousin, stylishly arranged beneath a hat that had succeeded in arousing a covetous urge in her breast for the first time, and she wondered somewhat bleakly if she were as out of place in this marvelous room as her nightdress obviously was.

Just then a light tap sounded at the door to the hall, and upon her bidding the caller to enter, the door opened to admit her smiling hostess, charmingly gowned in olive green silk.

"Good morning, my dear." The marchioness stopped on spotting Marianne, and put her head on one side like an inquisitive bird. "You look about twelve-years-old in that costume with your hair loose," she declared mischievously. "Now I see what Justin meant, though, about your hair."

Marianne put up an impatient hand and flicked the long tresses behind her shoulders. "I was just thinking about Claire's hairstyle," she confessed. "There is nothing one can do with a yard of poker-straight hair. I fear I must be a sore disappointment to your ladyship," she added anxiously. "I know nothing at all of current fashion."

"Pooh, nonsense!" declared her hostess roundly. "You are most attractive even without fashionable aids, and I shall hugely enjoy helping you to attain a more modern look, but it would indeed be a mistake to cut that marvelous hair of yours. We shall simply have to contrive a style that is somewhat less severe than a tight knot. In this respect, at least, it would be a grievous error blindly to follow fashionable dictates. You have the height and bearing to carry anything off, I daresay." The marchioness sat on the edge of the dressing table bench and looked with flattering approval at the slightly embarrassed Marianne.

"I am going to love having you here, my dear," she said gently. "It has been a very long time, too long, since I have done anything that greatly interested me. But you interest me, and I hope we shall become good friends."

"Oh yes, my lady," Marianne replied hastily, "you are so very kind to take a stranger into your home. I cannot be grateful enough for your interest." Her brow furrowed and she went on more slowly. "I do not wish to pry, but I did not perfectly understand . . . have you been ill recently? Will having me here be too much of a strain on you?"

"Oh no, my dear child. Has not Justin told you much about our family then?" She looked curiously at the puzzled girl.

"No, nothing at all, Ma'am. We . . . we did not have much opportunity for conversation of a personal nature."

Looking at the slightly flustered girl from beneath gold-tipped lashes, the marchioness wondered what they had found to talk about on a three-day trip without touching upon personal matters eventually, but she merely addressed herself to the question at hand.

"I was widowed four years ago, quite suddenly. My husband and I were very close, so very close," she murmured, almost to herself before becoming brisk again. "At the time, both Justin and Harry were in the Peninsula with the army and Andrew was up at Oxford." At Marianne's uncomprehending look she explained, "We had three sons . . ." Marianne's eyes widened at the use of the past tense, but the marchioness was continuing with careful control, "Justin and Harry were twins, but Harry was the elder by fifteen minutes. They had decided Justin would be the one to come home first to see to the estate, because Harry had a very important mission to undertake for the duke. He planned to sell out afterwards but was killed at Salamanca before he could do so." She squeezed Marianne's hand in appreciation for the distressed sympathy so evident on her guest's mobile features.

"I am afraid I am a coward, my dear. Oh, yes," she insisted, placing a finger on the young girl's mouth to prevent her uttering the instinctive protest rising to her lips. "The double blow prostrated me for far too long. I have not had the heart to resume my life, and I fear I have rather neglected the other two in my grief. Andrew was much younger, of course, but Justin and Harry were very attached, in the manner of twins, you understand. Each seemed to know what the other was thinking, and one would often finish a sentence the other had begun." She sighed deeply. "Justin greatly misses Harry still. I do not think the void in his life will be filled until he takes a wife and has a son of his own. And I had almost begun to despair of that happening, but now . . ." She broke off abruptly, and when she resumed speaking it was to reiterate that she was sincerely delighted to have Perry's daughter to stay with them.

Marianne murmured a suitable response, but

could not help wondering what the marchioness had been going to say about her elder son's matrimonial intentions and why she had, in her own words, "despaired" of his marrying until recently. Was this last a hint that he was now contemplating marriage? She wondered who the girl might be, and a vision of her lovely cousin smiling at the marquess suddenly filled her mind. They would undoubtedly make a very handsome couple, suitably matched in birth and lifestyle, she thought dispassionately. For some obscure reason she suddenly felt restless and had to force herself to remain seated while her hostess got down to practical matters concerning her wardrobe. A few moments ago she had been eager to discuss fashions. Surely it did not matter to her in the least whom the arrogant marquess took as his bride, but she pitied her cousin if he intended to treat his wife with the same slightly belittling charm he had displayed the previous day, almost as though she were an amusing child to be played with affectionately and even spoiled, but not considered seriously when matters of importance were involved. However, perhaps Claire was content to be admired and amused, then dismissed when the men wished to talk seriously. She knew that she herself could never accept such a subservient role in her husband's life. How nonsensical she was becoming, she thought impatiently, giving herself a vigorous mental shake. She had no thought of marriage in any case. She had her grandfather to look after in his declining years.

Resolutely she put aside any concerns but the

immediate one of what she was to wear that night at dinner. The marchioness, after a cursory examination of the few items hanging in the huge wardrobe, stated frankly that it was imperative to drive that very morning into Bath, to obtain a gown for dinner and make a start toward selecting fabrics and designs for a complete new wardrobe.

A few minutes previously a tiny young chambermaid had brought chocolate into the sitting room. They had been sipping it leisurely but now, after a glance at the silver mounted mantel clock, the marchioness declared they must waste no more time, but bestir themselves in preparation for a busy day. Exhorting Marianne not to dawdle over her toilette, but to come to the breakfast parlor as soon as possible, she returned to her own rooms to change the green silk for a carriage dress, only pausing at the door to say softly, but imperatively:

"Marianne?"

"Yes, my lady?"

"May I beg a favor of you on such short acquaintance?"

"Of course, Ma'am. Anything."

"That cap you were wearing yesterday . . ." She twinkled mischievously as her guest colored up and dropped her eyes in confusion. "I believe it has served its purpose, do not you? A decent interment is indicated."

A reluctant echo of mischief lit the young girl's eyes, but she answered with deceptive meekness. "As you wish, my lady."

Left alone, Marianne gulped the rest of the delicious chocolate, then repaired to the bedchamber where she set a new record for quick dressing, speedily twisting up her hair and securing it with ruthless jabs of the pins. As she entered the corridor outside her room she looked around with interest. Obviously the interior of the house had been altered since its construction, for in Elizabethan days the rooms would all have opened off each other without the amenity of corridors. Her appreciative eyes admired the deep Turkey red carpet on the floor, and she promised herself a better look at the few paintings on the wall when she would not be so pressed for time.

As she soundlessly approached the staircase, a door opened on the right and the marchioness issued forth, wearing a lovely pearl gray outfit. She was busy tucking something into a black reticule so was unaware of Marianne's presence until the girl called out just as she reached the staircase. Startled, her hostess spun around lightly and smiled approvingly.

"That was quick, my child. Now we may go down together."

How it happened Marianne was never quite able to say. They were descending the stairs together. One moment her hostess was gaily predicting that Marianne would admire Bath with its hilly streets; in the next she uttered a gasping cry and seemed almost to dive forward down the stairs, crossing in front of the girl. Marianne acted instinctively, grasping the railing with her left hand while her right clutched frantically at the older woman's gown. For an instant they remained poised in these supremely awkward positions. Marianne, unbalanced, was unable to shift her feet or get a hold on the marchioness' person. She hung onto a handful of dress stuff with grim persistence but her face reflected her fears that the other woman would be unable to seize something to break her fall before the dress slipped inevitably from her guest's frantic grasp. The Archangel Gabriel himself would not have been more welcome than the sight of the marquess, alerted no doubt by his mother's cry, charging white-faced up the stairs. He scooped his mother's helpless form into strong arms, and knelt down on a stair until he could be sure of his balance. Marianne, relieved of her burden, plopped onto a higher stair for a second to still the trembling of her limbs.

A quick glance assured the marquess she was unhurt, and he bent all his attention to his mother who was protesting weakly that he was crushing the breath out of her. He gave a shaky laugh as he settled her firmly on a stair and anxiously surveyed her pale countenance.

"What happened? Are you hurt?"

"I wrenched my knee. I don't know how, but I do know I should have pitched down the whole flight of stairs if Marianne had not grasped my dress."

"Can you put any weight on the leg, my lady?" queried the young girl who had descended to their level and was now kneeling and gazing anxiously up at her hostess.

"I think so. It doesn't hurt much." The marchioness was about to put a cautious foot on the stair below when her grim-faced son gathered her back into his arms.

"You are certainly not going to make the attempt here, however. Back to your room, Mama, until we are sure of that knee."

"My reticule, it's spilled everything down the stairs," protested the marchioness, trying unsuccessfully to look around his broad shoulder.

"Marianne will gather it all up. Stop wriggling. You might injure that knee again."

When Marianne joined them with the refilled reticule a few minutes later, she was immensely cheered to find the hard, anxious expression gone from the marquess' face. His very evident affection for his charming mother was the nicest thing she knew of him, she thought fleetingly, before turning her attention to the victim.

The marchioness, though slightly disheveled as to hair style, and crumpled from being carried, was sitting with color restored in a small cane chair. One leg was resting upon a needlepoint footstool, but she smiled cheerfully at Marianne and waved away the hovering dresser.

"I shan't need you for a few minutes, Norris." After she had expressed fervent gratitude for Marianne's quick action, she cried regretfully: "I am so sorry, my dear, to be so careless. I'm afraid I've spoiled our plans for a day's shopping. I can walk with just a bit of discomfort and there is no need to cancel our dinner party, but I fear the hills of Bath would be too much for my knee today."

"Should you try to entertain at all tonight, my lady? There is a chance, you know, that the knee will stiffen up a bit after a few hours. Would you not be better advised to postpone the dinner for a day or two until you are quite recovered?"

"That's what I told her but she refuses to listen to good advice." This from the scowling marquess.

"Now, Justin, do not be making too big a thing of this stupid accident."

The eyes of the two young persons met in the first look of complete understanding they had ever shared, but their combined protests were sweetly but firmly set aside by her ladyship whose daintiness and gentle manner attractively concealed a will every bit as strong as her son's.

"As I told Justin, Lord Melford and Miss Carstairs are due to pay a house visit of at least a fortnight to friends in Kent. They may not return to Maplegrove much before Christmas. It would be a pity to deny you this opportunity of becoming better acquainted with your cousins." She sighed. "It is unfortunate we are not of a size, so I might lend you something for tonight."

"It does not signify, Ma'am," Marianne assured her kind hostess smilingly. "I can wear the green velvet."

"As far as today's proposed excursion to Bath is concerned," the marquess put in smoothly, "why should we not ask Miss Carstairs to deputize for you, Mama? I shall willingly offer my services as driver and escort for the girls."

"Oh, I don't think . . ." began the marchioness, then bit her lip as she saw the swift pleasure light Marianne's face, and the rather mocking lift to her son's brows. "A splendid idea," she managed gamely, "if Miss Carstairs has no other plans."

A message was dispatched forthwith to Maplegrove, and it seemed Miss Carstairs did not have other plans and was, according to the reply that arrived less than an hour later, delighted to put herself at her cousin's service for the day.

And so the small party set out for Bath in high spirits. To the initial amusement of the marquess, his impossible ward displayed a rather endearing shyness in the presence of her pretty cousin, seemingly content to follow Claire's lead in conversation. On the other hand, Claire's attitude to her newfound cousin, though affectionate in the extreme, struck the marquess as having more than a touch of patronizing charm. He waited in uneasy anticipation for fireworks, but Marianne showed none of that quiet resistance with which she had greeted most of his sorties over the past few days. However, with a fine perversity he discovered he was not grateful for her almost humiliating eagerness to please her cousin. Did the chit have *no* instincts for danger where her own sex was concerned? She was quick enough to take umbrage at any supposed slight on his part. Could she not sense that Claire was cleverly reinforcing an image of a country mouse that no more fitted his spirited ward than the awful black dress she had worn that first night? Although false, it would be convincing in company that had not spent much time with her. He became increasingly thoughtful as they neared Bath. If indeed Marianne's only association with another female was with the essentially simple and direct Margery, it was providential that her period of mourning precluded any rash attempts to pitchfork her into the Ton before she had learned something of the nature of womankind. Ultimately, of course, his mother would hint her into the way of things, but for the moment he would do his possible by engaging Claire's attention.

In this exercise he proved so successful that Marianne received a bare minimum of attention from her cousin for the remainder of the drive. Perforce, she witnessed her first lesson in genteel flirtation from two whom she shrewdly guessed to be experts in the art. Although aware that both relished the thrust and parry of extravagant compliments and equally extravagant disclaimers, she wondered how Claire could endure his attitude of lazy amusement. His very air of patent willingness to play games to amuse a pretty child was an insult in itself. Though puzzled not for the first time by this, she soon gave up wondering about their relationship as the scenery attracted her attention. The air was crystal clear and the view over the rolling hills quite lovely.

And suddenly they were in Bath. Marianne was suitably impressed by the scale and sweep of the Royal Crescent and the Circus, and approved the light effect created by the extensive use of the honey-colored Bath stone for buildings. The marquess set down his passengers outside an unpretentious establishment on Milsome Street with somewhat the air of a man deprived of a treat.

Marianne was unsure whether the laughing regret in his eyes was due to the necessity of parting company with her lovely cousin for an hour, or disappointment at being unable to witness her own awkwardness in a situation that no doubt formed an integral part of the existence of all the women of his acquaintance. Once again she schooled her features to blank politeness as she thanked him for his escort and followed Miss Carstairs into the creative arena presided over by that expert on the latest fashions, Madame Louise. She glanced about the clean but bare interior with no little disappointment, although she could not have put into words just what she had expected. Fortunately her preoccupation with the physical setting caused her to miss the comprehensive glance of disdain that crossed the haughty countenance of the proprietress, emerging from a curtained alcove, as her eyes fell on the black-clad figure. Her expression became one of polite inquiry on catching sight of Miss Carstairs, delightfully attired in an emerald green pelisse trimmed in black fur with a matching cap. Marianne did note the quick interest and speculation in the shrewd black eyes as Claire made her cousin known to Madame Louise, however, and her own deep blue eyes became a trifle guarded. Evidently the disclosures of the earl's will were already common knowledge in Bath.

Certainly she could not fault Madame's manner, which nicely blended formal courtesy with pride in her own position as one of the leading modistes in Bath. From the moment of hearing Marianne's name, Madame Louise became blind to the obvious sartorial deficiencies of this new source of potential income. She hastened to show the young ladies to surprisingly comfortable chairs while she begged to know how she could serve them. Claire rushed into a sweetly apologetic explanation of the spur-of-the-moment dinner party that demanded an immediate purchase of a gown for her cousin to wear that very evening. Marianne observed the slight dimming of Madame's suppressed excitement with an amusement she hoped was better concealed than Madame's hopes of good custom.

The modiste was explaining regretfully that there were, alas, but two suitable gowns in an advanced stage of construction that might be expected to fit Lady Marianne, but she trusted one might be made to suit admirably. A young girl of fourteen or fifteen years was summoned from the inner recesses and ordered to fetch the appropriate gowns. In the interim the dressmaker laid stress on the fact that she created original designs to flatter her customers, as well as being able to reproduce any costume featured in *La Belle Assemblée* in strictest detail. Before she could produce any of the aforesaid designs, however, the minion returned, carefully carrying a sapphire blue velvet gown draped over one arm and a stiff yellow silk over the other. She was so tiny it was necessary to hold her arms high to prevent the garments from dragging on the floor and her sweet little face was flushed with the effort required. Madame herself condescended to assist her newest patroness to try first one and then the other, adjuring Miss Carstairs to remain seated and pronounce judgment on the results. Marianne, whose fingers could not resist stroking the heavenly velvet, elected to try this first, and obediently followed Madame behind the curtains to the dressing alcove. She stoically bore the measuring look the seamstress cast at her chemise clad figure and allowed her to arrange the folds of the gown more becomingly.

"Oh, it's lovely!" she exclaimed involuntarily, watching the play of shadows among the folds with each movement of her body in the glass.

"Ah yes," Madame allowed with smug satisfaction. "Your ladyship has the type of figure that enhances the simple lines, slim and smooth, and with a naturally regal carriage. The length must be adjusted, but otherwise it is perfect."

She pulled aside the curtain and preceded Marianne into the other room, assured that the gown would find favor with the fashionable Miss Carstairs.

In this assumption however, she was proved over-confident. For a long moment Miss Carstairs simply stared at her cousin, her lovely eyes widening briefly, then narrowing slightly as Marianne pirouetted at Madame Louise's direction to display the gown from all angles.

"What do you think, Claire?" Marianne asked eagerly.

"Well, it is indeed a lovely color, my dear, but do you not think it a trifle tight-fitting and, ah, revealing?" She paused delicately, but went on almost immediately, before Madame could express the protest so obviously rising to her lips. "Your situation is rather . . . tenuous at the moment, is it not? Though of course I perfectly agree with the marchioness that it is unnecessary to wear black amongst the family, the vicar and his wife will be among those present tonight, and you would not wish to give any least hint of disrespect. But you must use your own judgment, of course," she finished apologetically.

"Oh, no, I am persuaded you are quite correct," Marianne said quickly, concealing her disappointment. "You will know the thing to do. I'll try the other one now."

The yellow dress, though a bit fussy in Marianne's private judgment, with a triple frill descending from the moderately cut neckline and another at the hem, met with Claire's unqualified approval. Certainly there was no question of a too snug fit, in fact the bodice tended to hang a bit loosely around the high waistline, but when Madame Louise indicated a simple alteration to make it lie more smoothly, Claire laughingly declared it perfect as it was, and reminded Marianne that the dress wanted hemming also and must be ready by the time they had finished the luncheon the marquess had promised to provide, or they would be guilty of abusing his generosity. Not surprisingly, this decided Marianne to take the dress with the minimum of adjustment deemed necessary. She cast a lingering glance at the blue velvet while changing out of the silk, and was heartened to hear Madame Louise promise to save the gown until Lady Marianne should return with Lady Lunswick. In quiet accents she confided her intentions of making any adjustments the marchioness should require.

"The gown was meant for your ladyship," she finished, still in that confidential tone with a rather enigmatic expression on her face.

Marianne gazed thoughtfully at the modiste for a long moment, then smiled with unaffected friendliness and agreed that she would like to try the gown on for the marchioness' viewing the following week when they should have more time to begin ordering a complete wardrobe.

The girls took their leave then, hastening to a shop where Marianne might purchase a new reticule to carry with the yellow dress, before it was time to meet the marquess. Claire chatted away animatedly, pointing out places of interest. She made a lovely picture in her deep green pelisse and Marianne, noting the number of admiring glances her graceful figure drew, felt utterly drab beside her sparkling cousin. She reflected wryly that for someone who had not given her appearance a second thought until that pregnant moment scarcely a sennight ago when the marquess had glanced at and through her as though she were invisible, she was rapidly becoming immersed in a condition of personal vanity to the total exclusion of all other concerns. She took herself to task and began to concentrate on her surroundings, appreciating, as the marchioness had predicted, the charm and cleanliness of Bath. The air was crisp and the sunshine enhanced her favorable impression of the city. While they walked up Milsome Street to George Street where the hotel at which they had agreed to join the marquess was located, she listened to Claire's mingled snippets of gossip and opinion on current fashion as represented by the people they passed, with a show of courteous attention that left the better part of her mind free to form impressions of the passing scene. There was not time to stroll by the famous Pump Room, but she was quite content to await another visit in the company of the marchioness.

Claire was nothing if not lively company, and as the two girls entered the hotel, the marquess, rising from a chair to saunter indolently toward them, noticed that despite her dowdy clothing, Marianne's flushed and laughing countenance was vibrant enough to warrant her legitimate inclusion in the low-voiced compliment of the old gentleman with whom he had been chatting idly while he awaited their arrival.

"An attractive pair, by Jove!"

"By Jove, they are!" he thought, grinning to himself as he led his guests to the private parlor he had engaged. If his smile had an element of smugness in it, this was due to the fact that his tiresome ward had so far forgotten her determinedly aloof politeness in the excitement of the shopping trip as to greet him with absentminded affability. Deciding to test the depth of her forgetfulness, he turned a smiling face to her when they were comfortably seated and quizzed her gently.

"By the air of satisfaction emanating from the two of you may I venture to guess that your excursion proved fruitful?"

96

"Oh . . . yes, yes, of course."

It was slightly disconcerting to see the carefree smile fade as she replied a shade too quickly, and his gaze sharpened as Claire said gaily:

"We were fortunate enough to find the most ravishing dress and Madame Louise promised to have it delivered here within the hour, so we need not impose on your good nature any longer than necessary."

He bowed gracefully. "It is a pleasure, my dear Miss Carstairs, not an imposition, to be of some slight service to my ward." His voice remained suave as he turned again to the latter, but the golden brown eyes were watchful.

"And are you equally thrilled with your purchase, Lady Marianne?"

"I trust it will prove suitable and that Lady Lunswick will approve," she answered composedly, but his increasing sensitivity to her moods detected a shade of doubt.

Claire's laughter was slightly edged. "Of course it is suitable, Marianne. Madame Louise is the best modiste in Bath."

"And since it is widely known that Miss Carstairs has exquisite taste," Lord Lunswick inserted smoothly, "your ladyship may rest assured that your gown will be both suitable and attractive."

Apparently tiring of the subject of feminine apparel, he inquired pointedly into Marianne's impressions of Bath, and the conversation became general for the remainder of the luncheon. And since in the art of entertaining young females,

97

the marquess was an experienced and charming host, it was indeed a pleasant interlude for both young ladies.

It was not until early evening, when Marianne made her appearance in the saloon wearing the new gown, that Justin recalled that his compliment to Miss Carstairs' taste in fashion had been received by that young woman in uncharacteristic silence, accompanied by a swift lowering of long lashes.

As he stared expressionlessly at his ward, attired in the one color absolutely guaranteed to cause a fading tan to appear sallow, he wondered somewhat grimly if it would be his fate to spend his life protecting this strong but strangely vulnerable girl from the disingenuous attentions of her relatives. Although the gown could not be faulted as *démodée,* a subtle excess of fabric in strategic areas completely disguised the graceful curves of what he knew to be a perfectly balanced figure as thoroughly as though she were enveloped from head to toe in a cloak.

He had to concede a grudging admiration for Claire Carstairs' singleminded determination to dim her cousin's light, as he appreciatively witnessed the effect of her own tardy entrance a half hour later. She swept into the room on a wave of French scent and pretty apologies, wearing a softly draped gown that clung lovingly to her exquisite form. Justin quirked one eyebrow in a mocking tribute to her choice of color. The dense rich jonquil hue completely cast into the shade Marianne's pale buttercup yellow while softly flattering Claire's white skin and red-lit curls. His eyes gleamed with amusement as he observed his mother's comprehensive study of her young guest, and he acknowledged the rueful twist of her lips as she turned involuntarily to him with a wicked half-wink of his own that prompted an unwilling smile and a somewhat hasty greeting to the earl who had entered behind his sister.

The marquess, although genuinely appreciative of the humor of the situation, was aware of an instinct he dimly recognized as protectiveness toward this awkward, faintly hostile, but unaffectedly genuine ward of his, and this hitherto unknown force derived a fierce satisfaction from the fact that no calculated spite on her cousin's part could diminish the glory of that magnificent quantity of black hair skillfully arranged by someone who had seen its possibilities as a lovely frame for her incredible violet-blue eyes. It was drawn back smoothly from that center point on her forehead that caused her face to appear heart-shaped. The unusual length allowed of its being twisted into a shining coronet around her head, lending a regal air to her naturally graceful carriage. Two shorter locks had been curled and permitted to fall free in front of flat, well-shaped ears, softening the effect of the severe classical style. A magnificent setting for diamond clips, he mused idly, and wondered if the earl of Melford's thoughts were running in the same direction. Certainly he had not taken his eyes from his cousin since entering the room a moment before, and the tinge of pink creeping over Marianne's cheeks did not go unremarked by her trustee, who decided to bestir himself and initiate a general conversation while they awaited the call to dine.

The only other guests, the vicar and Mrs. Huntingdon, were accompanied by their daughter, Miss Sophia. Marianne found herself drawn to this quiet girl whose retiring manner did not quite conceal a thoughtful active mind. Everything about Miss Huntingdon's appearance was moderate—average height, slightly plump as to figure, neither dark nor fair as to hair and coloring. Until she smiled a severe critic might dismiss her as nothing out of the ordinary, but her rare smile illuminated her pleasant face, perfectly revealing the essential sweetness of her nature. She was talking serenely now with Marianne, who was curious as to the countryside immediately surrounding the Hall which she had so far had no time to explore, when the marchioness' light voice floated into a sudden lull in the nearby conversation between the marquess and the earl and his sister. Mrs. Huntingdon had expressed concern over her hostess' slight limp and the marchioness had been describing her morning mishap:

"I shudder to contemplate the results if Marianne had not had the presence of mind to act swiftly," she concluded seriously. "She hung on tenaciously until Justin appeared to catch me."

Miss Carstairs turned impulsively to her cousin. "How fortunate for her ladyship that you are so strong," she declared, gazing with exaggerated respect at the taller girl. "I never could have saved her." She looked helplessly at her small, beauti-

100

fully kept white hands, sparkling with rings, and all eyes followed the direction of her gaze.

"Yes, my hands are unusually strong for a woman," Marianne conceded coolly. "It comes from milking the cows and handling the reins."

In the small silence this non sequitur gave birth to, Justin fixed his thoughtful gaze on the ceiling. Well, that was one vague worry he need not have entertained. He had recognized the shuttered blankness of his ward's face when answering her cousin as her habitual expression when dealing with himself, and knew she had taken the measure of Claire's spuriously affectionate pose. However, his original concern that this tiresome girl would contrive to resist efforts to introduce her successfully to the Ton was reinforced by the deliberate reference to her past life on the farm. The marchioness had gracefully filled the conversational breech, but her son, transferring his gaze to his ward's expressionless mien, was uncomfortably aware of a challenging gleam in the dark blue depths before she lowered her eyes.

The numbers were necessarily uneven, but as this was by the way of introducing Marianne to the people she would be most intimate with for the present, it was not allowed to matter. She was seated at the right of her host and found her attention nicely taken up by him and by Mr. Huntingdon on her other side. Although a younger and more vigorous man than the dear rector to whom she was sincerely attached, the vicar obviously possessed the same gentle human kindness, and by the time the ladies left the gentlemen to their port, her initial stiffness had relaxed considerably. The smallness of the party had assured that in some measure the conversation would remain general, and this circumstance plus the duty she owed her other partner adequately concealed the fact that her attentions to the marquess were confined to half smiles and minimal responses to direct questions.

Later the marchioness skillfully promoted an amiable discussion among the ladies while they waited for the gentlemen to join them in the saloon. Although she devoted herself principally to Mrs. Huntingdon, she was unobtrusively aware of the easy chatter of the three young girls. Miss Carstairs was doing the lion's share of the talking, but as it was perfectly obvious by their eager faces that the other two were enjoying her tales of London parties, their hostess tactfully left them undisturbed. The arrival of the men after a very reasonable interval should have been a welcome interruption had not their attention remained on a topic evidently begun in the dining room. As the gist of the rather heated discussion between Mr. Huntingdon and the earl became clear, Marianne's attention left the ladies and focused intently on the gentlemen.

"How can you say that so callously?"

The Misses Huntingdon and Carstairs, unaware that Lady Marianne's interest had strayed from their conversation, jerked up their heads in surprise at the sharp exclamation. Their startled eyes flew to their companion's face to find her own magnificent orbs flashing tempestuously at the equally startled earl.

"How can you sit here in this comfortable room and dismiss the problems of huge numbers of people so callously?" she repeated, controlling her voice with a visible effort.

"Oh, but really, my dear cousin," he protested, "although your tender heart does great credit to your womanly nature, this is a matter of economic and political necessity. A mere woman cannot be expected to understand that the state must make an example of these rioters and root out all the troublemakers or there will be anarchy in the factories and in the streets whenever a measure is unpopular. It is necessary to squash this Luddite movement now and make an example of it."

"I beg your pardon, cousin, but as a mere woman I find no difficulty at all in comprehending the situation. The Combination Act purported to forbid associations of employers and employees alike, but can you deny that there have never been any real efforts to curb the employers? Only the workers have been prosecuted for attempting to organize, and why should they not? Do the magistrates ever exercise their authority in fixing a fair minimum wage? Does the government show any concern over the high price of bread or the starvation wages or wretched conditions existing in the majority of manufactories?" Her eyes challenged her cousin's as she paused to gulp some air, suddenly uneasily aware that she had the full attention of everyone in the room, although the two elder ladies had not heard the entirety of her remarks and were looking expectantly at the group surrounding the guest of honor. Ah, well, she shrugged, preparing to further expound her views on the plight of the great army of underpaid factory workers.

"Bravo, cousin! Your eyes are absolutely magnificent when you are enraged, are they not, Lunswick?" the earl blurted admiringly, turning to his host for confirmation of this irrelevant observation.

Absolutely astounded at his evasion of her challenge to defend his position on governmental handling of the Luddite violence, she simply stared at him as though he represented a strange new species, unaware of the appreciative twitch her unbelieving disdain had brought to the lips of her trustee.

"What would you advocate, Lady Marianne?" the latter slipped in quietly.

"Repeal of the Combination Act of 1800," she replied promptly, "and the legalization of trade unions. What other recourse do the workers have but to use the strength of their numbers to bargain for better conditions?"

The vicar mentioned Sir Robert Peel's efforts to alleviate the distressing conditions of children and apprentices in industry, deploring the greed and lack of conscience that prevented more than a handful of employers from following his enlightened example. Soon he and Marianne were immersed in a discussion of Robert Owen's New Lanark mills which might serve as a model for others, if only the government could be persuaded to accept its responsibilities to its poorer citizens.

They had long since lost the attention of the others. Miss Carstairs had declared with a charming pout that she and Miss Huntingdon were in danger of being neglected for the ubiquitous poor, and her host had laughingly acquiesced to her demand for a change of topic. Although he was debonairly attentive, from time to time Miss Carstairs had the distinct impression that he was straining to follow the quiet conversation of the vicar and this amazing new cousin who actually seemed to prefer talking politics with an old man to conducting a pleasant flirtation with two handsome young ones.

She might be a lot better looking than she had first appeared, but with that attitude she just won't take, Claire concluded complacently. Of course that huge fortune made her decidedly eligible, but thank heavens the marquess did not need to repair his fortunes by making a rich marriage. She experienced no difficulty in dismissing her cousin from her mind in favor of continuing her attack on this flatteringly responsive but so far infuriatingly unimpressionable prize on the Marriage Mart. Miss Carstairs, after two seasons, was far too shrewd to attach any real significance to his willingness to follow her lead; indeed, she suspected he would encourage her to any desperate degree of flirtation and calmly accept any and all favors while remaining untouched emotionally. Strangely enough, this impregnability to feminine wiles only stiffened her determination to capture this matrimonial prize, whether or not she captured his heart, if indeed he possessed such an organ. Someday he must marry to provide an heir. No matter how cold-blooded he appeared, she had no doubts as to his eventual carrying out of his clear duty, and she meant this to be sooner rather than later. Such bad luck that she and Aubrey were to be away paying a tiresome visit just at this particular time when their new cousin provided the perfect excuse for her to see the marquess more frequently. Ah, well, they would be back by Christmas and by then he should be grateful for a change from the company of this bluestocking ward of his. Having observed them together on two occasions today, she was easily able to dismiss an initial fear that Marianne's patent indifference to his charm might pique his interest and bring out the hunter in his nature. Men like responsive females and this girl seemed to have a cold disposition, at least as far as the masculine persuasion was concerned.

Thus did Miss Carstairs dismiss one who might have become a potential rival as she drove home with her brother, moderately satisfied with the small amount of headway she felt she had gained in the past two days.

In the room the guests had so recently graced, the marchioness regarded her son and her charge warmly.

"Well, that went off quite well, I think. Did you enjoy yourself, my child?"

"Oh yes, Ma'am. Everyone was so kind and I enjoyed talking to Mr. Huntingdon and Sophia,

Miss Huntingdon, I mean. She has invited me to call, and has promised to show me the most pleasant walks in the neighborhood—if you have no objection, Ma'am?"

"Of course not. I am pleased you will have some companionship of your own age and sex while you are here. Sophia is a sweet girl and very sensible. Now off to bed with you. It has been a very long day."

Marianne murmured a grateful good night to the marquess and his mother, and headed for the door her host was holding open for her, but paused, remembering something as she reached him. She turned quickly back to the marchioness.

"Before I forget to mention it, my lady, Mr. Huntingdon told me where the nearest Catholic church is. If it will be convenient for you to send a groom with me, I may easily ride the distance each Sunday."

Justin's brows jerked together. "You are a Catholic?" he demanded incredulously. "Your father was not."

Marianne's silky brows rose slightly. "It is simply another instance of my father's lifelong disinterest in me that he made no requests about my religious upbringing to my grandparents. My grandmother was French and my grandfather is Irish." She added sweetly, "Naturally I was raised as a Catholic."

Justin remained, looking thunderous, as Marianne turned her glance expectantly to her hostess, who hastily promised there would be no problem in arranging transportation each Sunday.

When the girl had again bidden them good night and passed through the door he still remained by the entrance for a time staring moodily at nothing in particular, then abruptly coming to himself, walked back into the room to kiss his mother and absently wish her good night.

She made no effort to detain him, but when she was quite alone, abandoned the unequal struggle against the laughter bubbling up inside her.

"Oh, dear! Poor Justin!" she gasped on a quiver of mirth, addressing the small portrait of her late husband on the fireplace wall, "A bluestocking, a political radical, *and* a Papist!"

CHAPTER SIX

Saturday was spent in a delightfully lazy manner after the rather hectic first day of Marianne's stay at Lunswick Hall. The marchioness guided her leisurely through the impressive structure that had been in the Raymond family for over two hundred years. The Great Hall and a few of the older bedchambers still exhibited beautifully maintained linenfold paneling and intricate wooden ceilings, but the Hall had been continually repaired and renovated down through the years, and boasted delicate Adam ceilings in some of the newer rooms as well as a plethora of exquisitely carved marble fireplaces in every conceivable shade of the rainbow. Marianne's practical mind boggled at the expense of maintaining some two dozen or more guest chambers in a condition to be employed at a moment's notice, and her hostess ruefully admitted to staggering costs in fuel alone. While her husband was living and her sons growing up they had been accustomed to entertaining large numbers of friends and relatives upon the slightest excuse for weeks on end, she confided in a reminiscent vein, but in the last few years guests had been rare. Marianne, not wishing to see her kind hostess brooding over her near seclusion of the immediate past, hastily expressed a desire to examine the kitchens, and they repaired to the heart of the house where a small army of servants could be mobilized to cater for anything from an invalid diet to a large scale feast on public days.

Everything from the open ovens to the newest model in closed cookers by Mr. Bodley was there, kept in spotless condition. It was a rather gray day, but there were no dark corners in these kitchens. Huge ceiling chandeliers were augmented by wall lamps in strategic places, casting a glow over the shining utensils hanging on the white walls. Enormous dressers displayed plates and bowls for every conceivable use, and well-scrubbed tables bore mounds of vegetables awaiting preparation for the evening meal. She could hear cheerful conversation and splashing from the scullery where the kitchen maids were engaged in washing up the luncheon dishes. A cook paused over decorating tiny pastry cases to bob a brief curtsy to the women. Marianne was introduced to the dour Gallic chef who presided over this interesting kingdom. He greeted her with cold politeness, his piercing dark eyes alight with swift suspicion. Later, back in the marchioness' small sitting room, she apologized for the chef's barely concealed hostility, explaining that though a culinary artist of the highest degree, Christophe was something of a misogynist. She confessed to an abject dread of upsetting him lest this should lead to his final resignation, detailing for the benefit of her guest's puzzlement that he resigned on an average of twice a month and was only to be dissuaded by Justin's diplomacy and, she suspected, outrageous bribes to soothe his ruffled feelings. Marianne rather doubted the validity of her hostess' self-confessed inability to deal with the irascible Frenchman. In her brief experience of the marquess' young and vital mother, she already felt it inconceivable that anyone could resist her potent charm, allied as it was to a genuinely warm-hearted interest in those about her.

Of her trustee she saw nothing at all that day. His mother attributed his absence from the breakfast parlor to a desire to get an early start in catching up with the affairs of the estate, which he had neglected for better than a sennight. Evidently he was still engrossed with the aforesaid estate matters at lunch time, because he did not put in an appearance. His mother must have had some communication with him during the interval Marianne spent resting in her room in the afternoon, because at dinner the marchioness casually explained that Justin was spending the evening with friends in the neighborhood. Marianne had not mentioned her trustee once during the long day in his moth-

110

er's company and did not do so now, contenting herself with a polite acknowledging smile at this announcement.

It was not until she exited from the huge front door the following morning at Coleman's announcement that a carriage awaited to convey her ladyship to church, that Marianne encountered her trustee for the first time since the dinner party. The guilty knowledge that she had rather gloated over his chagrin at learning of her religious preference, combined with an unacknowledged little spurt of pleasure on discerning the identity of her driver caused a slight increase in color in her cheeks but she greeted him coolly.

"Good morning, my lord. It is most kind of you to engage to drive me to church, but I do not wish to abuse your hospitality and would feel easier in my mind with one of the grooms." She made no move to climb into the open phaeton, ignoring the hand he reached down to assist her.

"Get in," he replied briefly. "We must talk before I leave for London tomorrow, and this is as good a place as any in which to be private."

She obeyed without another word, digesting this unwelcome bit of news in silence. A sudden lump in her throat had to be swallowed before she could manage briskly:

"Indeed yes, I have not yet asked you about banking arrangements. At the modiste's on Friday your mother sent a message to Madame Louise requesting the account to be sent to her, but naturally this imposition cannot continue. Shall I use a bank in Bath, my lord?"

"Naturally you will continue to have all bills sent to the Hall for my settlement," he replied, glancing at her in surprise. "What other arrangements had you contemplated?"

Marianne frowned in puzzlement. "I assumed, of course, that you would deposit my income in a convenient bank so that I might draw upon it to meet my expenses."

"As your trustee it is my duty to manage your income, and except for your wardrobe, you will incur no expenses while my mother's guest under my roof."

She resented the hint of arrogance in his tone and plunged recklessly:

"I planned to purchase a riding hack and . . . and perhaps even set up my carriage. I like this phaeton, by the by, but naturally I would not dream of increasing your stable expenses with my cattle."

"How gratifying that you should admire my choice of conveyance," he drawled, "but," and the smooth tones hardened and became less equable, "understand that you will purchase no horseflesh and commission no vehicles built while I am away. I will mount you during your stay. In fact, after church I planned to introduce you to a two-year-old black I acquired yesterday for your use. He's smallish but with plenty of spirit and a good mouth. As far as a carriage is concerned, you may drive the gig while I'm gone, and on my return I'll take you around and show you the finger points of handling a phaeton and pair."

As the girl by his side sat silent, torn between fierce resentment of his high-handed actions and a grudging appreciation of his thoughtfulness in immediately selecting a special horse for her use, he hesitated and then went on more slowly:

"I will make available a certain amount for your personal use, pin money as it were. You will have no need to deal with banks."

"Pin money!" she echoed in bitter accents and turned a rebellious face toward him. "My grandfather, bless his heart, has no conception of money, neither has he any interest in it. I have handled the household accounts since my grandmother died and for the last five years I have had the sole management of the farm accounts as well. Grandpère's income is deposited quarterly." A thought struck her suddenly. "I apprehend my father was the source of that income?" At his nod of confirmation she continued in the same even tone, "I paid the wages, if money was needed for repairs I bargained with the workmen, hired them, and paid them for the work. When stock was bought I handled the selection, with Jonathan's assistance, and paid for the purchase. If a crop failed I saw to it that economies were made, and negotiated any loans necessary to tide us over the bad period. And you tell me I shall be given pin money like some schoolroom child to spend on my small pleasures? Should I thank you, my lord?"

For a time the only sound in the quiet morning was the rhythmic clopping of the horses' shoes, but the challenge in the air was almost tangible.

113

"No, I do not expect thanks from you, my child, but . . ."

"I am not yours, nor am I a child!" she almost spat out.

"Then you will not subject me to childish displays of rudeness!" he snapped back, suddenly as incensed as she. "I am well aware of both circumstances," he went on in an aggravatingly reasonable tone after a dangerous interval when brown eyes clashed with purple. Although ashamed of her outburst, she refused to lower her gaze and had the ultimate satisfaction of seeing him, of necessity, turn back to the horses without having subdued her.

"You have accepted grave responsibilities at an age when young girls should be going to parties and thinking of nothing more serious than the season's fashions," he began in a preoccupied tone and raised an absentminded hand to quell any remarks from her. "This is an unnatural situation, no matter how capably you have carried out the role thrust upon you. You are past due for some light relief and good times, and in any event, your capabilities do not alter the present situation. By law I have control of your income until you marry, though naturally I am anxious to accede to all reasonable requests."

"Until I marry? I have no intention of marrying, but for the sake of argument, what happens to my fortune if I do marry?"

"Naturally your financial affairs would then revert to your husband's care."

"You mean my problematical husband would control my income?"

"Of course, and the capital as well; that is the law."

She bit off a furious exclamation to demand, "As a mere chattel am I permitted to inquire just how great a matrimonial prize I might be, my lord?"

His face reflected his distaste at this plain speaking but he answered evenly, "Your father's estate was in the neighborhood of a quarter of a million pounds."

He heard her swiftly indrawn breath, though she made no comment, and turned to meet the somewhat bleak expression in the lovely eyes with a burning fierceness in his own.

"You need have no fear that I would ever permit a fortune hunter to address you."

She smiled at that but the violet eyes did not lighten as she replied quietly, "I thank you for your concern for my future, my lord, but with such a huge fortune I shall never be sure, shall I?"

"Yes, you *will!*" he ground between clenched teeth.

The force of the brief repudiation struck her silent, and try as she might she could discover no light remark with which to reopen the conversation, though it was suddenly of tremendous importance to learn why he was so sure she would not be married for the sake of her fortune.

Having delivered himself of this conviction, however, the marquess seemed disinclined to pursue

115

this or any other subject, and they arrived at the stone church without another word of conversation passing between them.

To Marianne's great surprise the marquess did not drive away after assisting her down from the phaeton, but proceeded to accompany her inside the church. He remained by her side throughout the Latin service, seemingly quite at ease in the unfamiliar setting, his unreadable face composed and thoughtful. Still shaken from their unsatisfactory financial discussion and embarrassingly aware that she and the splendidly attired marquess were objects of much covert speculation among the dozens of fellow worshippers present, Marianne was too *distraite* initially to give much attention to her surroundings. Seesawing between bitter resentment of the control her titled trustee had over her life, and an equally uncomfortable churning sensation that resembled—inexplicably—elation at his presence at her side, contributed to her unreceptive state, but eventually the solemnity and peace attending the age-old celebration of worship seeped into her being, calming her spirit and soothing her turbulent emotions. She realized with a guilty pang that the marquess, high-handed though his actions might appear to someone accustomed to making all decisions for herself, as well as all practical ones for her unworldly grandfather, was sincere in trying to do his best for her, and had received up to this point scant appreciation for his unremitting efforts on her behalf. It was not his fault that her unorthodox upbringing had not fitted her to play the role so suddenly assigned to her. Where was her sense of fair play that she should mentally castigate him simply because her nature rebelled at being treated as an incompetent child, which was, after all, exactly how unmarried women were dealt with by long right of custom and law.

At this point in her musings she sent a troubled glance at the silent figure by her side and received a cool but strangely reassuring little nod in return. Suddenly she experienced a lessening of the tension that had hitherto existed betwen them, accompanied by a corresponding lifting of her spirits.

When at last they exited into the sunshine, she was feeling more in charity with her companion than at any time in their short and stormy acquaintance, and an air of mild comradeship hung over the sports phaeton as they wended their way past the Hall to the stables, where Marianne was immediately captivated by the strong sleek beauty of the newest addition to the marquess' stable. She had first paused to bestow a friendly pat on the nose of each occupant of the several stalls they passed on their way to the location of the new black, artlessly declaring her disinclination to arouse jealousy among the other horses.

"For they are like pampered children, you know, going into the sulks if they are overlooked." She failed to note the fleeting look of indulgent amusement that visited her guardian's face at this engagingly uttered confidence, so absorbed was she at that instant in her initial delight at the appearance of the horse he had acquired for her use.

117

"Oh, what a beauty! Yes, I do mean you, you darling," she laughed, as a coal-black head turned immediately in her direction, nudging her shoulder and demanding his share of attention.

"Aye, he's a right fine young'un," agreed Melstead, his lordship's head groom as he led the black out into the yard for a thorough examination. "Smallish, but strong, with a nice turn for speed and no bad habits. I reckon your ladyship will find him a comfortable ride."

"Oh, I am sure I shall," Marianne enthused. "He looks a speedster for all his quiet manners. We shall have some glorious rides together, you magnificent creature," she added, petting the inquisitive nose lovingly. "What is his name?"

It was her trustee who answered. "He's called Thurgood's Choice, but you may rename him to suit yourself."

"Well, he is choice indeed, but I think I shall call him Ebony instead. He's blacker than black, isn't he?" she inquired, obviously in a rhetorical spirit since her attention never left the animal to whom she continued to address a stream of loving nonsense in crooning tones while the two men gazed indulgently at the attractive picture made by the two healthy, vibrant creatures engrossed in mutual admiration.

When at last a reluctant Marianne had been persuaded to return to the Hall, the tentative rapport that had come into existence with the marquess was reinforced by her sincerely expressed appreciation for his thoughtfulness in acquiring Ebony.

"I hoped you would like him," he replied simply, and initiated an amiable discussion on the points of the black that lasted until they had entered the Hall. Only at the last moment did anything occur to lessen the complete accord in which these erstwhile antagonists now found themselves.

"I thought it advisable to remove you from Ebony's side before you considered it your duty to croon him to sleep," the marquess declared with a teasing smile that brought a slight flush to Marianne's cheeks and a responsive quiver to her lips. "From your lovely speaking voice I would hazard a guess that you sing delightfully," he added, and watched with chagrin as the familiar closed expression wiped the animation from her features.

"You would be mistaken in your guess, my lord," she replied stiffly. "I have no accomplishments at all." Before he had recovered from this snub, she had murmured an excuse and retired to her room to remove her bonnet, leaving the marquess to indulge some sour reflections on the unpredictability of the female of the species.

Despite this rather daunting episode, the rest of the day passed quite pleasantly. The marquess and his young ward did not meet again until just before dinner, and for the duration of this excellent repast and the remainder of the quiet evening he exercised his practiced charm of manner to insure that the conversation flowed smoothly and amicably, and never once touched upon anything but the merest commonplace. Every mild attempt on the part of the marchioness to turn from strictly impersonal subjects was parried gently but inexorably by her son. After this performance Marianne could scarcely have been criticized for suspecting that her enigmatic trustee deemed women quite ineligible for any but the most superficial conversation, had she not already gleaned this from his demeanor at Friday's small dinner party, and his customary attitude toward Claire and his mother. With Claire his manner was condescendingly flirtatious, and although it was patently obvious to the meanest intelligence that he adored his lovely mother, in his ward's view at least, filial respect was a good deal diluted with the type of affectionate indulgence one might display toward a precocious child. He organized her life with just the right touch of deference, but whether or not Lady Lunswick automatically accepted his control or merely *allowed* him to manage her was an intriguing point upon which Marianne did not yet feel able to pass judgment. Although fully conscious of the marquess' adroit handling of the conversational ball, she could not deny that this was the first time she had felt comfortable during a prolonged period in her trustee's exacting presence. His descriptions of the immediate locale and of Bath proved both interesting and enlightening. She was itching to begin exploring the area both on foot and on her beautiful Ebony. Altogether it was the pleasantest evening she had spent since leaving her grandfather's house and she went to bed glowing with eager anticipation of her first ride on the neat little black, which made more inexplicable the slight heaviness of mood that settled on her within minutes of awakening the following morning.

When Marianne entered the sunny breakfast room a bare half hour later, it was to find a determinedly cheerful hostess as its only occupant. A crumpled napkin at one end of the table gave mute evidence that the marquess had already eaten. She closed her eyes briefly on the sight, and after clearing her throat slightly, turned a smiling face to the marchioness with a bright inquiry as to the hour of his lordship's departure.

"Oh, Justin would not leave without bidding you good-bye, my dear child. He just stepped into his study for a moment to retrieve something or other."

Despite her efforts to achieve nonchalance the marchioness was already regretfully conscious of the void her son's absence would make. "Thank goodness for your visit, Marianne. I must confess I find myself sadly cast down whenever Justin goes up to Town, though of course, I *wish* him to lead a life of his own. I detest possessive mothers. For a time after Harry's death he did not care to see any of his old friends, and that was truly awful. He seemed *haunted*. Had not Andrew fallen into a scrape at Oxford that necessitated Justin's intervention, I do not know how long this state might have lasted. The necessity for action snapped him out of that frightening mood." She chuckled softly. "I vow I must have been the first mother to *welcome* her son's peccadilloes, and I was hard pressed to present a properly disapproving air to Andrew when he came home, so relieved as I was

121

to see the change in Justin that I had to constrain myself from casting myself on Andrew's neck in gratitude."

The subject of her remarks entered the room at that moment, clad in a fawn-colored driving coat that must have borne upwards of a dozen capes. A brown beaver set at a jaunty angle provided a dashing contrast to carelessly waving gold-streaked hair. He was wearing one immaculate kid glove and carrying the other as well as an envelope, which he proceeded to lay on the table at Marianne's right hand.

"We had a bit of unfinished business to attend to," he explained smoothly, in response to her puzzled glance at the envelope. He extended the ungloved hand and clasped hers firmly for a brief instant, wishing her an enjoyable visit in a friendly impersonal tone to which she replied with an equally cool wish for his safe journey.

The marquess had reached the door after a last embrace for his determinedly smiling mother, when he paused momentarily and pinned his ward with a sardonic shaft from amber eyes.

"Be sure to read your daily quota of improving literature while I am away, Lady Marianne, and don't miss me too much."

"Oh dear, and I had so looked forward to reading nothing save trashy novels from the lending libraries in Bath while I pined for your return, Lord Lunswick," she replied in disappointed tones, and could not repress a smile at his delighted shout of laughter. With a friendly wave of the hand holding the glove, his large athletic figure disappeared through the doorway.

After an instant of suspended animation both ladies resolutely tore their eyes from the empty door frame and turned to each other with some bright remark.

CHAPTER SEVEN

In the spinney the late afternoon stillness was rudely shattered by the thunder of rapid hoofbeats approaching, not from the tree-bordered lane, but from across a meadow which still showed faint traces of green amongst the yellowed grass. A squirrel furiously chattered his annoyance at this potential interruption of his labors and scooted swiftly up to a safe perch in an oak tree. In the next moment any appreciative eyes amongst the woodland denizens could have been gladdened by the impressive spectacle of a magnificent black horse clearing the hedge dividing the lane from the meadow in a soaring leap. Not until the proximity of the spinney made such speed dangerous did the thunder lessen, as if both horse and rider shared an equal reluctance to abandon the wild gallop. As the sunshine of the field dissolved and was consumed in the dusky glow of the woods, Lady Marianne Carstairs bent over the neck of her now sedately trotting mount and crooned appreciation into his perked ears, reflecting exultantly on the advantages of having given her groom the slip for once. Certainly Brownley would have roundly condemned that last exhilarating stretch. At heart, the girl strongly suspected, the marquess' trusted groom stringently disapproved of any gait faster than a sober trot for those persons laboring under the disadvantages of being born into the feminine gender. Only Marianne's very real devotion to her considerate hostess prevented her from forthrightly dispensing with the groom's escort and allowing the chips to fall where they might, but it was unthinkable that she should repay the great kindness of the marchioness by becoming the object of censorious conjecture amongst the local populace.

Unconsciously she sighed deeply, guiltily aware that despite her affection she was quietly resisting certain aspects of her hostess' design for her education as a lady of quality. Certainly she was enjoying the resumption of instruction on the pianoforte being provided by Mrs. Huntingdon, a talented performer and patient teacher, and was, after a mere four weeks, experiencing some return of her former proficiency on that instrument. In addition to sponsoring the challenge and joy brought about by the resumption of her protégée's musical education, the marchioness had introduced her to a completely new world of pleasure with the introduction into her household of a dancing master from Bath. Marianne, who had never so much as witnessed a performance of any save country dances, was enchanted with the waltz and more complicated quadrille. It would have been an impossible task to decide who was the more delighted to discover her aptitude for this graceful pastime, Lady Lunswick, playing the music for the lessons with an air of a proud parent displaying her offspring's precocity, or Marianne herself. The latter's pleasure in this new accomplishment was appreciably augmented by sharing the lessons with Sophia Huntingdon. The two girls, much of an age, had quickly discovered in each other a certain mutuality of interests, as well as an agreeable similarity of tastes, and were already fast friends. Both were indefatigable walkers, delighting, whenever the uncertain weather permitted, to spend hours out of doors rambling over the estate. Marianne found Sophia the perfect companion on these outings, and was continually amazed and entertained by the encyclopedic knowledge of the local flora displayed by the vicar's shy daughter. So reluctant was Sophia to push herself forward that several weeks elapsed before Marianne was allowed a glimpse of a few of the exquisitely detailed drawings her friend delighted in making of the plants that so intrigued her. Utterly devoid of artistic talent herself, Marianne could yet appreciate the skill that raised Sophia's lovely sketches and watercolors out of the ordinary class of nature studies. She was firmly convinced that her friend's work was of exhibition standard, but Sophia merely smiled and disclaimed any extraordinary degree of skill, and quickly returned her work to her portfolio over Marianne's protests.

Both Mrs. Huntingdon and Lady Lunswick took

pleasure in promoting the sisterly comradeship that had sprung up between the girls, realizing that circumstances had denied to both the privilege of growing up in a good-sized family. Sophia, to be sure, was possessed of a brother, but as he was some dozen years her senior and had married while she was still in short coats, she could not be said to have profited by the give and take of ordinary family living, while for her part, Marianne had been raised entirely by elderly grandparents, and with the single exception of Jack Richmond had never been exposed to members of her own generation. When Jonathan and Margery came to live on the farm, Marianne had taken a friendly interest in the welfare of the young family, but Sophia was the first female friend of her own order, and she was vastly enjoying the experience. The dear marchioness gladly supplied another commodity that had been sadly lacking in Marianne's life for many years—maternal affection. The girl had blossomed in the warmth of her affection. She honestly felt she could never repay her hostess' many kindnesses, so why then this nagging restlessness, the occasional burst of rebellion that overcame her good intentions to be tractable and obedient to the wishes of her hostess? Marianne's face reflected her troubled spirit as Ebony daintily picked his way through fallen leaves and small branches.

Young ladies of quality did not ride *ventre à terre* through deserted meadows without the escort of a groom, neither did they regret the curtailment of the satisfying physical labor connected

126

with managing a farm. Before the marquess' sudden appearance, her life had been too full of tiring daily chores to encourage serious reflection on her future. Though the hours spent with her grandfather and the rector had been devoted to abstract philosophical or literary discussion, the topic of her own personal future had somehow never seemed vital. Now she had too much time for reflection, and she derived no comfort from her thoughts. The marchioness seemed to take for granted her entrance into London Society and eventual marriage, but to Marianne any extended period away from her grandfather was unthinkable. At eighty-two he could not be uprooted from the placid existence he enjoyed in Yorkshire or deprived of the stimulating companionship of his old friend. The obvious solution was to bring her visit to a close in a perfectly amicable fashion and return to the farm, but in exercising the honesty of intellect embedded in her by her grandfather, she could no longer deny that her earlier reluctance to embark on an adventure apart from the secluded life she led at home had been eroded by the pleasures of her visit to this luxurious estate. Despite her very real longing to see her grandfather and assure herself of his welfare, she had to acknowledge that she would be reluctant to relinquish the companionship of Lady Lunswick and Sophia, and even, to her eternal discredit, the proximity of a large city full of frivolous attractions such as theaters and fashionable clothes. Somehow she had become filled with nebulous longings and a restlessness she could not account for. Although her grandfather's rather abstracted communications did not alarm her about his circumstances, she could not be entirely content away from him. Nor could she accept the marchioness' unstated, airy assumption that her visit was of indefinite length to be terminated by a hypothetical marriage some time in the vague future. A frown wrinkled her brow. She should, of course, muster up enough resolution to confront her trustee and demand that he agree to a time for the termination of her visit. Her frown deepened as she admitted to herself that this action would not be entirely agreeable, although she was persuaded it was the proper decision.

Not that she had been granted an opportunity to confront her trustee about anything at all, for he had been on an extended stay in London since a few days after her arrival in Somerset. It was already the first week in December. She had received two cheerful letters from her grandfather that dealt more thoroughly with conditions in the Eighteenth Dynasty in Egypt than those in rural Yorkshire at present. She also had more prosaic communications from Jack and the rector conveying comfortable tidings of her grandfather's health and spirits, but she could not be entirely easy in her mind about leaving him to Clara's ministrations for any extended period of time. Not that he required a degree of perfection of service beyond Clara's talents—far from it indeed. When engrossed in his studies or writing, he was very apt to forget about irrelevant matters such as meals and the proper clothing to suit the climate, and had to be bullied into following a healthy regime. Though Clara was capable of overriding his mild protests at being disturbed in his scholastic endeavors to harry him to the table, she was never so successful as his granddaughter in inducing him to make a good meal once there.

With Christmas fast approaching, the marchioness was making festive plans, taking Marianne's continued presence in her home for granted. Something must be said soon about bringing her visit to a close in good time to reach the farm before inclement weather made traveling difficult. Surely they would understand that her grandfather should not be alone at this season.

Her unsatisfactory musings were brought to an abrupt cessation by a sharp command uttered from disturbingly near at hand:

"Hey there, rider! Stop! I require assistance."

Surprise caused her to jerk the reins suddenly and Ebony snorted. Marianne patted him apologetically, peering about her in search of the owner of that peremptory voice.

"Over here! Why are you so slow? I cannot help this poor animal by myself . . ."

The impatient voice halted in mid-sentence as horse and rider became visible, picking their way between two enormous bushes. The owner of the voice rose slowly to his feet from a squatting position beside a whimpering, twisting creature, his impatient frown giving way to a somewhat glazed expression as he beheld the apparition before him. A magnificent black horse carrying an equally magnificent black-clad rider with creamy complexion and snowy stock providing the only contrast to the unrelieved black. A tide of dark color surged to the man's cheeks as he realized from the lady's slightly amused expression that he must have been staring like a mooncalf. He darted forward to assist her but she was too quick for him, having taken in the scene immediately and dismounted with an economical swiftness, to stride to the side of the writhing animal.

"Do not touch him, he's crazed with pain!" the man warned.

"Nonsense, he knows we are here to help him," the girl retorted, gentling the animal's head briefly, a look of concern replacing her earlier amusement. "I'll hold him while you pull the horrid things out. You poor darling, you've had a run in with a hedgehog, have you not, and are totally vanquished." This last was addressed to the canine victim in soothing tones, as she suited her actions to her words by firmly gripping the wriggling creature.

The stranger hesitated briefly, still fearful that the dog might savage the girl, then as she directed a mildly questioning glance at him, dropped to his knees beside the animal and commenced removing the sharp spines from various parts of its anatomy. He worked in silence with steady, determined motions, while Marianne crooned soft-voiced encouragement to the whimpering pup and shifted her grip as it became necessary to aid the extraction of the spines. Except for a terse, "Keep him steady," from the man when the pup renewed his efforts to escape, no conversation passed between the two during the delicate operation.

"Stay, Ebony, quiet!" the girl directed at the black horse as he edged closer to the large chestnut contentedly nibbling the sparse grass.

Although he kept his eyes on his task, the man was aware that the girl had bent several curiously intent glances at him during their collaboration. The panting dog grew quieter as the lengthy process slowly rid him of the torturing quills. At one point he turned his head and licked feebly at the girl's black-gloved hand. The man forbore to comment on the suspicious drop of moisture that fell on the same glove a second later, methodically continuing his labors until he could say with a ring of triumph:

"There, that's the lot!"

Marianne heaved a heartfelt sigh of relief and stretched her cramped muscles, thankfully accepting the aid of a strong arm in struggling to her feet.

"Do you think he'll be all right now? He seems so weak, poor little thing." She stood staring compassionately down at the now still body.

"He'll do once we've seen to cleaning him up and having basilicum salve put on the worst patches. He's young but I daresay he's learned a valuable lesson. If you'll allow me to assist you in mounting, Ma'am, I'll hand him up to you until I'm mounted myself, then I'll take him again."

This exercise was accomplished with a nice precision, thanks to the pup's weary acceptance of his fate, and now the two riders took stock of each other.

"Thank you very much for your timely assistance, Ma'am. I could not have managed him alone," he said frankly. "I fear it has grown quite dark while we labored, so you must allow me to escort you to your home." He executed a graceful half-bow despite his burden and continued, "Allow me to present myself. I am—"

"Lord Andrew Raymond, unless my eyes have deceived me, and I'll wager we are heading in the same direction, my lord."

"You know me?"

The young man had been gazing at his companion with frank admiration. Now his blue eyes widened with surprise for a moment, but he said with great firmness, "No, we have *not* met. Never tell me I could have forgotten such an event."

Marianne laughed at the unsubtle compliment and assured him cheerfully, "No, of course we have not, but you are very like your brother, you know."

And indeed Lord Andrew Raymond was a younger edition of the marquess, with the same lithe athletic build and streaky gold hair. Like his brother he was the happy possessor of a classic nose and slightly cleft chin with sun-bronzed skin, but this Raymond had inherited his mother's bright blue eyes, made even more spectacular by his coloring.

As she returned his assessing look with one of her own, he grinned engagingly, thereby dispelling the sense of twinship with his brother. Marianne wondered with an inexplicable pang if the marquess had looked just so boyishly open and friendly before that cynical smile had become part of him.

"You have the advantage of me, I apprehend, Ma'am, since I have the misfortune to look like my brother, while you, I feel certain, are an original, resembling no one else on earth."

Marianne threw herself into the spirit from whence came this theatrical speech, arranging her features in a pathetic cast. "Alas, sir, it is but too sadly true. I am an orphan with neither sister nor brother to succor me. It quite sinks my spirits." She bowed her head.

"An orphan and going in my direction? I have it!" Suddenly Lord Andrew snapped his fingers, causing the dog lying across his saddle to pick up his ears briefly before lapsing once more into lethargy. "You must be Perry's daughter, the girl Justin inherited."

"You make me sound like a pocket watch or some such thing," she protested smilingly, "but your surmise is correct, Lord Andrew. I am Marianne Carstairs. Was Lady Lunswick expecting you today?"

"Mama? No. I was at Chestnut Hill, my estate, you know, checking on things for the winter when I took a sudden decision to come home early."

"You have no baggage? You travel light, my lord."

"I sent my man along earlier today with my gear, enough for a nice long visit," he replied with an innocent air. "Was that not foresighted of me?"

Marianne shook her head in amusement, declining to follow his flirtatious lead. The marquess'

133

young brother certainly did not lack audacity, but already she felt quite easy in his company and liked him for his calm efficient action regarding the dog. By the time the stables were in sight, they were chatting together like old friends.

Lord Andrew insisted on escorting Marianne to the main entrance, promising to lead her horse back to the stables since he wished to make arrangements for the dog in any case.

"You go in and prepare Mama for the return of the prodigal son, Lady Marianne. Tell her I expect the fatted calf."

So Marianne went in, smiling at his nonsense, to seek out her hostess which was not a difficult task. She found Lady Lunswick bouncing with anticipation, prowling about in the Great Hall so as not to miss her son's arrival. She looked up and smiled brilliantly at her young guest.

"Marianne! The most marvelous thing! Andrew is come home, at least his baggage has arrived and I expect him momentarily."

"I know it, Ma'am. I have just left Lord Andrew this moment. He will be here in a trice."

"You have met my son? But how is this?"

Lady Lunswick listened attentively to Marianne's tale of the encounter in the spinney, nodding in absent agreement when the girl described her first glimpse of the youngest Raymond.

"Yes, they are very like, and Harry and Justin were as two peas in a pod, of course. All my sons seemed to be stamped from the same mold."

Marianne smiled sympathetically at the unconscious maternal pride in the older woman's voice.

"And a very nice mold it is too, Ma'am," she twinkled.

"Naughty girl!" laughed her hostess. "Overfond mamas are a type with which I have no patience." She spoiled the effect of this firm pronouncement by adding compulsively, "But they are rather splendid, are they not? It is not simply my partiality?"

Marianne solemnly reassured her on this point and Lady Lunswick's dimples deepened. "You are roasting me, my dear child, but never mind. You shall see how our state shall improve. We have grown sadly dull this past week with the uncertain weather, but any house containing Andrew can expect to be alive with interest. Things just seem to happen when he is around."

Just then a mild commotion was heard at the door and she broke off what she was saying to dart forward, throwing her arms around her son's neck as he entered. He staggered momentarily, then lifted her clean off her feet and swung her around, grinning wickedly.

"Still on your dignity, I see, Mama."

"Andrew, you wretch," she scolded, "put me down this instant."

He meekly complied with this maternal command, but not before dropping a butterfly kiss on her nose while lowering one eyelid in the suspicion of a wink directed at Marianne who was watching appreciatively. Suddenly she was as firmly convinced as the marchioness that Lord Andrew's presence in the Hall would indeed insure against any gathering *ennui*.

The difference in the atmosphere of the well-run household was apparent in the breakfast parlor the next morning. Marianne entered to find Lord Andrew the only occupant, industriously doing full justice to a gargantuan repast while Coleman anxiously hovered over him, possibly laboring under the delusion that the younger son of the house fasted between visits. He pressed platters of ham and cold roast beef upon the victim of encroaching starvation, his anxious expression lightening only upon a repeated assurance that Lord Andrew would be delighted to partake of these offerings when he had made room on his plate by finishing several of the eggs that reposed temporarily thereon. Marianne, who had frequently undertaken the Herculean task of providing a sustaining meal for her old friend Jack Richmond, was less awed by the spectacle of a healthy young man consuming enormous quantities of food than intrigued by Coleman's obvious concern. Ever the perfect butler, in the month of her residence at the Hall, he had not, to her certain knowledge, betrayed his calling by permitting so much as a flicker of emotion to cross his craggy countenance whatever the provocation. She had wondered idly whether, in the unlikely event of someone's having the temerity to stick him with a pin, he would bleed at all, though firmly convinced that any necessary blood would be shed with unmoved calm. Now, having discovered the younger Raymond son to be his Achilles' heel, she murmured a response to Lord Andrew's cheerful greeting but fixed her interested gaze upon Coleman, who at once held out her chair, his features again composed in their habitual wooden cast. This did not change as she wished him a bright good morning, but undaunted by his imperturbable reply, she smiled at him rather saucily as he presented silver-covered dishes with the air of one performing a thankless task. Despite his expressionless mien, Lady Lunswick and Marianne were never left in any doubt of his opinion of females who, in the face of the best efforts of the chef, preferred to do no more than drink coffee and nibble at a piece of toast in the morning.

Formality not having survived the hilarious dinner meal the previous evening, Lord Andrew had merely paused between mouthfuls to issue a cheerful, "Hallo, Marianne," but she had no expectation of receiving his full attention until the inner man had been replenished, so she applied herself to her own breakfast after a smiling greeting. As she pushed aside her plate and allowed Coleman to pour another cup of coffee, however, her companion tore his eyes from his plate long enough to demand incredulously:

"Is that all you are going to eat, one paltry slice of toast?"

Marianne thought she detected a slight pursing of the butler's lips as he left the room. She serenely informed her companion that her breakfast was sufficient for her requirements.

He eyed her thoughtfully. "Women have some dashed queer notions, starving themselves to stay thin. A few more pounds wouldn't hurt you any."

She took this advice in good part, merely reminding him that she had made an excellent meal the night before. "Have no fear that I am headed for a decline, but I find I need less food here than on the farm where I was used to be much more physically active."

"How about riding with me this morning?"

"If your mother can spare me I should like that, thank you."

Lady Lunswick had entered the breakfast parlor as they spoke and now replied that she could certainly spare Marianne. "I know it chafes you to ride always with a groom, my dear child. You will enjoy your rides in Andrew's company much more."

Guilty color rose in her guest's cheeks, but as she opened her lips to confess that she had evaded her groom the previous day, Lord Andrew came to her rescue.

"That's a vastly fetching cap, Mama. Whom are you trying to dazzle?"

She dimpled at his teasing. "I ordered a new supply the last time Marianne and I were in Bath. They arrived yesterday." She waved away the platter Coleman was presenting to her. "Just bread and butter please, and not a word from you, Andrew," she stated firmly. "I shall not be bullied into eating more than I like."

Marianne smiled at Andrew's rueful grimace. Evidently this scene had been played many times before. Coleman, impassive as ever, had departed, expressing his disapproval only by the rigid set of his shoulders.

"By the way, Marianne, I saw our patient when I visited the stables earlier this morning. You'll be pleased to hear he is one hundred percent improved, frisking around making an absolute nuisance of himself among the stable hands. They were not thanking me for adding him to the household."

"Nuisance!" laughed Marianne. "The name suits him; but I am relieved to hear he is better. That was a horrid experience for the poor creature."

"May I bring him to see you, Mama?" asked her son casually.

The marchioness eyed him warily. "Andrew, I will not have an untrained dog brought into the house. Be assured that if the grooms do not care for his antics the house servants will be even less amenable to his disturbing presence."

"Oh, I just meant to bring him so you might see what a professional job Marianne and I made of his injuries," he said hastily.

As Marianne excused herself to change to her riding dress, she heard her hostess reiterating that the dog was not to stay in the house.

"Of course not, Mama, just for a visit," agreed Lord Andrew.

Less than fifteen minutes elapsed before Marianne returned, running lightly down the back staircase that was the more direct route to the breakfast parlor. She peeked into this apartment but found it deserted. Before she could turn toward the main hall, however, her ears were assailed by a series of sharp excited barks and, repressing a smile at what she strongly suspected to be Lord Andrew's customary promptness in pursuing an advantage, pushed open the door to Lady Lunswick's morning room. And now the smile could not be suppressed at the scene that unfolded before her appreciative eyes. Their late victim, apparently unaware of the standard of behavior expected of canine visitors, was planted firmly in front of the marchioness resisting all her entreaties that he release the workbag he held in his teeth. Several skeins of rainbow-colored silk lay about in a wild tangle, the colorful results of earlier attempts to separate him from his prey.

"You abominable dog, you will ruin that bag!" Lady Lunswick protested, scolding distractedly as she tried to retrieve the various items from the floor. Bag in mouth, the pup paused with head to one side and tail furiously wagging to indicate his enthusiasm for the fine sport being offered by the lady addressing herself to him. He dropped the bag to bark his appreciation but seized it again before Lady Lunswick could reach it. She stamped her foot in frustration and directed a quelling look at her son who was too overcome with mirth to be of any use.

"Drop it, sir!" commanded Marianne in a nononsense voice as she advanced on the culprit after laying down her gloves and whip on the mantelpiece. Pleased to welcome another participant into his game, the pup wagged his tail even more furiously and offered one end of the bag to the newcomer for a session of tug-of-war. She ignored this in favor of scooping him up bodily.

"Bad dog! Drop it I say!"

Perhaps it was surprise at this new turn of events or something in his captor's tone, but the dog complied meekly with this order and ventured to lick Marianne's hand ingratiatingly as she placed the workbag up on the mantelpiece before setting him down again.

"No, do not think to win me over, sir; your behavior is disgraceful," the girl said sternly, turning her back on him to begin winding up a strand of yellow silk before giving it to Lady Lunswick, who had paused in this endeavor and was examining the needlepoint bag for damages. "I don't think he has harmed it, Ma'am," Marianne offered.

"And look, Mama, he is attempting to make amends," added her unhelpful son, indicating the dog who, very willing to participate in this new game, was holding out to his harassed hostess a tangled red skein with the air of one always eager to be of assistance.

"You are aptly named, Nuisance," she declared tartly, accepting the silk and removing his paw from her green skirt.

He woofed softly, ingratiatingly, and tentatively placed another paw on her skirt.

"He's apologizing, Mama."

"And well he should," retorted his mother, unmollified, though Marianne noted that she was absentmindedly scratching behind the dog's ear while she rated Lord Andrew for introducing a barbarian into her house.

"He will soon learn to mend his ways, Mama.

141

Only see how intelligently he is regarding you."

At this point the intelligent hound gave a weary sigh and succumbed into a heap, comfortably establishing his head against one of Lady Lunswick's slippers. This elicited a spontaneous chuckle from her, but she argued, "He is the stupidest creature in the universe and do not think, Andrew, that he shall be allowed to remain in the house. I shudder to contemplate the havoc he would wreak in the kitchens or butler's pantry. You must remove him to the stables when you go out."

"Of course, Mama, but he'll sleep for a good while now. The horses have been waiting out front." He blazed a smile at his parent and wheedled, "Shall I get him when we return?"

Marianne intervened hastily, "What kind of dog is he? I do not recognize the breed."

Lady Lunswick emitted a sound that was dangerously close to an unladylike snort.

Lord Andrew laughed. "His ancestry won't bear looking into I fear. He's a rank commoner but goodnatured and definitely intelligent."

This last was addressed to his mother who had snorted disbelievingly again, but she looked amused also and urged them to run along.

"But if this stupid animal causes another disturbance in the meantime, Andrew, he will not be here when you return," she threatened.

Marianne settled her charming black beaver more firmly on her head, gathered her crop and gloves from the mantel and preceded Lord Andrew to the main entrance where a groom held their horses.

"Should we leave Nuisance inside, do you think? You would not wish to cause your mother any annoyance, and there is no denying he is unfit for a house dog as yet."

Andrew's grin was conspiratorial. "Mama adores dogs, indeed all small animals. She has not had a special pet since old Bess died last winter. She will be most happy with Nuisance."

"Happy?" Marianne's silky brows mounted dramatically, but Lord Andrew merely laughed.

"Wait and see," he promised as he tossed the girl up into the saddle, then mounted his big chestnut, nodding dismissal to the patient groom.

As they headed down the carriage drive he ran an experienced eye over the black. "He's a prime young 'un all right, and built for speed if I'm any judge."

Marianne proudly patted the silky mane of her favorite, thrilled as a fond mama at praise for her child. "Ebony is an absolute darling and the smoothest ride imaginable, aren't you, old boy!"

The neat black pricked up his ears and tossed his head.

Andrew chuckled. "And likes compliments obviously. Did you bring him with you?"

"Oh no, your . . . that is, Lord Lunswick selected him for me before he left for London."

"There's no one with a better eye for a horse than Justin. How do you two get on together?"

There was the tiniest pause, then Marianne said casually, "I told you, marvelously. Ebony is a perfect mount."

Lord Andrew trained a bright blue stare on the

composed face of his companion. "Doing it up much too brown, my girl," he said mildly. "You know I meant Justin."

"Well, if you will have the unvarnished truth, we disagree on almost every subject."

The touch of defiance in this bald pronouncement was not lost on Lord Andrew. His lazy glance sharpened for a moment. "Now I find that most interesting," he drawled, then leaving the subject despite its stated fascination, challenged: "Let's shake the fidgets out of the horses with a gallop, shall we?"

The last view anyone watching from the Hall would have had was of two riders going neck or nothing over the first low hill past the gate house.

CHAPTER EIGHT

Marianne immensely enjoyed her initial ride with Lord Andrew Raymond, and all the others that succeeded it. As his fond mama had predicted, life was never boring when her younger son was in residence. Shopping excursions to Bath took on additional pleasure, Marianne discovered, when the ladies had the escort of an obliging young man who, though he might leave them to their fittings at Madame Louise's, was always willing to meet them at the Pump Room and later to arrange a luncheon at one or another of the town's hotels, often with a small party of his mother's friends. On all visits to the Pump Room he thoughtfully insisted on procuring a glass of the famous waters for both ladies, despite his mother's repeated protests that since nothing ailed her she had no need to take the nasty stuff. Her careful son would solemnly recite the maxim about an ounce of prevention, never taking his eyes from his mother's expressive countenance until she had swallowed a token amount, not without many a grimace of distaste. Marianne, who had recognized early in their acquaintance his lordship's propensity for unmerciful teasing, managed to drink her portion with no change of expression by judiciously holding her breath and concentrating fiercely on something else while swallowing the potion. She never omitted to thank his lordship politely and took pains to conceal her dislike of the drink, thus denying him his little triumph. That he suspected her duplicity was attested to by his persistence in supplying her with the health-giving liquid and the inevitable bland but close scrutiny while she drank it. However she always met this look with an innocent one of her own, savoring his disappointment. The marchioness was too intent on her own reaction to note the byplay in the beginning, but as the two women walked down Stall Street one day she confided her dread of the coming ordeal.

"I'd almost rather go directly home than be compelled to drink another dose of that detestable water," she declared rebelliously. "How *can* you actually like it?"

At this Marianne was betrayed into a gurgle of

laughter, though she managed to control her features almost immediately and murmur something to the effect that she did not find the water intolerable. However the giggle had been sufficient to rouse Lady Lunswick's suspicions. She stopped dead outside the Pump Room and confronted her young guest, reading the mischief in the blue eyes above the prim mouth.

"Why, you hate the nasty stuff as much as I do!"

"Yes, but do not, I implore you, inform Andrew of the fact."

"But why? Oh, you naughty girl! It is too bad of you to make a May game of my poor Andrew!" These righteous words were wholly belied by an expression of unholy glee on her charming face.

"Rather 'poor Lady Lunswick' and 'poor Marianne,' " retorted her unrepentant companion. "Andrew is a sad tease."

His indulgent mama was forced to admit the justice of this accusation. "Yes, I fear Andrew has always had too much levity in his make-up. Even as a youngster he could never resist a prank, no matter what it might cost him later in punishment. But what is to be done?"

"I do not know, Ma'am, except it occurs to me that we have yet to see Andrew drink the waters."

"But that is because Andrew is always here first."

"Not today, though. Look who is approaching," said Marianne as Andrew came toward them. "Well met, Andrew. Since we are here before you today, your mother and I shall wait upon your comfort for a change." She smiled enchantingly up at him.

"I could not think of it, Marianne," he replied smoothly. "It is for a gentleman to perform that office for his companions. There is always such a crush around the fountain."

"Nonsense, Andrew," inserted his mother, grasping his arm and turning him firmly away. "It is our turn today. Marianne shall procure you a glass. We insist, do we not, Marianne?"

"Yes indeed, Ma'am. It is our pleasure, Andrew."

And Lord Andrew had given in gracefully, heroically swallowing the water under the solicitous eyes of his doting relatives, for Marianne had become one of the family by this time. The marchioness had treated her as a daughter right from the beginning, of course. Lord Andrew had shown a marked inclination to flirt lightheartedly with his mother's guest initially, but had gained no like response from one of her direct nature. Indeed, after a series of extravagant compliments on their first ride together, she had tartly ordered him to stop throwing the hatchet at her, an unromantic remark guaranteed to quench the ardor of any gentleman not absolutely sunk in love. After an instant of disbelief, Lord Andrew had shouted with laughter and thereafter had paid her the sincere compliment of according to her conversation and opinions the same attention and respect freely given to his male acquaintances. They spent many companionable hours outdoors, riding and inspecting the estate, and contrived to enjoy each other's company in the saloon in the long winter evenings. While Lady Lunswick industriously worked on

147

the complicated embroidery patterns for which she was justly renowned amongst her friends, immense imaginary fortunes were won and lost as her son and houseguest engaged each other at piquet. When the vicar and his family spent the evening at the Hall, Lord Andrew would make a fourth at whist so Mr. Huntingdon might indulge his fondness for the game. On these occasions Sophia and Marianne were left to amuse themselves, neither girl being deemed a worthy enough opponent to earn a seat at the whist table. This they were quite content to do. In Marianne's opinion, the only liability in having Lord Andrew at home was that she now saw less of Sophia than formerly. Andrew was forever suggesting an outing and though he was perfectly willing to include Sophia at any time, the vicar's shy daughter was not the enthusiastic rider Marianne was, much preferring to find her enjoyment in walking. In fact Marianne had great difficulty in persuading her friend to join any of their activities. Though Sophia and Lord Andrew had been acquainted since childhood and Lord Andrew treated her with the casual affection a young man might accord a female cousin, in his presence Sophia seemed to lose all her ease of manner. Marianne had realized at their first meeting that the vicar's daughter was shy and reluctant to push herself forward, but this was quickly overcome as their friendship developed, and Sophia, with her fine mind, proved a good conversationalist. With Lady Lunswick too she was always quite at ease; therefore, her stiffness when in Lord Andrew's company had Marianne

148

in a puzzle. She mentioned the matter to Lady Lunswick who confessed herself at a loss.

"Andrew and Sophie were the best of friends until he came down from Oxford a couple of years ago. There are only three years between them, you know, and Sophie was always Andrew's slave in the days when he was home from Eton. Harry and Justin were more than six years older than Andrew and would not often tolerate his company; then of course they joined the army and were not often home at the same time as Andrew. He appears not to have noticed how silent Sophie has become; he seems pleased to see her as always, but I cannot help wondering if he has done something to wound or offend her in his careless fashion, though there isn't an ounce of harm in his pranks. Boys never seem to realize that the females they played with as children *do* grow up, and sometimes develop exquisite sensibilities in the process, though to do her justice, Sophie has always been such a level-headed girl. Lately she actually seems more comfortable in Justin's company than Andrew's, and she was always used to go in awe of the lordly twins."

"I could understand it if Andrew teased her unmercifully, but he never does tease Sophie—that is, hardly ever," Marianne amended laughingly. "Andrew's manner is generally bantering, but he is sometimes gentle with Sophia and always looks after her comfort."

"Well, unless you feel able to question Sophia indirectly, I fear there is not much to be done at present," confessed the marchioness. She paused with her needle halfway into her embroidery and looked questioningly at the young girl, then resumed her stitching.

Marianne's hands, which had earlier stilled at her task of sorting the silks for Lady Lunswick, slowly resumed a rather aimless movement amongst the colorful array. The ladies were cozily ensconced in the marchioness' small morning room since Lord Andrew was away visiting friends in the district. Tonight her eyes were unaware of the charm of this favorite apartment, as they roamed unseeingly over the crimson velvet chairs with their oval backs and carved frames—small chairs to insure the comfort of a tiny lady while she plied her needle or cut out intricate paper patterns from *The Ladies' Amusement Book* that she carefully colored and later applied to various small objects to achieve a look of painted or inlaid decoration. There was a fine large console table of satinwood at which she generally worked at this craft, and candle stands strategically placed to light her efforts. The white marble fireplace with its carved floral swags glowed in the light of a brisk fire and many candles. Two large wing chairs upholstered in red, blue, and gray stripes were invitingly placed near the fire to tempt her sons. The fine needlepoint fire screen had been worked by Lady Lunswick. The red, blue, and gray was repeated in the patterned carpet and the same soft gray was used for curtaining the windows. Marianne thoroughly approved of this restful color on the walls, making as it did a neutral background for a few landscapes and family portraits. The ceiling and delicate plaster trim were a sparkling white. A delightful room in which to pursue one's artistic interests, and Marianne enjoyed keeping her hostess company, though she had steadfastly refused to pursue any creative endeavors of her own. At the moment, however, her mind was far removed from the restful room. An idea had taken possession of it with the force of a thunder clap, an idea both startling and unrestful.

The silence lengthened as Marianne stared into the low flames until it penetrated the marchioness' concentration on her fancy work.

"Are you concerned that any probing would call for great delicacy?" she inquired. "One would not wish to pry into Sophie's private thoughts."

"No, nor would I wish to be guilty of causing her embarrassment," Marianne answered slowly, "especially if there is any basis for an odd notion that just came to me." She lapsed abruptly into silence, seemingly unaware of the older woman's questioning look.

After a pregnant moment Lady Lunswick could bear the suspense no longer: "An odd notion?" she prompted.

"Yes," Marianne began hesitantly, but any explanation she might have made was interrupted by the ecstatic barking of the formerly recumbent shape nestled near Lady Lunswick's chair. Nuisance, who had been napping peacefully, got to his feet with his customary awkwardness and dashed toward the open doorway.

"Look at that idiotish animal," Lady Lunswick laughed. "He must hear Andrew."

"Not so very idiotish, Ma'am. After all it is a wise pup that knows his own savior," Marianne paraphrased lightly.

"That is true enough. He must know it is thanks to Andrew that he spends most of his time comfortably established indoors despite the prejudices of nearly the entire household."

"Oh, but you must concede that his manners have improved out of all recognition this past week or so."

Lady Lunswick was not about to concede any such thing, but just then her son entered the room with Nuisance madly circling his tall figure and thereby endangering his benefactor's balance.

"Good evening, ladies. What a sad thing it is indeed that a man's most fervent welcome must come from a mere four-legged creature."

Marianne chuckled softly. "I would be most happy to oblige, Andrew, except that panting is so undignified and so wearying."

He grinned appreciatively. "Well, I shall simply have to take the thought for the deed." He turned to his mother who was smiling at their nonsense. "I was at the receiving office in Bath today, love, and picked up this letter for you." Lady Lunswick extended her hand for the missive. "It is from my Aunt Aurelie," he added, and leaned forward to place the large blue envelope in the small hand that had stilled its movement.

"Aurelie?" echoed his mother blankly. "I cannot conceive what she could have to say to me."

"There is only one way to discover that," replied her son mildly.

"Oh . . . yes, to be sure."

Marianne, idly watching this tableau, wondered at the slight reluctance she sensed in her hostess with regard to the obviously unexpected letter. Andrew began a conversation about the friends he had been visiting, but the girl gained the impression that his attention, like her own, was divided, some part of it intent on the silent woman in the red chair who was now reading her letter with frowning concentration. She might have found the handwriting difficult, for it seemed an inordinately long time before she lowered her hands, still clutching the tinted sheets to her lap, and raised her eyes to the fireplace.

"Well, Mama, and what has my Aunt Aurelie to say?" Andrew's voice was curiously expressionless.

"She . . . she wants to come here for Christmas with Richard and . . ."

"Here! Does Justin know?"

"I . . . I do not know, but I should say it is unlikely. She writes from Northumberland. What is the date, Andrew?"

"Today? It is the nineteenth. Why?"

"Well, it will take at least three days for a letter to reach Castle Mauraugh. Aurelie writes that she will arrive on the twenty-second. She will already have left." Catching Marianne's curious eye, the marchioness closed her lips firmly against whatever else she had planned to say. When next she spoke, the sense of urgency had gone from her tones leaving them somewhat flat.

"You must know that Aurelie is my sister-in-law,

153

the widow of my only brother who died last year. Now that she has put off her blacks she plans to reside in London, but the town house is undergoing extensive renovations at the moment. She writes that she feels Richard, my nephew, would benefit from contact with his relatives. He has been too much alone since his father's death."

Here Lord Andrew interrupted to say, "Aurelie has two married sisters and a mother, has she not? I should think it more likely that she would go to them while the house is torn up."

"She feels Richard has had too much of petticoat rule just lately and should be exposed to his male relatives for a while."

"How old is Richard?" Marianne scarcely cared but felt constrained to make some innocuous comment to ease the atmosphere.

"His fourth birthday was in October, I believe."

"Only four? I . . . I apprehend his father was your younger brother, Ma'am?"

"William was seven and forty when he died."

The brevity of Lady Lunswick's answers argued against further questions and Marianne cudgeled her unresponsive brain for something noncommittal to say. The situation was saved by the arrival of the tea tray, but although Lady Lunswick's inherent social sense enabled her to guide the conversation into a pleasant discussion of some new music, nobly abetted by Lord Andrew, and though the prospective visit of her sister-in-law was not mentioned again, Marianne had no doubts that this was the topic uppermost in the mind of each.

The next few days saw preparations for guests

set in motion throughout the great house. Rooms were prepared for the countess of Mauraugh and the old nurseries aired and cleaned to receive her small son and his nurse. Curtains and draperies were taken down and cleaned, rugs were beaten, silver and brass polished to spotless brilliance. The kitchens were a hive of activity at this season in any case, as Lady Lunswick presided over the organization of gifts to the tenants and numerous dependents. Marianne saw much less of her hostess during this period. She and Andrew undertook the pleasant task of gathering holly and seasonal greens to decorate the various reception rooms and the Great Hall. The weather held cold and clear throughout the preparations, and an air of anticipation hung over the great house. If her hostess appeared a trifle preoccupied when they met at meals, Marianne laid the cause to her busy schedule and did her best to relieve Lady Lunswick of as many details as possible.

Despite her preoccupation with her duties, Lady Lunswick was aware of her guest's efforts and she was generous in expressing her appreciation as the ladies drank tea in the blue and gold saloon while awaiting the arrival of Lady Mauraugh and the little earl.

"Is this the first Christmas you have spent away from your grandfather, my dear child?" she inquired.

"Yes, Ma'am. I have never been away from him before." For a moment she blinked furiously to hold back the sudden silly tears. "But I love being here with you. And I know Grandpère is enjoying his stay at the rectory. I had a most reassuring communication from him only yesterday. Still it seems so . . . strange to think I shall not see him at Christmas . . ." Her voice trailed off at this point and her sympathetic hostess attempted to give her thoughts a happier direction by describing the activities that centered around the Hall during the Christmas season. She said finally:

"I am sorry, dear child, that the trip to Somerset was thought to be too much for your grandfather at this time of year. You know I'd have been delighted to welcome him here. Much as I would have regretted your absence at this holiday I'd have allowed you to return to Yorkshire, had it been my decision to make, but it is Justin, you know, who is responsible for your actions. It is most unfortunate that he has been delayed so long in London. When I first mentioned your desire to be with your grandfather he made me promise not to make any travel arrangements for you until his removal from Town."

Out of deference to her hostess, Marianne kept her opinion of her trustee's high-handed assumption of authority over all her actions to herself, inquiring merely:

"Will Lord Lunswick be unable to return home for Christmas, Ma'am?"

"Good heavens, I trust I may count on Justin to arrive in good time." The marchioness looked alarmed at the mere thought of her son's absence, but just then Andrew poked his head around the double doorway leading to the hall.

"I hear carriage wheels, Mama. You will not

wish to miss my Aunt Aurelie's arrival, Marianne," he said with a curious little smile. "She always travels in the first style of elegance. Come outside."

Lady Lunswick rose with an air of decision. "I shall come, too, as Justin is not here to welcome them."

"Take this shawl, Ma'am." Marianne hastily pulled a soft white wool wrap from the back of a chair and placed it over Lady Lunswick's shoulders.

Coleman had the huge door open and was already deploying his minions as the ladies reached the main entrance. Marianne gazed in fascination at the size and style of the entourage that was coming to a halt in front of the shallow steps. First to arrive was a smart traveling carriage drawn by a team of beautifully matched chestnuts that elicited an admiring gasp from Lord Andrew. The chaise itself was painted almost the same red-brown with shiny black wheels, trim, and center pole. A golden crest was emblazoned on the door panel. The rich gold-colored livery of the coachman was equally splendid. The second carriage now drawing up behind was obviously a job carriage and not to be compared with the first, but the massive amount of baggage strapped on behind and loaded in a precarious pile on the roof insured that it would not go unnoticed through the countryside. No less than three outriders accompanied the cortege.

Marianne was still assimilating the grandeur of the arrival when the door to the crested chaise opened, and the steps were let down. Immediately Coleman was tendering assistance to the widowed countess in descending, and now it was Marianne's turn to emit an involuntary exclamation, but hers expressed as much surprise as admiration as she beheld the vision now bestowing her hand and a sweet smile on the butler before turning to greet her hostess.

"Is that your *aunt*, Andrew? How can this be? Why she is no older than I."

Lord Andrew, after his first look at the horses, had concentrated his attention on Marianne and was openly enjoying her stunned reaction.

"Close your mouth, my girl. You are at present giving a splendid imitation of the village idiot. I see my Aunt Aurelie has made her customary first impression. You are not quite correct, by the by. She *is* older than you. She is four and twenty, the same age as your obedient servant. Do you find her moderately attractive?"

"Are you quite mad? She is the most beautiful creature I have ever clapped eyes on," Marianne said flatly, and she turned to study the new arrival.

It was her coloring that created an immediate impression of rare beauty in those seeing Aurelie St. Claire for the first time. Masses of glorious red-gold hair were beautifully arranged beneath a leaf-green hat that deepened the green of long narrow eyes set at an intriguing slant in a face with a complexion of rose petal perfection. Nowhere had nature erred in assembling the various parts that made up the lovely countess. Delicately chiseled nose, beautifully shaped mouth, small perfect teeth, her face a classic oval—everything contributed to the exquisite whole. Her voice was just as lovely as her appearance as she eagerly greeted her hostess.

"Georgina, my dear sister, it is so lovely to see you again, and looking so well too. I hope you do not think me presumptuous in daring to address you thusly, but dear William always insisted that our close relationship overrode the difference in our ages."

Marianne goggled, but the marchioness was equal to the occasion. She returned smile for smile.

"And William was quite correct as usual, my dear Aurelie. The similarity in our circumstances also wipes out artificial barriers."

"Our circumstances?"

"Both widowed with our lives centered in our children," replied Lady Lunswick sweetly, glancing from her sister-in-law to the open chaise. "Where is little Richard? Not too shy to come out and meet his aunt and cousin, I trust?"

Lady Mauraugh gave a tinkling laugh. "Oh, Richard is in the other chaise with his nurse who is absolutely devoted to him. Selwyn, my dresser, rode with me. I am such a poor traveler you are aware, dearest Georgina, and Selwyn knows how best to make me as comfortable as may be under the circumstances. Such terrible roads and scarcely decent accommodations en route, I declare my wretched head never ceased aching for an instant. So bad for the boy to see his mama out of frame, do you not agree? He was much happier traveling with Nurse."

Lady Lunswick intervened hastily, hoping to forestall a recitation of the sufferings undergone by her delicate sister-in-law on the journey.

"You remember my son Andrew, Aurelie?"

"But of course. How very like Justin you have become, Andrew. Where is Justin, by the by? I have been longing to thank him for being such a support to me when dear William died." She turned back to her hostess with a sadly sweet air. "He was all kindness and devotion. Indeed I scarcely know how I should have survived the initial ordeal without his sensitivity and understanding."

Andrew smiled and said easily, "I am afraid you will have to postpone your thanks for the time being, Aunt. Justin is in London at present."

"In London? At Christmas?" For an instant the countess looked absolutely taken aback and her well-modulated tones lost a trifle of their sweetness, but she dazzled a smile at Lord Andrew as he ceremoniously raised her gloved hand to his lips.

Marianne had been a silent spectator to the scene being unfolded, but now a faint, uncomfortable sensation she could not readily define ran down her spine, and she slanted a quick look at the lovely widow.

"We expect Justin any day now," Lady Lunswick inserted smoothly, then determinedly drew attention to the silent girl at her side. "Allow me to present our houseguest, Lady Marianne Carstairs, Aurelie. The countess of Mauraugh, Marianne."

The countess turned limpid green eyes in the

younger girl's direction that nevertheless summed her up in one swift glance. Marianne received the full benefit of that high-powered smile.

"How do you do, Lady Marianne. My sister wrote that Lord Melford had a daughter. I am delighted to make your acquaintance."

And she probably was delighted, thought Marianne, as she murmured a conventional response. Knowing herself to be a nonpareil, those green eyes had taken everything in about Lord Melford's daughter and dismissed her as competition. Immediately she was ashamed of the thought and rather appalled too at the direction her mind was taking with regard to the young widow. It was a relief to turn her attention to the other members of the party now assembling on the steps while Coleman deployed his troops in removing the awesome amount of baggage into the house.

A smallish stout woman with a pleasant face and an unbecoming puce bonnet holding tightly to the hand of a small boy as though to protect him was undoubtedly Nurse. A tall, spare, sour-faced creature clutching a large tooled leather jewel case must be Selwyn, who knew how to make her mistress comfortable, though one might be forgiven the suspicion that unless her nature belied her expression there could be little comfort in her presence. The little boy, now being presented to his aunt by his proud mama, held her sympathetic interest longest. He was the same age as Margery's young son Jamie, but not nearly so sturdy-looking. Like his mother, he possessed a head full of red-gold curls and perfect skin, but the whiteness that

161

so enhanced the countess' fragile beauty was less appealing in a boy. In fact, Marianne's thoughts were running along the lines of more outdoor activity and good nourishing food when it came her turn to meet Richard. The child offered his hand with unusual self-possession in one so young, and looked straight at her from candid blue eyes fringed with long lashes that put Marianne in mind of the marchioness. Those eyes must have come from his father, she concluded, as she returned Richard's interested stare with a friendly smile. The smile widened as she observed his somewhat awed appraisal of his splendid cousin. Obviously he was more at ease among women but she suspected it was Lord Andrew he found most appealing.

There was to be no immediate opportunity to pursue the acquaintance, however, for the small party that presently assembled to take tea in the blue and gold saloon did not include the young earl. In response to Lady Lunswick's invitation to her nephew to join his relatives, Richard's parent had explained that Nurse felt strongly that the boy should be kept quiet for a time to recover from the journey.

"Richard is not so robust as I could wish," she confided with a sweet wistful smile. "Although in general he enjoys good health, he quite often succumbs to infectious colds, particularly if he becomes fatigued or overexcited."

Privately Marianne wondered how the taking of tea with his newfound relatives could be classed as an activity likely to overstimulate even the most delicate child, but of course his nurse and his mother must be allowed to know Richard's constitution best.

Both Lady Lunswick and the countess possessed such supurb social sense that the conversation then and later at dinner was never allowed to flag. The countess related all the news pertaining to any old friends of her sister-in-law who still resided in the locale of Castle Mauraugh. She touched lightly on the renovations currently in progress on the London establishment belonging to her late husband. Since the marchioness had married from this house she was most interested to hear the plans in greater detail. The evening passed most pleasantly. Though the two widows dominated the conversation they courteously included Lord Andrew and Marianne in everything, and Marianne, in any case, was quite content to listen quietly while she readjusted her ideas of widowed sisters-in-law and aunts to include quite young and staggeringly beautiful redheads. Andrew too was rather less loquacious than usual, seemingly more interested in listening than in initiating any conversation himself. Marianne was surprised to discover when they retired relatively early that she was more weary tonight than after the quite strenuous days that had preceded the arrival of their visitors. Only as she climbed tiredly into the inviting bed did it strike her that in the midst of a plethora of social chatter, no one had touched on any subject that might be construed as even slightly personal. Frowning a little, she tried to cast her mind back over the evening but found she could recall little that had transpired beyond a description of the new fabrics and wall coverings destined for the London residence of the lovely countess. It was slightly puzzling but she was too tired to conjecture, and in minutes was fast asleep.

CHAPTER NINE

The next day was spent fairly quietly by all. Marianne, despite her tiredness, had not passed a restful night. Vaguely menacing dreams had troubled her slumbers and she arrived in the breakfast parlor slightly heavy-eyed to find only her hostess at the table. She was frowning thoughtfully at the coffee cup in her hand when Marianne entered but looked up with a smile and an affectionate greeting. Judging from a glimpse of Coleman's wooden countenance as she slipped into a chair, Marianne concluded that Lady Lunswick must have refused all offers of sustenance. She sighed slightly. Much as she hated to add to his burdens, she felt totally unable to cope with the butler's idea of a light breakfast.

"Just coffee and toast please, Coleman," she begged, and was greatly relieved when he accepted this without demur. She carefully avoided his censorious eye as he withdrew.

The marchioness chuckled. "Poor Coleman. We are a sad trial to him." She inclined her head to one side and considered her guest. "You look slightly down pin this morning, my dear. Do you not feel quite the thing?"

Marianne hastily denied any symptoms and asked about the rest of the household.

"It seems Aurelie has not yet recovered from the effects of the journey. She sent word that she'll be remaining in her room this morning and hopes to join us for lunch. Andrew breakfasted early and went off somewhere, so Coleman informs me."

"And the boy?"

"In the nursery, I presume. Shall you object if we have him with us for luncheon since we are not expecting guests?"

"Of course not. He will soon grow bored with just the companionship of his nurse. He is probably a lonely child and will think it a treat to be in company."

As it materialized, Lady Mauraugh joined her hostess and Marianne for lunch, but her son did not. She explained that Nurse felt it was not a good idea to push a child forward too much.

"Neither is it good for a child to be too much alone. He needs companionship," said Lady Lunswick.

"You are quite right of course," agreed her sister-in-law with her wistful smile. "I hope to find playmates for Richard among my acquaintances in London."

"Meanwhile, after his evening meal his nurse may bring Richard to us for a visit before we dine."

There was the slightest pause, then the countess

smiled. "How very kind of you, Georgina. Richard will be delighted."

And Richard had indeed been delighted to go amongst company, Marianne was recalling later as she slowly descended the great staircase after having excused herself to find some extra pins to secure her hair, which had come loose from its heavy coil. The weather that had remained cold but clear for over a sennight had rapidly worsened as the day wore on, limiting Richard's walk with his nurse to a few tame turns about the shrubbery before lunch. Rain had begun shortly thereafter and had turned to snow before dusk had set in. For the past hour Lady Lunswick had been going from window to window bemoaning the fall and wondering aloud if Justin would be forced to lay up somewhere on his way from London. Richard had created a welcome diversion, coming sedately into the room with Nurse. He had greeted everyone politely at Nurse's bidding, lingering near his mother to inquire anxiously if her head felt better. His mother had not been able to come and see him in the nursery, he informed the assembled company, because her head ached. Upon his mother's reassurance that her head now felt fine, he smiled for the first time, revealing twin dimples like his aunt's, and was easily persuaded to go to his cousin Andrew, whose large watch he proceeded to examine at some length. At Marianne's suggestion he was allowed to go with her to visit Nuisance in the morning room, a visit subsequently enjoyed by all parties. Richard had been inclined

166

to hang back timidly at first, but Nuisance's friendly overtures were impossible to resist, and soon the child was laughing delightedly while the pup frisked about him. It was during this play time that repairs to her hairstyle had become imperative if Marianne was to dine at the same table as the exquisite countess.

She was halfway down the final flight when Coleman and a footman hastened to open the big door. A whirl of cold, damp air rushed in and with it the elder son of the family, accompanied by another gentleman. He had greeted Coleman and was laughingly allowing himself to be divested of a snow-covered greatcoat when he glanced up and caught sight of the silent girl on the staircase. She had no difficulty in recognizing the mocking smile that appeared presently, but for an instant there had been an unfamiliar gleam in his eye that had halted her progress on the stairs. The smile released her from this temporary paralysis.

"Good evening, Lord Lunswick," she said quietly, continuing her descent.

He had strolled over to the staircase and now extended his hand to assist her needlessly in descending the last two steps. As his approving eyes summed up the picture she presented, Marianne knew a fleeting satisfaction that she was wearing the blue velvet gown she had coveted on that first trip to Madame Louise, and she met his look serenely.

Lord Lunswick spoke finally, lightly dispelling the enchantment of the unexpected meeting.

"What a very welcoming sight—a lovely lady to

greet two weary travelers, eh, Martin?" Suavely he presented his companion to his ward. "Sir Martin Archer, Lady Marianne Carstairs."

Sir Martin, who had been eyeing Marianne with flattering attention, blushed as she turned her eyes to him and stammered that he was her humble servant.

Marianne's equally frank appraisal of the newcomer left her well disposed in his favor. She smiled and extended her hand. Sir Martin, who appeared to be a year or two younger than Lord Lunswick, was of medium height and wiry build. His features were pleasantly unremarkable, but the light brown hair, brushed carefully careless in the popular Brutus style, and his very high, stiffly-starched shirt points surmounting a wide, complicated arrangement of his cravat proclaimed that Sir Martin aspired to moderate dandyism. Like his host he was neatly attired in light pantaloons, shining Hessians, and superbly cut dark coat, but his waistcoat sported two fobs and a quizzing glass hung by a black ribbon about his neck.

Gently Marianne withdrew her hand from his convulsive clasp, barely restraining an urge to wriggle her fingers to insure that they still functioned. Seeing Coleman at the closed doors to the saloon patiently waiting to announce Lord Lunswick's arrival, she smiled at both and led the way forward.

Before Coleman had uttered two words, Lady Lunswick had jumped up from her chair and was halfway across the room to greet her son.

"Well, Mama, did you fear I'd have to lay over somewhere on the . . . Aurelie!" His voice had trailed off as he caught sight of the smiling countess sitting in a gold brocade chair wearing a shimmering gown no less golden than her setting.

Marianne had been gently tugging to no avail to release the hand he had caught up in his on entering the room. For an instant his grip tightened unbearably, then she was free with no effort required on her part. Unnoticed, she slipped away from the small group standing stock still in the center of the room, seating herself at a little distance. She dragged her eyes from the marquess' thunderstruck countenance, surprised to find her brain was functioning well enough to record the puzzlement on Sir Martin's face and the anxious look in Lady Lunswick's eyes as they rested upon her son. Andrew too was intent upon his brother and his teeth were clamped on his lower lip. Only Lady Mauraugh seemed smilingly at her ease in the gold chair.

"You appear very surprised to see me, Justin. I trust it is not an unpleasant surprise?"

"It is always a pleasure to gaze upon you, Aurelie," the marquess answered, and now both voice and expression were flatteringly cordial. "You look lovelier than ever. You must forgive my astonishment but I was unaware that my mother had invited you to spend the holiday with her." Did she detect a faint question in his tones? Marianne wondered.

The countess was all pretty confusion as she laughingly confessed that she had begged dear

169

Georgina to allow her to bring Richard to visit his father's relatives because he stood greatly in need of masculine company. The marquess' face expressed exquisite politeness, but one eyebrow escalated slightly and his mother intervened.

"I had no idea Aurelie had formed the intention of removing from Castle Mauraugh."

"And have you formed such an intention?" inquired the marquess gently.

"Yes, but the house in Portman Square is in such a state with builders and decoraters everywhere that it is simply uninhabitable at present. But enough of my silly affairs; we are keeping your companion standing," said Lady Mauraugh, bestowing a brilliant smile on the man in question.

"Ah yes, forgive me, Martin. Mama, Aurelie, may I present my friend, Sir Martin Archer. Andrew, you and Martin are already acquainted, are you not?"

In the flurry of acknowledging introductions that followed, Marianne strove to gather her scattered wits together. Justin (somehow she had come to think of her trustee by his Christian name in the wake of his mother's numerous references to him) had been completely taken aback to find his uncle's widow comfortably established in his home. Certainly she was an unexpected sight, but whether an unwelcome one as well was the question she would pay dearly to have answered. The concern evidenced by his mother and brother would seem to support this theory, but Justin himself had quickly recovered his equilibrium and not only paid his surprise guest a pretty compliment, but

170

was now devoting his entire attention to her conversation while his mother graciously made *her* unexpected guest welcome.

Andrew brought Marianne into a desultory discussion of the weather conditions the recent arrivals had encountered on the road that lasted until Coleman announced dinner, the ladies all having agreed that the hour being so advanced, it would be a crime to make weary travelers change before dining.

Conversation sparkled at dinner. Sir Martin proved to be a most entertaining raconteur who was not loath to tell a story against himself. Lady Lunswick and Andrew were bent on drawing him out, and the marquess, at the head of the table, divided his attention equally between his ward and his uncle's widow. Unlike Andrew, he did not persist in calling the young woman aunt, but addressed her quite naturally by her given name. He still gave Marianne her title and, though he was a perfectly charming and attentive host, the girl felt that the magic interlude in the hall could not have happened. She told herself sternly that she must have imagined the warm look in his eyes earlier, and was unable to prevent her manner toward him from appearing rather stiffly formal. It was a relief to withdraw with the ladies to the music room, where she gave a good imitation of being totally absorbed in the countess' renderings of several selections by a fine new composer from Germany named Beethoven. Not that one was obliged to *pretend* approval of Lady Mauraugh's playing. As well as being beautiful, she was highly accomplished. Marianne had sat silently through a discussion with Lady Lunswick that afternoon that had thoroughly covered all the finer points of creative stitchery, and she had already learned that Lady Mauraugh did "little watercolors" for her dearest friends.

When the gentlemen joined the ladies, the countess graciously obliged with one additional selection, looking graceful and ethereal with the candle glow turning her hair to rich fire. Sir Martin, confessing himself to be tone-deaf, gravitated toward Marianne during this interlude, and when the music ended remained attentively at her side. Marianne, thoughtfully observing Sir Martin's attempts to keep her own attention though the gorgeous widow was at her most charming, wondered idly if he had learned of her father's fortune, then promptly hated herself for the uncharitable thought. Truth to tell, she was more than a little dismayed by her own reactions ever since the arrival of Lady Mauraugh. She knew herself to be deficient in the attainments expected of young ladies of quality and was well aware that her looks were not in the accepted style of fashion, but these facts had not caused her any significant anxiety before the advent of the countess. Lady Lunswick and Andrew had always made her feel they truly valued her acquaintance, and she was now shocked and ashamed at the jealous tumult within her breast when she was in the company of a lovely, accomplished woman. It did not occur to her, mentally squirming in an excess of self-contempt, that she had never experienced the least

172

stab of jealousy in the face of Sophia's very real talent. If this degrading emotion was going to overcome her in London where the assemblies were thronged with lovely, accomplished women, she would do better to retire immediately to Yorkshire, she conceded ruefully. But at least she could now put a name to the disturbing lowness of spirits with which she had been struggling ever since the arrival of Lady Mauraugh. Certainly her reaction was not very admirable and was exceedingly foolish as well, for the presence of the countess was most unlikely to have any effect on her own life. Indeed the chance of their ever meeting again after this visit was so slight as to be negligible. Meanwhile a charming man was doing her the honor of preferring her company, and she had best bestir herself to respond with something slightly warmer than mere civility. Refusing to think about herself any longer, she set out to entertain Sir Martin and succeeded to admiration if his air of absorption and frequent gusts of laughter were anything to judge by.

At least that was the strong impression received by the marquess as he glanced their way, not for the first time, after one such burst of merriment. Noting that his mother was fanning herself lightly, he excused himself to move the fire screen to shield her somewhat from the heat. He returned her appreciative smile affectionately and wandered over to take a seat near the blue sofa upon which Marianne sat with Sir Martin.

"Martin, old chap, Lady Mauraugh was inquiring about Sarah Grensham just now. Did you not mention that you had bumped into Mrs. Grensham last week at Somerset House? I told her ladyship your information would be more current." He smiled lazily at his friend who looked startled. At the same moment Lady Mauraugh's green eyes turned toward Sir Martin inquiringly, and he rose with what good grace he could muster, murmuring an excuse as he changed to a chair nearer the countess.

Marianne glanced uncertainly at Lord Lunswick from under curling black lashes to find him studying her at his leisure.

"Tell me, Lady Marianne, do you still think of yourself as a farmer?"

Those fantastic eyes, more blue than violet tonight, widened and her lips quivered into an unwilling smile which he noted with bland satisfaction. Good! Whatever she had expected, he had succeeded in surprising her.

"Of course, my lord," she answered demurely, then at his quizzical look, conceded honestly, "but I do not think about the farm very often these days."

"Allow me to tell you that you do not look like anyone's idea of a farmer."

She smiled slightly in acknowledgment of the implied compliment, but remained silent.

So much for attempted flirtation. Obviously there had been little progress along these lines during his absence; Andrew must be losing his touch. He tried another tack. "How have you been spending your days since I have been away?"

This proved a more productive vein. At first

hesitantly, then with more confidence as she noted his attention, Marianne described her recent activities, unaware how revealing her comments on Lord Andrew, Sophia, and Lady Lunswick were of her affection for these persons. He did not interrupt and asked only a few questions, but they were enough to elicit the story of her meeting with Andrew in the spinney, and she found herself telling him about Sophia's paintings also. He chuckled over the adventure with Nuisance and even more when she related the gradual introduction of the dog into the household, seemingly over the strenuous objections of the marchioness.

"Mama possesses the feminine trait of allowing her men to make for her any decisions that might prove unpopular with the staff. She'd have made a good diplomat."

Marianne took mild umbrage at this provocative remark. "That can scarcely be termed a feminine trait, my lord," she said somewhat drily.

But his lordship refused to be led into a general discussion on the failings of human nature as typified by either sex. He smiled at her, a different, more intimate smile than his customary cynical quirk, and it brought a faint rise of color in her cheeks.

"You have been having an enjoyable time here?"

"Oh, yes, my lord."

"Then, may I be permitted to hope that you no longer hold me in such deep dislike for coercing your removal from Yorkshire and your presence in my home?" He spoke lightly but was regarding her intently, and a wary look came into her eyes.

"I . . . I don't dislike you, Lord Lunswick," she managed at last. "It was just that the *manner* in which you—"

He held up a silencing hand. "Unnecessary to say more. I think I know how your independent spirit rails against any authority I may have, but I do not wish to quarrel, at least not on my first night home." He watched with satisfaction the smile that began in her eyes and gently tugged at the corners of her mobile lips as he added this qualifying phrase. "I am content, at present, to know I no longer have your enmity."

"Oh, never enemies, my lord," she cried, rather distressed at the harsh sounding word.

"Then may I hope, friends, Marianne?" he asked, deliberately dropping her title for the first time. His amber eyes were very compelling, holding hers with a deep seriousness.

She smiled at him shyly, but whatever she might have said was forestalled by Lady Mauraugh's clear tones, raised to reach the marquess, as she called to him to settle a question. For a second longer he continued to hold Marianne's glance, the line of his mouth suddenly much firmer, but the intimacy between them was shattered. The girl beside him had been startled into awareness of the general company by the countess' voice and was no longer attending to him. He turned toward the other group with a smiling answer to the question.

The conversation remained general until the ladies retired for the night. Fortunately for Marianne's peace of mind she had been unaware of the

176

long speculative stare trained on her by the countess after the latter's question had succeeded in breaking up a duet she had found too cozy-looking for her liking. The narrowed look had not escaped the notice of the marquess, however, and when the green eyes shifted at last to his face they met an enigmatically smiling regard.

Marianne went to bed in happy ignorance that she was being reassessed by Lady Mauraugh, with the cautious hope that the increased size of the house party might not after all spell disaster.

CHAPTER TEN

Despite the lack of cooperation by the weather, which remained determinedly damp and dismal, the family and guests gathered together at the Hall for Christmas continued to have a very enjoyable time indeed. The comfort of their surroundings must be held greatly responsible, Marianne thought, and this was surely the achievement of Lady Lunswick, who was indeed a notable housekeeper. In the most unobtrusive manner imaginable she held all the reins of household management in her capable hands. The domestic machinery of the huge estate seemed to run along on greased wheels. If there did exist those intra-household clashes that enlivened other great houses from time to time, no echoes of such reached the ears of the guests, whose comfort was insured with no apparent effort. Beds were always warmed, hot water for shaving and washing appeared almost before a guest realized his desire for same, and visiting servants, even those like Selwyn whose deepest instinct was to find fault in everything, could discover little to repeat to their employers, every facility being afforded them to cater to the idiosyncrasies of their respective masters. Had Marianne been acquainted with the world of Society from birth, she would have known of the reputation of Lunswick Hall for hospitality and an excellent table. As it was, she was learning to admire the marchioness all the more for the manner in which she catered to increased numbers and remained unflurried in the face of her sons' occasional capricious behavior which, Marianne was convinced, must necessitate changes in her prearranged schedule for meals. That this superb adaptability was possible with no guest the wiser must be due to the devotion in which Lady Lunswick was held by all her staff. Certainly it entailed much planning and work behind the scenes, yet their hostess seemed always to be available to her guests. It was a source of very real satisfaction to the young girl that Lady Lunswick permitted her to be of some assistance in the planning and carrying out of the domestic arrangements as though she were in fact a daughter of the house.

The success of the house party might also be ascribed in part to a nice mixture of congenial people. Certainly Sir Martin Archer was a man to gladden the heart of any hostess. His secure social position and wide acquaintance among the great families had given him a broad repertoire of anecdotes, and his amusing nonconsequential manner assured his welcome in any group. Gregarious and good-tempered by nature, he was never above being pleased, and was always most willing to enter into whatever plans were being put forth for his entertainment. He could be counted on to dance with the wallflowers, to turn the pages for a young lady performing upon the pianoforte or harp, or to make up a fourth for whist; and his non-demanding personality made him adept at soothing away the attack of nerves and shyness that often rendered new debutantes tongue-tied in their initial appearances on the social scene. True, he might never be able to hold his own amongst the ministers and orators who belonged to the Melbourne House set, nor would he have anything original to contribute to the stimulating literary and artistic conversations taking place at Charles Lamb's "Wednesdays," for his intellect was not of a high order and his conversation could scarcely be said to be brilliant, but his amiability and shrewd social sense made him an asset to any mixed gathering.

The Countess of Mauraugh was another who would be welcomed to decorate any scene even if she never opened her mouth. But the lovely widow had not earned her designation as an Incomparable before her marriage on her beauty alone. She was accomplished, conversable, and charming, exuding a potent appeal that most men found irresistible. Naturally, a woman so abundantly endowed with every attribute to attract the opposite sex was bound to have detractors amongst her own, but whatever might be said of her in tonnish circles, prompted no doubt by jealousy, here in Somerset she was taking pains to be universally agreeable company. Marianne, firmly repressing the instinctive unease she experienced in the widow's company, stoically did her social duty by their guest, though it was an unprofessed relief to escape to Andrew's undemanding society whenever he found an hour to resume the fencing lessons, begun as a joke weeks ago, but now quite seriously pursued by a very apt pupil and a proud instructor.

The assembled company saw very little of the young earl. Apparently his devoted nurse held a strong conviction that a child's place was not among the adults. Because Lady Lunswick insisted, her nephew made a token appearance in the saloon each evening after his meal. After greeting everyone with a poise that was quite remarkable in one so young, he would sidle by degrees to a spot close to Lord Andrew, a process that Marianne watched with some amusement. Obviously he had elevated that young man to a status of hero, but still he was quiet and well-behaved, thrilled with any notice Lord Andrew took of him but never demanding attention. In comparing Richard with the only other child of this age with whom she was acquainted, Marianne found him to be much more self-possessed among adults but less spontaneous than Jamie. Only with Nuisance did Richard seem to approach the gaiety and enthusiasm that characterized the Yorkshire child, so Marianne formed the practice of bringing the pup up to the nursery for a short time each day for a playful session with the little boy. The two were boisterously delighted with each other. At first Marianne had been a bit apprehensive lest Nurse disapprove of the shrieks that emanated from Richard during these uninhibited romps, so she was relieved to observe Nurse's complacency amidst the uproar. Evidently her strict theories on raising children did not preclude a judicious amount of noisy, physical fun-making.

During the week between Christmas and the New Year, the company was pleasantly augmented on several occasions by neighbors exchanging visits. By this time, Marianne had met several of the genteel families in the immediate locale, and had found them to be quite friendly and welcoming, though she remained most drawn to the Hunting-dons, who had become the kind of friends from whom it would be a wrench to part. They formed part of the company tonight, along with her cousins who had driven over from Maplegrove.

Aubrey and Claire had returned early in December and now called at Lunswick Hall with some regularity. Marianne had enjoyed—or endured— (she was not of one mind on this point) the experience of being shown round the ancestral home of her father's family, including the room where he and his two brothers and one sister had made their entrance into the world. She had gravely studied a portrait of her father done when he had been at home between naval engagements, just before the period when he had met her mother, she had guessed. It showed a laughing young man with merry brown eyes and a devil-may-care insouciance about his bearing that both intrigued and slightly repelled her. She admitted that she would have liked to have known her father, but felt again the pain of his not sharing the same desire with respect to herself. How desperately he must have loved her mother to have been so completely shattered at her death, but why had not this love, in later years, been transformed into at least a curiosity about the daughter they had produced? Since she would never know the answer to this riddle, it did not bear dwelling on, she concluded sadly, and resolutely turning her back on the painting, inquired about the rest of her father's family.

She learned she had two more cousins, the sons of her Aunt Margaret who resided in Kent, but somehow she did not feel quite the eager sense of anticipation at the prospect of meeting the rest of her family as she had experienced on learning of the existence of Claire and Aubrey. Lady Lunswick and Andrew were held much closer in her affections than her Carstairs cousins, though she enjoyed Claire's vivacious company in small doses and found Aubrey mildly amusing. However, his attentions to her had been growing increasingly more marked lately, and she was somewhat at a loss to know how to deal with this unlooked-for development. While conceding him to be pleasant and eager to please her, as well as undeniably handsome, she could not help thinking that his intellectual growth had ceased completely at an unusually early age, especially since he never had a word to say for himself should the conversation chance to touch on subjects of more serious content than gossipy *on-dits* of the privileged class of society or the newest fashions in clothes, sports, or entertainment. Moreover, she well remembered their first clash over the actions of the factory workers and wondered, despite his charming attentions to herself, whether he was not *au fond* of a basically unfeeling nature. He had been beside her since Mrs. Huntingdon ceased playing some twenty minutes previously, and she was beginning to experience a slight *ennui* in his company. She replied to his most recent query rather mechanically and fell to studying the other occupants of the saloon with the greater portion of her attention, since Aubrey did not require too much in the way of positive response to keep him rambling on in his usual inconsequential fashion.

At the finish of the musical interlude, a card table had been set up in a corner of the large room for the elder members of the company and Lord Andrew, who had good-naturedly offered to complete the foursome. That his mind was not quite so set as usual on the bloodthirsty contest was attested to by an occasional agonized wail from his unfortunate mother who had drawn him as a partner. Marianne noted with amusement that, though he charmingly begged his long-suffering mama's pardon after each misplay, his attention continued to stray to the group in front of the fire that included the Misses Carstairs and Huntingdon and Lady Mauraugh, who were laughing immoderately at an anecdote Sir Martin had related concerning Poodle Byng, a gentleman who was rarely seen unaccompanied by his pet poodle. The marquess added a sequel to the story that increased the general hilarity, except that Sophia suddenly looked blank. Quietly Lord Lunswick explained to her the relationship obtaining amongst the principals and succeeded in winning a delighted smile of comprehension from Sophia, while the conversation flowing around them took a more sober turn.

Marianne rested a thoughtful gaze on the marquess as he devoted himself to Miss Huntingdon. What an accomplished ladies' man her trustee had proved to be, and how completely he adapted himself to the company in which he found himself. There were four young, unattached females present, she mused, and the marquess wore a different face with each.

Earlier in the evening he had been engaging her provocative cousin Claire in a light flirtation, egging her on to explain the significance of various signals a lady might convey by the skillful use of her fan, though his ward entertained a shrewd suspicion that *he* might as competently have instructed her cousin in the art of flirting with a fan. With Sophia he talked gentle platitudes and took pains to ease her shyness by an air of kindly benevolence and interest in her conversation. Marianne conceded the necessity to combat Sophia's innate reluctance to draw attention to herself in any way, but felt that after an acquaintance covering many years, her trustee should have discovered that he had no need to descend to common-

184

places with the well-read daughter of two intellectually superior parents.

Following this line of thought further, after an encouraging smile that kept the earl of Melford prating contendedly at her side, she considered Lord Lunswick's attitude toward the beautiful countess. This was more difficult to characterize. He did not play the laughing cavalier with Lady Mauraugh, though he never failed to compliment her on her appearance and always requested the favor of some musical selections. He appeared rather more gravely attentive than light-heartedly flirtatious, and invariably displayed exquisite courtesy when addressing his uncle's widow, but even while formulating this opinion Marianne wondered why it should strike her thusly. Lord Lunswick displayed perfect manners in all his dealings with the fair sex, but there was some additional quality in his attitude toward Lady Mauraugh—formality perhaps? No, she must be mistaken. It was obvious that they were very well acquainted, but she could detect neither the ease of comfortable friendship nor the warmth of courtship, not at least in Lord Lunswick's demeanor. Now that she dwelt on the subject it struck her forcibly that Lady Mauraugh *did,* for all her ubiquitous charm, display a well-bred but decided preference for Justin's company. What was more to the point, if this preference was apparent to one who amongst those present was least equipped by the experiences of her life to assess the nuances of male-female relationships, it must be only too

185

obvious to Lord Lunswick. Suddenly convinced beyond any doubt that the Countess of Mauraugh had come here to Somerset for the express purpose of permanently attaching the marquess, Marianne was forced to admit to complete ignorance of her trustee's feelings in the matter. So far he gave nothing away to any interested party, least of all his ward.

Which unsatisfactory conclusion brought her to the last eligible female of the party: herself. Again her thoughtful gaze searched the unrevealing face of her trustee. How did he regard his troublesome ward? Was there a distinctive manner that he reserved for her company? Her intense concentration on the marquess must have reached him where he sat a few feet away, because he glanced up and caught her staring. In the second or so before she managed to avert her gaze and turn with apparent interest to Lord Melford, she was aware of being thoroughly studied. This awareness became acute as she felt rather than saw him rise and saunter over to the plush sofa on which she sat. When he spoke it was to give her a report on a recent speech made in the House of Commons by a member from the midlands addressing himself to some proposed new taxes, and she supposed she had an answer of sorts to one at least of her questions. Perhaps he regarded her as a disembodied intellect, she thought with detachment, as he calmly continued his report in the face of the earl's poorly concealed annoyance at the interruption. However she was inclined to dismiss this notion as incompatible with the evidence of ad-

186

miration in his expression at times when he looked at her. She was beginning to recognize that warm look in a gentleman's eyes now, and to experience a little thrill of gratification at being able to arouse the sentiment, shallow and transitory though it might be. How very pleasant it must be to be beautiful like Lady Mauraugh and know oneself a constant target for such admiration! Another less pleasant notion presented itself for consideration. Perhaps the admiration was solely for her excellent understanding and not her appearance after all. And if this *were* so, why should that sit so ill with her? Had she not been most annoyed in the early days of their acquaintance at the tendency of the marquess to dismiss the mentality of most women as inferior? That he no longer did so, as far as she was concerned, should be a source of great satisfaction, and of course it *was*. But the rueful thought persisted that she was hoist with her own petard.

"Did I not express myself clearly, Marianne? You appear a bit—perturbed perhaps?"

The mild inquiry jerked her back to the present and there she remained, because, as usual, Justin could capture her interest and hold it. In fact, she was forced to admit, though quite privately for she had no slightest intention of pandering to her trustee's vanity, that he was proving a fascinating companion, and one moreover whose company she welcomed wholeheartedly, though she persisted in her refusal to seek him out at any time. The wry thought intruded that this made her unique amongst the present company, the fem-

187

inine part that is, because even Sophia shyly invited his presence with her eyes, but Marianne had her own theory as to why Sophia preferred Justin's company.

When the hotly contested card game eventually broke up, Lord Andrew rose and stretched his arms behind his back to relieve the cramped muscles, then strolled over to the long windows which gave onto the rose garden. He twitched the drape aside and stood studying the sky for a moment.

"The stars are very bright tonight," he tossed over his shoulder before wandering back to the center of the room. "It is my guess it will stay clear for a while now, so we may get in some riding at last."

"Oh, delightful!" cried Lady Mauraugh enthusiastically. "I have not been on horseback since I arrived. Do say we might ride tomorrow, Justin." The green-eyed beauty smiled at her host, confident of her powers of persuasion.

"Of course, Aurelie. I think we'd all welcome the opportunity of a good ride. Marianne, I have yet to see you put Ebony through his paces. Would you like to ride tomorrow?"

"Yes, I'd love to."

The gentlemen agreed that an outing was a splendid idea, and the earl and Miss Carstairs were easily persuaded to join the riding party.

"And you will come too, will you not, Sophie?" coaxed Marianne with a smile for her friend.

"Oh, no! I mean, I thank you but I beg you will hold me excused."

"Oh come, Sophie, be a sport," said Andrew in

wheedling tones. "I'll see you get a nice placid mount. Gretel will carry you in armchair comfort. You'll enjoy it."

Painful color surged to the young girl's cheeks but she kept her eyes on Marianne. "Another time perhaps. There were things I planned to do tomorrow."

"Why not join the party, my dear," inserted her father genially. "You've been cooped up inside for the better part of a sennight."

Mrs. Huntingdon, after a swift glance at her daughter's face and a speaking look for her husband, apologized gracefully for having already committed Sophia to some parish plans for the morrow. She began to make her thanks for a delightful evening, and the Huntingdons departed shortly thereafter. Once they had agreed on a time for the riding party, the earl and Miss Carstairs also took their leave.

Marianne turned to Lord Andrew. "Did Sophia never enjoy riding then, Andrew?"

"She was used to come with us on occasion. It is not that she rides badly, only that she tires more quickly than most."

"Oh, then I apprehend she feared to hold us back tomorrow. We must plan a nice easy ride soon."

"Yes, but not tomorrow," said the countess gaily. "I am longing for a good gallop on Diamond."

"Is that the white mare you brought with you?" inquired Lord Andrew with interest.

"Yes. Is she not beautiful? Justin selected her for me last year."

Involuntarily Marianne's eyes flew from Lady Mauraugh's smiling countenance to her trustee's face, but she could read nothing there. She realized suddenly how very tired she was and was deeply thankful that the marchioness suggested an early night for the riding party.

The sunshine streaming through her window next morning confirmed Lord Andrew's weather prophecy. A combination of welcome sunshine and pleasurable anticipation lent spring to her movements. With the maid's help she coiled her heavy black hair low on her neck to make room for the dashing black-plumed beaver hat. She paused for an instant to admire the snowy frills at her wrists and throat, and accepted her gloves and crop from the maid with a smile.

The party assembled at the main entrance scarcely ten minutes past the appointed hour, except for the countess who arrived just late enough for everyone to be mounted. She trilled a breathless apology and all eyes turned to survey the picture she made in her light blue riding dress, daringly styled à la Hussar with navy braided trim. The large hat in a matching navy blue with three curling white ostrich plumes set off her red-gold curls to perfection. Sir Martin dismounted to take the groom's place in assisting her to mount and was rewarded with a brilliant smile.

Lord Andrew, mounted beside his brother's large bay, noted the marquess' attention on the three ladies of the party who were clustered together, waiting while the groom adjusted Lady Mauraugh's stirrup. He drawled lazily:

"What would you wager on the chance of assembling three more beautiful females in one spot at the same time?"

"Not a groat," was the prompt reply.

"All so different too," mused Andrew, pursuing his theme. "Miss Carstairs sparkles with vitality, looking like a woodland creature herself in that leaf-green color. My Aunt Aurelie is of course the very embodiment of classical perfection, wouldn't you say?"

"Oh, indubitably."

"And then there is Marianne. How can one characterize Marianne in a few well-chosen words?" He paused to consider, but the marquess spoke first.

"Beauty without artifice," he suggested quietly, his eyes on his ward's face as she acknowledged a remark of Sir Martin's with a quick appreciative smile.

"Very good, Justin," approved his brother. "You have hit her off exactly. Marianne practices none of the usual female tricks on a fellow. A very comfortable girl to have around, do you not agree?"

Whether the little smile on his brother's lips signified agreement or not was left unspecified as the party began moving off. At first they kept more or less together, going at a slow pace and chatting amongst themselves, but this tame activity quickly palled on Lord Andrew.

"Marianne!" he called imperatively. "Let's *go!*"

The girl needed no urging. She let Ebony have his head and the two rapidly left the laggards behind.

Lady Mauraugh was cantering beside the marquess, whose eyes were trained on the flying figures far ahead.

"Your ward rides very well, though her style is perhaps not best suited to Hyde Park," she remarked sweetly.

"You ride well yourself and your style *is* suited to the Park."

"Do you remember the wonderful rides we used to have, Justin?"

"I remember everything," was the cryptic rejoinder. "Shall we give the horses some real exercise now?"

He turned to include the rest of the party in the invitation and soon they were all galloping over the hilly field. They caught up with Lord Andrew and Lady Marianne where they awaited them beside a gurgling stream. After the horses had drunk, the party moved off again, more slowly this time through a delightful stretch of trees whose bare branches allowed the sun's warming rays to penetrate. The ranks had shifted again and now the earl and the marquess rode slightly ahead with Lady Marianne.

"Justin!"

At Andrew's imperative call the three riders turned and saw a scene of confusion behind them. Sir Martin appeared to be supporting the collapsed figure of Lady Mauraugh with one arm while he controlled his own horse. Lord Andrew had the reins of the white horse, but his attention was on Miss Carstairs who was attempting to bring her horse under control again. Evidently he had taken exception to something on the path and was rearing.

The marquess, reacting immediately, galloped back, leaving the others to follow within seconds.

"What happened?" He brought Mountain right up to Miss Carstairs' mount, leaving Andrew free to give Diamond's reins to Sir Martin who was still supporting the countess. Lord Andrew jumped down and received the hatless figure into his arms a moment before his brother felt it safe to leave the excitable gray Miss Carstairs was riding.

Lady Mauraugh was indicating that she was able to stand, but it was Sir Martin who answered the marquess' question in a voice full of puzzlement.

"She must not have seen that low hanging branch because she rode right into it."

The countess was standing unaided now except for Andrew's arm. One gloved hand was rubbing the back of her head lightly. Her color was good but she winced slightly at the touch and laughed shakily, "I don't know how I can have been so stupid. I fear I was wool-gathering."

The marquess removed her hand and gently explored her scalp with his own fingers. "Thank heavens the skin is not broken and there is merely a very slight swelling. Is there much pain?" he inquired, looking concernedly into the green eyes.

"No, at least just a very little, less than I deserve perhaps." She glanced round at the others apologetically. "I am so sorry to spoil your ride with this stupid accident. Please do go on. Justin will see me home."

"Yes, of course. Are you able to ride?" On receiving an affirmative answer, the marquess lifted her into the saddle amidst a chorus of comments from the others to the effect that they should all return together.

"Oh, please!" Lady Mauraugh looked distressed. "I should feel much worse if I thought I had curtailed everyone's pleasure. Please do go on."

"I have had enough riding for today," declared Miss Carstairs. "I'll come along with you, my lord, in the event Lady Mauraugh becomes faint."

He smiled his approval at her. Lady Mauraugh's lips compressed.

"Really, I shall be quite all right with Justin," she protested strongly. "I shall feel I have ruined your morning."

"No need of that," Lord Andrew declared bracingly. "The air has grown more chill in the last half hour. It is time for all the ladies to return to the Hall for a welcome cup of coffee."

During this exchange Marianne had dismounted and retrieved Lady Mauraugh's hat from the path. Evidently that had been the object that had frightened Claire's mount. Back in the saddle, she was brushing the dirt from the white plumes when Claire edged close and said for her ears alone, "The only pain her ladyship is suffering at the moment is disappointment that her scheme failed in its object."

The violet eyes widened and studied her cousin's

face, alight with malicious amusement. "What are you saying?"

"That she deliberately rode into that branch, of course, so she might lure Lord Lunswick away from the party."

"You must be mistaken."

"I saw her," replied Claire calmly. "I would wager my mother's pearls that her hat is the only thing to sustain an injury."

Marianne made no reply because the men had all remounted, but her cousin's words had given her plenty of food for conjecture on the return trip, which was a strangely quiet one. When Lady Mauraugh attempted to initiate a conversation, the marquess suggested quite kindly that talking would only increase her headache. He rode almost silently by her side, and the others seemed to be absorbed in their own thoughts for there was very little conversation exchanged.

Marianne's thoughts were concerned with the intelligence conveyed to her by her cousin. Though there wasn't much for which she would take Claire's word, she did not disbelieve her in this instance. Claire had been quite convinced in her own mind that the countess had contrived the accident, so Marianne was not alone in thinking the beautiful widow was hunting the marquess in earnest. He accorded her all the consideration due to a guest, but to Marianne's eye he did not appear to seek out her company. Did this morning's incident indicate desperation? The countess could not realistically extend her visit much past the

Christmas season except at the specific request of the marquess. Despite her efforts there was only a superficial cordiality in the relationship with her sister-in-law, and little Richard's presence at the Hall went virtually unnoticed though his need was the ostensible reason for the visit. As they entered the carriage drive to the main entrance, she decided it was time to shelve the question for the present. Doubtless all would come clear in due course.

She was to have those sentiments recalled strongly to mind later that same night. The marquess was hosting a sizable reception and all the neighboring gentry had been able to attend thanks to the clear weather. Two reception rooms were given over to accommodate the guests, but even so by eleven o'clock the crowd of constantly moving humanity had raised the temperature to uncomfortable levels in both. Lady Lunswick, unlike the majority of her contemporaries, did not fear the night air, but it would have been unthinkable to throw open a few windows for a moment to let in a cooling draft. Marianne, in the vicinity of her hostess momentarily, suggested she slip into her morning room and relax for a short time in private.

"For you are looking flushed, Ma'am, and I suspect you have the headache a trifle, or will have if you continue here."

"You are quite correct, my child. I shall be glad when this evening is over, but hospitality is expected of us at this time of year. I find I no longer have the same pleasure in huge gatherings as when

196

I was younger. Let us step into the conservatory for a short spell. It will be cooler with all that glass, and I love that damp earthy smell."

There was only one wall light near the entrance and the conservatory itself was lit only by the silvered moonlight. The two women stood close together, quietly savoring the damp cool air and odor of greenery for a time while their eyes adjusted to the relative gloom. Almost immediately, however, Marianne became aware of a murmur of voices somewhere to their left.

"There is someone here already," she whispered, touching her companion's arm lightly. "Perhaps we had best not . . ."

The whisper died in her throat as her seeking eyes made out two figures in intimate conversation. Even as she recognized the gentleman by the set of his shoulders, the white-garbed feminine form raised her hands to those same shoulders and her lips invitingly to his. For an instant the man seemed to hesitate, arms at his side, then he bent his head to hers and encircled the slight form in strong arms. The marchioness emitted a small gasp and stiffened under the hand that had tightened involuntarily on her arm. As she made an instinctive movement forward, Marianne gently but firmly drew her back through the doorway by which they had entered the conservatory. In the dim light of the single wall sconce they stared at each other. Noting the older woman's pallor, Marianne led her unprotestingly down a corridor and, opening the door to her morning room, gently pushed her hostess inside. She closed the door softly, then sped to the room where the buffet was already spread. Casting a hasty eye over the food that would be served quite soon now, she settled for a claret cup, pouring a good-sized glass with hands that shook slightly.

CHAPTER ELEVEN

When Marianne returned to the morning room shortly thereafter, having safely negotiated the route with claret cup intact, one glance assured her that the ghastly pallor that had frightened her had gone from the marchioness' face. Her relief was short-lived, however, for Lady Lunswick was seen to be suffering a great agitation of spirits if her incessant pacing of the small room was a true manifestation of her mental state. As the young girl stood hesitating just within the room, Lady Lunswick swung around again furiously, her soft lilac skirts whipping about her.

"How could he—how *could* Justin be so stupid as to allow himself to be entrapped by *that woman?*" she almost snarled, baring her even white teeth. Caring nothing for any sort of response, she resumed the erratic pacing and her hands were clenching and unclenching at her sides. On her next swing by Marianne, the girl stopped her and thrust the glass into her hand, folding her own firmly on top. She gentled the older woman into the nearest chair.

"Drink this, please. It will steady you. It is almost time to serve supper, and you will be missed shortly."

Suddenly all the fight went out of the marchioness. Meekly she drank from the glass and handed it back to the anxious girl kneeling by her chair. Their eyes were almost on a level and Marianne saw tears shining in Lady Lunswick's.

"How could he, Marianne?" she repeated, this time without the fury.

"You wished him to marry, ma'am," the girl reminded her softly, averting her own eyes from the despair mirrored in the other woman's face.

"Yes, but not *that woman!*" her hostess declared passionately. "Any other, even that baggage, Claire, would do better."

"Surely, ma'am, you must have suspected that Lady Mauraugh felt—that she was greatly attached to the marquess?"

Lady Lunswick waved an impatient hand. "Oh, *her!* Of course I knew what her game was before she came here, but I would not credit that Justin could be such a fool as to let himself be attracted by such a woman, not after what she did!"

There was a palpitating little silence while rampant curiosity warred with well-bred reserve in Marianne. Curiosity won.

"I do not perfectly understand, ma'am. Do you feel Lady Mauraugh is being disloyal to your brother by contemplating another marriage so soon after his death? She has observed the period of mourning."

"Oh, William! William got what he asked for—

and paid for," she replied bitterly. "I am referring to what she did to Justin."

"What did she do to Justin?"

Lady Lunswick's eyes came back to her guest's face in a considering look. "I thought you must have heard the story by now, from Andrew, or Sophia perhaps. Everyone knew, the whole world knew."

Marianne contented herself with a negative shake of her head.

Lady Lunswick held out her hand for the glass and drained it before embarking on her tale.

"It happened over five years ago. Justin was home from the Peninsula to recover from a troublesome wound and he met Aurelie, who was one of the Incomparables of her season. Well, you may guess what effect she had on him. He was five and twenty, restless at being out of the fighting, handsome in his regimentals, and ripe for falling in love, which he proceeded to do at first sight of Aurelie. And she gave him every encouragement to do so, Marianne. They were taking bets on the date of the match in all the clubs in town. Then, just before he made the offer, Justin presented his uncle to Aurelie. When he proposed she stalled for time, said they had not known each other very long and a lot more in the same vein which I shall spare you. To end the story, within a week Aurelie was engaged to William and Justin had gone back to Spain. I got the whole story from Harry later. Justin refused all comment and he changed from an open, smiling young man to the guarded cynic you see now."

"She may have found she loved your brother, Ma'am," Marianne offered tentatively, not that she believed it.

"Rubbish! A man four and twenty years her senior and a victim to the gout into the bargain! As much as Aurelie could love another person than herself she was in love with Justin, or at least it deeply gratified her vanity to be courted by such a handsome and popular young man. Wealth and a title, weighted against a second son's prospects, swung the decision in William's favor. It absolutely sickens me to think she will now achieve a higher rank and greater wealth, and ruin my son's life a second time."

"But if she loves him and he still loves her, his life will be far from ruined."

"Aurelie is much too spoiled and selfish to make any man happy for long. She thrives on the adulation of all men. For Justin I want a woman who will love him deeply, not one who is merely gratified to be loved *by* him."

"And who shall blame you, Ma'am? But perhaps Justin prefers to marry a woman whom *he* deeply loves and chance that the match will prosper."

The marchioness sighed. "You may be right, my child. In any case there is nothing I can do save put a good face on the situation. Justin is a man grown. But I had so hoped he would see . . ."

Marianne waited but Lady Lunswick evidently thought better of what she had been about to utter and merely sighed gustily again. She rose from the chair and squared her shoulders. She smiled, albeit a trifle wearily at Marianne.

"It is high time I went back to my guests. Thank you, my dear child, for staying here with me during this time. Forgive me for crying on your shoulder as it were."

She went out then, but the girl did not follow immediately. She dropped into the chair vacated by Lady Lunswick and rested her head against the high back. She sat there with her eyes closed for several minutes while she recovered, or sought to recover, from the effects of two dramatic events she could well have done without. It was difficult to say which had been more distressing—witnessing the embrace between the marquess and the widow, or being the recipient of his mother's bitter confidences. She might tell herself with cool logic that it was none of her affair whom the marquess kissed or whom he married, but she was unable to carry the thought one step further and agree that it was *nothing* to her whom he might kiss or marry, for the uncomfortable truth was that the sight of that embrace had produced an almost physical ache somewhere deep within her that the subsequent disclosures by the marchioness had increased tenfold. It was a minor consolation to know that she had revealed none of this to Lady Lunswick. Stubborn pride had its value at times, and she could not have borne the older woman's sympathy at that moment. Why had she not realized earlier that she had succumbed to the charm and physical attractions of her trustee? It wasn't love, she reminded herself bleakly, because she was not even sure she *liked* the marquess very much, but even in the beginning when she had disliked him quite

intensely there had been an equally strong awareness of his physical magnificence, which had culminated tonight in a stabbing desire to be in Lady
Mauraugh's place in the conservatory. The fact
that this burning sensation was only infatuation
should make it easier to overcome. And from this
moment forward, the concealment and eventual
eradication of this degrading infatuation would
become her single-minded pursuit until she could
escape from Lunswick Hall.

To this end she walked over to the mirror above
the fireplace and unnecessarily straightened the
black sash of her gray satin gown. She smoothed
one of her silky black brows with a damp fingertip
and tucked a stray lock of hair back into the
braided coronet, all the while practicing her smile
which would have to be judged a rather wavering
effort at first. The smile became real, though rueful, as she acknowledged that these maneuvers
were nothing more than a form of stalling, so great
was her reluctance to rejoin the party. She promptly turned her back on her reflection and strode
purposefully to the door.

Even with pride to the rescue, the remaining
hour of the reception seemed to drag out inter-
minably for Marianne. She smiled and chatted with
acquaintances though she could not have told anyone the topics covered, and made a pretense of
eating some unidentifiable concoctions. She noted
that Lady Lunswick performed her duties as
hostess with her usual grace, though her smile appeared a bit set. When she spotted the marquess'
tall figure wending its way rather purposefully in

her direction, she slipped unobtrusively into the other reception room and joined a laughing group clustered around the pianoforte. Somehow she could not contemplate the possibility of a conversation on literature or politics with her trustee tonight, and as for Lady Mauraugh, who was surrounded by admiring cavaliers as usual, Marianne took care to avoid catching even the merest glimpse of that beautiful, satisfied countenance. Hopefully, by tomorrow she would be able to look at the countess without displaying the dislike and jealousy that were presently gnawing at her spirit.

By dint of careful maneuvering that would have done credit to a field general, she managed to avoid contact with the two people who could threaten her hard-won composure, but this and the effort required to produce the spurious affability with which she met all others, took its toll in nervous energy. By the time the last guest had departed she was thoroughly exhausted. The blessed oblivion of sleep was not quickly summoned, however, because she was also restless, unhappy and, despite her earlier resolutions, unsure of her ability to meet the challenge she had set herself with all flags flying. It was close to the false dawn before she fell into a heavy slumber, from which she was awakened abruptly by the maid bringing in chocolate. She eyed the drink with disfavor and the dark-colored morning gown the girl laid out with an even more jaundiced eye.

The pleasant anticipation with which she had greeted each new day during the visit had increased with Lord Andrew's arrival and intensified further with the return of her trustee. Now it was gone, dispersed by an embrace she had not been meant to witness, and she needed something to counteract the sense of foreboding that pressed on her like a physical weight. Dismissing the maid with a smile, Marianne studied her wardrobe with a concentration she would have characterized as ridiculous two short months ago. But lovely clothes were a protective shell for a woman, and since last night's disaster there was no denying she needed all the armor she might gather about her, especially today if there was to be a betrothal announcement. Her searching eye fell on a heavy soft cotton gown that she had ordered on impulse but never as yet worn. It was neither pink nor red but a delicious shade somewhere between, delicately patterned with a tracery of white leaves and flowers. Made in a simple style that closely followed the lines of her figure, it had long, tight sleeves dripping with snowy lace over the hands. An inserted yoke of the same exquisite Belgian lace below the high collar was allowed to take the shaping of its design over the bodice. There was no other ornamentation. Seriously considering her reflection in the silver-framed mirror, Marianne made the pleasant discovery that nothing had ever been more becoming to her coloring. It enhanced the natural color in cheeks and lips and made a lovely contrast to her dark hair. She wasted a few seconds wishing for bouncing curls like Claire's as she secured her smoothly coiled locks. Lady Lunswick generally acceded to Marianne's wishes regarding her wardrobe, but for some unexplained reason she was adamant about retaining the unfashionably long hair. Oh, well, since nothing would serve to change its color in any case what did it matter how she wore it? At least the smooth style spared her the necessity of resorting to nightly curl papers and irons to achieve a popular look.

The morning was well advanced before she descended to the breakfast parlor, but any hopes of avoiding the marquess who invariably ate early, or the countess who just as invariably remained in her room after a social evening, were dashed even before she had crossed the threshold, as she distinguished their voices amidst the muted sounds of china and metal. Perhaps it would be best to get the announcement over with and end the doubts—hopes?—that persisted. She raised her chin and stepped through the entrance with a serene smile and a general greeting to the assembled company. Evidently everyone had risen late because all residents both permanent and temporary were present.

"You win the prize for lazing today, Marianne," quipped Lord Andrew. "Even my aunt is up before you. By Jove, I like that getup, though. You look like a nice tasty dish of strawberries and cream."

Amidst the chuckles that followed this saucy remark, Marianne wrinkled her nose at him but could not prevent herself from slanting a quick peek at the marquess. He had already returned his attention to his plate, and she promptly hated herself for caring.

Sir Martin smiled at her warmly and pulled out the chair beside Lady Lunswick before Coleman could perform this office for the latecomer. Lady Mauraugh had given her one comprehensive narrow-eyed stare and a polite "good morning." Sir Martin and Lady Lunswick, however, vied with each other in assuring her that she looked utterly charming in her deep-pink gown.

"Do you confine your mourning dress to public appearances only, Lady Marianne?" If there was a slight edge to the countess' smiling inquiry, it would undoubtedly escape the masculine ear.

"That is correct," Marianne replied, looking straight at her questioner. "I wear black in public to avoid causing embarrassment to my hostess."

"You should wear this color more often. It suits you charmingly," her trustee inserted smoothly, and immediately inquired everyone's plans for the day.

The talk remained away from personalities for the remainder of the meal. Marianne contributed little beyond an agreement that she would ride with Andrew before lunch. She was forming polite phrases of congratulations in her mind as she sat tensely, awaiting an announcement that did not come. As the meal drew to a close she scarcely knew whether she was relieved to postpone the ordeal or frustrated because it was all to do over again. To her discerning eye, Lady Lunswick was experiencing unqualified relief as she rose to leave the breakfast parlor. She had been slightly abstracted during the meal and had rather avoided her elder son's eye. Marianne noticed the marquess glancing at his mother once or twice with a faintly puzzled air, but he made no remarks of a personal nature. Since

207

he and Sir Martin had made plans to inspect a promising colt owned by a gentleman residing some twenty or so miles away, they took their leave immediately. Marianne had caught the flash of disappointment in Lady Mauraugh's face as the gentlemen's plans were announced, and she held her breath lest Lord Andrew should feel constrained to invite the widow to join them. He, however, had calmly continued to eat his way through his customary sustaining repast as though he had heard nothing. The marquess had then smilingly suggested that Lady Mauraugh might enjoy joining his brother and his ward on their ride, but she had declined with cool civility.

"No, I thank you. My head still aches a trifle from yesterday's accident. I shall be pleased to spend a quiet day indoors."

Offering up mental thanks for small blessings, Marianne made her escape from the room before her trustee could carry his solicitous concern for his beautiful guest's comfort to the extent of perhaps requesting his ward to forego her ride in order to bear the former company.

However nothing of that nature intervened to spoil her outing with Lord Andrew. The weather had stayed brisk and brilliant and Marianne returned to the Hall in better spirits. At lunch she accepted his invitation to receive some fencing instruction, and in mid-afternoon joined him in the fascinating room set aside for the display of the magnificent collection of old weapons the Raymond family had amassed through the years. The walls were hung with battle axes and lances and gorgeously decorated swords. Tall, glass-fronted cabinets contained numerous examples of firearms from muskets to handsomely detailed dueling pistols, including some fine modern specimens by Joseph Manton. Marianne enjoyed coming in here and wandering around to examine the marvelously worked sword hilts and scabbards, some of them richly encrusted with jewels. She enjoyed her fencing lessons too, but the sport demanded intense concentration and today's lesson went badly at first. Whatever her mental state, her riding could not be faulted because it was so much a part of her, but the lowness of spirits oppressing her since witnessing that fond embrace in the conservatory robbed her of the concentration necessary for a creditable performance with her foil against Lord Andrew. Time and again he popped in a hit over or under her guard, calling out criticisms as the session progressed.

"You are too slow to disengage! Don't drop your point after that parry. Be prepared for another thrust in the same position."

Finally he stopped dead in disgust and glared at his erstwhile promising pupil. "Your mind is elsewhere today. I could have slain you a dozen times. Are you tired? Do you wish to stop?"

Marianne shook her head, stung by his criticism.

"No, no, let us continue. I shall do better." And her defense did improve, but Lord Andrew was still not satisfied.

"Where is your attack today? Do not forget the best defense is a good offense. Press me! Lunge! Pretend I'm my Aunt Aurelie."

This outrageous remark shocked a small choke of laughter from Marianne, but she resolutely remained silent and raised her foil menacingly.

"Ah, that's better. Press your advantage now. Very good. Be ready to spring back immediately when I parry and advance. Watch for an opening."

They were advancing and retreating about the large room. If there was still less skill than enthusiasm in Marianne's attack, it failed to diminish her pleasure in the exercise.

"Stop!"

Startled at the sharp command, Marianne obeyed instantly, but she was in mid-thrust. In righting her balance, her foil made accidental contact with Lord Andrew's chin and she was horrified to see a slight red line appear.

"Andrew! I have hurt you but I scarcely understand how." She dropped her foil precipitously and pulled a handkerchief from the pocket of her gown which she pressed to his face for an instant.

"Calm yourself, it is the merest nothing. I saw your button had worked loose. That's why I shouted. It stings a bit but I don't think it is bleeding." He examined the handkerchief and showed her that it was almost unmarked.

"Thank heavens," she breathed in heartfelt relief. "I do most sincerely beg your pardon, Andrew."

"You have little science as yet, but there is no denying you are a dangerous wench," he said lightly, retrieving her foil from the floor and replacing the button securely.

"Ah, but I can take away the pain I inflict," she

declared mischievously and placing her hand on his shoulder, she pressed her lips fleetingly to the scratch.

He grinned at her. "As I said, a dangerous wench."

"I take it congratulations are in order?"

The smiling couple turned toward the doorway from which the voice had issued. The marquess closed the door behind him with a deliberate air and advanced slowly into the room, his face inscrutable.

"Oh no," Marianne protested. "I do not deserve to be congratulated for that hit. Andrew was off guard and it was purely an accident."

At his brother's incredulous expression Lord Andrew burst into laughter. "He does not mean the hit, you pea goose. He's referring to the balm you so generously applied to my wound."

Marianne looked puzzled. "Congratulations?"

"I realize your social experience has been limited, but even in Yorkshire it is customary for a young lady to announce her betrothal after being discovered in an embrace." Instantly he wished the hateful words unsaid, as he watched the almost forgotten stillness come over her face, but before he might begin to frame an apology, she was answering quietly:

"Then for the sake of her reputation, I suggest you lose no time in repairing with Lady Mauraugh to the nearest church."

It was a magnificent Parthian arrow, he conceded, but he had no slightest intention of allowing her to get away with it. As she made to slip past him with her head held high, he detained her with a none too gentle hand on her elbow. After one pointed glance at the hand holding her arm, she stood quite still, facing him calmly. Neither was aware that Lord Andrew's initial amazement at the events of the last minute had turned to intense speculation as he studied the two cold faces before him.

"I think you will concede the necessity of explaining that remark before you leave this room." The marquess' voice was silkily smooth but his eyes were not.

Marianne assumed an air of perplexity. "As you wish, sir, though I confess I cannot see the necessity of detailing on which *particular* occasion you were observed." She allowed her voice to trail off.

Despite his anger and chagrin, the marquess' lips twitched at this readiness to offer battle. "You little shrew! You know quite well there was only one occasion . . ."

"I know no such thing!" The hot rejoinder belied her earlier cool calm and she bitterly regretted the lapse as his smile widened, but he was continuing thoughtfully: "So you were in the conservatory last night. Were you alone?"

"The conservatory, was it? Is that why you wished that henwitted Evans girl on me as I was heading for a breath of air? So you and my aunt might dally in the conservatory?"

The marquess' lips tightened but he ignored his brother's attempts to exacerbate the situation. His eyes never left his ward's face.

"Were you alone?" he repeated.

"Lady Lunswick was with me."

"So that accounts for Mama's strange behavior today. *Damnation!*"

Marianne displayed ostentatious outrage and made to remove herself from the room, ignoring the fact that *she* had experienced a strong desire to utter a few oaths herself in the last twenty-four hours. If it was war he wanted, war he should have.

"Don't be missish," he barked impatiently. "We must think what is to be done. I shall need your help."

"To attend the bride at your nuptials?" Marianne had paused near the door and she met his eyes steadily.

"Is it legal for my Aunt Aurelie to become my sister Aurelie?" inquired Lord Andrew pensively. "It sounds vaguely incestuous to me."

"Andrew! If you cannot refrain from such tasteless attempts at humor, then leave us." The marquess turned his back on his brother and walked slowly toward the waiting girl. He said quietly, "There is no question of my marrying Lady Mauraugh."

Her heart started racing at his words and the look in his eyes, but she ignored her heart.

"Then allow me to tell you, my lord, that I find your behavior last night utterly incomprehensible, and also your behavior on entering this room today."

He sighed in frustration. "I know how it must appear to you, but can you understand there are some things a gentleman does not do? When a

213

beautiful woman invites an embrace he does not spurn her, but neither is he compelled to marry her."

"Not even if the embrace is witnessed, and the lady's reputation is at stake? That is *not* what you implied ten minutes ago."

"You may count on me to do the correct thing, Marianne," offered Lord Andrew generously.

Marianne smiled at him perfunctorily, but her attention returned to the marquess, who ignored the interruption.

"The cases are completely dissimilar. You are a young, innocent girl. Conduct that might be dismissed in a more experienced female would brand *you* as fast, and ruin your chances of marriage."

"I see. Then you would advise me to accept Andrew's obliging offer?"

He glowered at her though his anger was directed mainly at himself for failing to note the trap. "Of course not! Very well. I apologize for my actions on entering this room; they were totally uncalled for. Are we now quits, you little spitfire?"

"*We* are, but if I were Lady Mauraugh I should be in the hourly expectation of receiving an offer from you."

"On the contrary, if you were Lady Mauraugh, you would know that you could not compel an offer by throwing yourself at a man's head unless he wished to make the offer in the first place."

"And you do not?"

"I do not."

Recalling that impassioned embrace, she looked faintly troubled and exclaimed bitterly, "Men have reserved every advantage to themselves in this life!" She turned on her heel and headed for the door for the third time. At least Lady Lunswick's mind might be set at rest. Again she was detained.

"Stay, Marianne! As I said, though I am in no way compelled to offer for Lady Mauraugh there is no denying the situation is a bit awkward while she remains my mother's guest."

"That is scarcely my affair."

"What you need, Justin, is another female in tow, to draw fire as it were."

For the first time the marquess looked with approval on his brother. Marianne's eyes narrowed but she remained silent.

"An excellent suggestion," agreed the marquess. "If I were seen to be paying court to another, Aurelie would soon realize that I have no intention of resuming—" He broke off, furious with himself for the slip.

"Of resuming your former *affaire*?" The faint hope that Marianne was still in ignorance of his earlier relationship with the widow was dashed by her quick interruption. "Why not? Obviously she wants to marry you. You offered for her once and she is no less beautiful now. Are you intent on punishing her a little before you accept her?"

"No! I offered once, but not twice. I am no longer young and impressionable. However I would spare us both the embarrassment of a direct confrontation. Aurelie is not slow to size up a situation; she will not require that it be spelled out for her."

Lord Andrew agreed heartily. "Now it only re-

215

mains to choose someone to be the object of your gallantry."

"Well, Claire would be the obvious choice," offered Marianne. "You pay her a great deal of flattering attention, and I have seen Lady Mauraugh observing you together."

Lord Andrew looked horrified. "Good grief, girl, do you not see that that would be tantamount to jumping from the frying pan into the fire? Don't be so idiotish!"

"Well, she should have to be told, of course, but I am persuaded she would cooperate enthusiastically," Marianne persisted.

Now the marquess intervened. "*Not* Miss Carstairs. In consideration for Lady Mauraugh, the fewer people who know about this the better." He was looking expectantly at Marianne whose color had risen slightly.

She did not pretend to misunderstand him. "I am sorry, my lord, but I have no talent for playacting, and in any case Lady Mauraugh is never going to believe you might actually prefer *me* to her."

"*I* shall do any play-acting required, and you are quite mistaken if you really feel Lady Mauraugh will experience the slightest difficulty in accepting such a situation." At Marianne's doubtful expression, he continued softly, "You may take my word for it that Aurelie watches *you* much more closely than she observes Miss Carstairs. Is this not so, Andrew?"

"Oh, absolutely." Andrew had no hesitation in

corroborating his brother's startling pronouncement. "Now, do not be a little marplot, Marianne. Simplicity is the key to a successful operation. All you have to do is refrain from giving Justin the cold shoulder and the thing is done."

For a palpitating moment Marianne stared from one brother to the other, her bottom lip gripped in her teeth, then she replied gravely, "I mislike the entire situation, but I shall not betray you." And this time she whisked herself out of the room before either of her tormentors could prevent her removal.

For a long instant there was no sound in the large room. The marquess' silence was brooding and his brother's expectant. Finally, the younger man broke it to say cheerfully:

"Well, thanks entirely to *my* ingenious efforts you managed to brush through that without being completely rolled up, horse, foot, and guns."

"If you are in the expectation of receiving gratitude for some of your more infelicitous comments during this regrettable interlude, you'll be sadly disappointed."

Undaunted by the censure in his brother's tones, Lord Andrew persisted. "I had to do my utmost to keep the channels of communication open lest your conversation degenerate into a pure slanging match. Is it not just like a woman, though, to be always where she should *not* be, hearing and seeing what was never meant for her ears and eyes?" As his brother continued to stare at nothing identifiable, he went on reflectively. "Though I must say, for a man who denies he wishes to wed a woman, you have some odd notions of how best to convince her of this fact."

Justin held up his hand in a fencer's gesture. "Touché! I was a fool to allow myself to be so neatly maneuvered but . . ." Here he paused before continuing with obvious difficulty, "I had a bad tumble over Aurelie once. Even last year when I went up to Northumberland for Uncle's funeral, I was not quite sure how I felt about her. Last night, in the conservatory, well, it was an opportunity to discover if there was any lingering—" he stopped abruptly. "And there was *not*," he finished briskly.

"Naturally, I am delighted that you have convinced yourself there's nothing deader than a dead love. I strongly doubt, however, that you have convinced Marianne of this, but perhaps it does not signify?" He paused suggestively and studied his brother intently.

Justin's mouth twisted in a wry grimace, and he said dryly:

"A knowing one, aren't you? Too quick by half." With that he turned on his heel and strode swiftly from the room, leaving behind a singularly unabashed young man who whistled a popular march tune while he put the foils back in their proper places.

CHAPTER TWELVE

With extreme reluctance Marianne closed her bedroom door behind her and headed down the corridor toward the stairway. She wished she'd had the sense to plead the headache so she might avoid going to dinner, however much it went against the grain with her to play the coward. The more she had dwelt on the way Andrew and her trustee had maneuvered her into taking part in this distasteful charade, the more resentful she had become. Heaven knew she held no brief for Lady Mauraugh, but it was quite odious to be scheming against the woman in this fashion. Not that this opinion was shared by Lady Lunswick! On the contrary, when Marianne had reported the conversation that had taken place in the armory to her hostess, the latter had all but danced for joy to learn her son did not wish to marry her sister-in-law. She brushed aside as excessively scrupulous Marianne's reluctance to participate in the farce of courtship to deter the countess from her pursuit of Justin; in short, she applauded the scheme whole-heartedly. Marianne was rendered speechless as it was clearly impossible that she explain to her hostess that the scene in the armory, following the one she had witnessed in the conservatory, had brought rushing back all her initial dislike of her ladyship's elder son. Since his return from London she had been liking the marquess all too well indeed, as witnessed by the distress she had experienced on seeing him and Lady Mauraugh in that embrace. But at least she could not have thought ill of him if he kissed the beautiful widow because he still wished to marry her. However, he had made it abundantly clear that he had no such intention, and in her eyes that put him smack in the ranks of the philanderers, a class of persons for whom she felt nothing save contempt. And it did not matter a bean to her if he labeled her a prudish provincial either, she thought defiantly.

The marquess, waiting unobserved at the bottom of the stairs, saw the little toss of her head and the set expression that robbed her of all animation and speculated gloomily that she was thinking of him. At least she had donned the blue gown she had worn the evening he had returned home. He had waylaid her an hour ago on her way to her room to change, and had requested this, but with something less than confidence. Her polite little nod had chilled him to the marrow. He had not needed Andrew's delicate hints to enlighten him as to how much that scene in the conservatory was likely to cost, but, he quoted mentally, "Let us mind, faint heart ne'er wan a lady fair." Suddenly it struck him that with this old saw he had capped Andrew's ridiculous performance this afternoon, and the thought tickled him momentarily.

At that instant Marianne raised her eyes from the stairs and became aware of his presence.

"Something about my appearance amuses you, my lord?" she asked coolly.

"Do not be so quick to sport your canvas, my child," he replied with maddening condescension. "You'd look excessively charming if your expression did not suggest that you were on the way to your own execution." Encouraged by the faint smile this sally evoked, he held out his hand to assist her down the last steps, and once there he retained hers for a moment, studying her face with serious eyes. "If I smile when I look at you, it is because looking at you gives me pleasure."

There was a quiet earnestness in this speech, but Marianne received it unblinkingly, hardening her heart against his blandishments. After a moment he said more briskly, "It has occurred to me that you never wear jewelry. Do you disapprove of jewels on some theoretical basis?"

This brought another faint smile. "Not theoretical, my lord, purely practical. I do not possess any jewels."

"You do, you know. Not many, but I discovered two necklaces and three rings among your father's effects. They are now yours."

"Did they belong to my mother?"

"Yes. One of the necklaces consists of some really lovely sapphires in a filigree gold setting." He took a jeweler's box from his pocket. "I have had it cleaned for you. It will be the perfect touch with this gown. Come over here."

Marianne suffered herself to be led down the hall to a large pier-glass over a console table. Obedient to his command, she stood facing the mirror while he placed the necklace about her throat and bent his head to fasten the tiny clasp.

"Oh, it's lovely," she breathed ecstatically, touching the sparkling stones with reverent fingers while she waited impatiently for a signal that the clasp was secure. His nearness was becoming too disturbing for comfort.

"There, it is fastened."

Two things happened almost simultaneously. Marianne started to turn impulsively to thank the marquess, when a dark flash in a corner of the glass drew her eyes to the figure of Lady Mauraugh revealed by the open door to the blue and gold saloon. Her reluctant gaze met the furious glance of the countess, not the least bit diluted by distance and mirror reversal, and all motion stopped for an instant while she fought against a slight wave of nausea and tore her eyes from that lovely, angry face. He planned this, she thought angrily. Even the passing on to her of her father's gift to her mother had been turned to good account in his campaign to discourage the woman who had jilted him. Such cold calculation sickened her, but it also stiffened her resolve not to become one of his victims. Accordingly, she turned a calm face to him and thanked him coolly for the necklace. She noted a shade of disappointment in the amber eyes and was repaid for her efforts. He bowed slightly in acknowledgment.

"Your father had good taste, especially if, as I suspect, you are the image of your mother. Now I think it is time we joined the others."

"Just a minute, my lord. I know I agreed not to betray you in this masquerade but there is one condition to be met if you wish my cooperation."

His eyes grew hard, but he merely inquired, "And that is?"

Marianne stared at him levelly. "That you agree to allow me to return to Yorkshire when I ask it of you."

His brows snapped together and the well-shaped lips thinned to a straight line, but her glance never wavered from his inquisitorial stare, and at last he capitulated. "Very well, but since you are not above blackmail—well, what else would you call this condition of yours?" he snarled as she opened her lips to protest—"I'll expect active, not merely passive cooperation from you, and that includes forgetting 'my lord' and 'sir.' My name is Justin and I wish to hear no other from you. Are we now agreed on the terms of our bargain?"

"Yes."

"Yes, what?"

"Yes—Justin."

He smiled but it was not a particularly pleasant sight. "And now, let us repair to the saloon. Everyone will be wondering what has occurred to detain us."

Despite her promise, Marianne found herself totally unable to oblige the marquess with an air of complacence, so the diversion provided by the appearance just then of the little earl accompanied by his nurse was timely indeed. Richard, walking sedately down the stairs, peered over the railing and caught sight of the couple heading for the saloon door. He jumped down the remaining three steps and skipped up to the young woman smiling a welcome to him. Although he unhesitatingly slipped his hand in her extended one, his words were a rebuke.

"Lady Marianne, you did not come to the nursery this afternoon."

"Say good evening to Lord Lunswick, Richard," put in Nurse austerely, before the girl could summon forth an excuse, though she was aware from the deep reproach on Richard's face that any attempts at self-exculpation would have to be inventive indeed to reduce her treachery to a minor offense. While watching the little boy's polite greeting to the marquess, she prudently decided on a policy of abject abasement and in due course was graciously forgiven. His good nature restored, Richard entered the room chattering gaily between the two, holding a hand of each while Nurse unobtrusively sought a chair away from the main group.

Their entrance, late as it was, could not go unremarked. Indeed Lady Mauraugh had already witnessed the tableau near the pier-glass, at least visually, but although she looked quickly at the sapphires, she made no comment except to welcome her host with a warm smile.

"Justin, I have scarcely laid eyes on you all day. Was the colt to your liking?"

While the marquess made her an easy answer and nodded to the assembled group, his mother's sharp eyes had taken in the gleaming jewels adorning her young guest's throat.

"Marianne, how beautiful! And so perfectly right for you."

Sir Martin and Lord Andrew added their voices to the chorus of admiration.

"Thank you. It belonged to my mother and I shall take great delight in wearing it." The girl released her hand from Richard's to approach her hostess so the latter might study the necklace at closer range.

Lady Mauraugh, who had come forward to greet her son, knelt in a graceful attitude by his side and offered a smooth, scented cheek for his kiss. Tonight she had chosen to wear black lace, which heightened her exquisite fairness and emphasized the red-gold hair. Marianne's covert attention had been on the widow from the shocked instant of meeting those green eyes in the mirror, and she wondered again how Justin could seem so oblivious to the lovely picture she presented with her arms about the child. She could not quite credit that a man who had once desperately wished to marry a woman might remain unaffected by her potent appeal a mere five years later, especially when the full battery of her charm was directed at his sensibilities.

"You are come just in time to secure this bracelet for me, Justin," Lady Mauraugh declared, disengaging her lovely arms from her son and holding out one from which a diamond bracelet dangled loosely. "I caught the clasp awhile ago and cannot seem to secure it with one hand."

"I'll do it, Mama, let me!" pleaded Richard eagerly.

Lady Mauraugh's smile disappeared as she almost snatched her arm away from the small, seeking hands. "Nonsense, Richard, your fingers aren't yet clever enough to do this difficult catch." She rose from her knees and held out the arm to her host who had made no move toward accepting this commission.

"I fear my fingers are too clumsy for such a delicate task. You had rather beg Marianne's assistance or my mother's." He turned to the girl in blue velvet with an intimate smile. "Marianne?"

The long bronze lashes swept down to conceal her expression as Lady Mauraugh silently surrendered her arm to the ministrations of the other woman, but Marianne could feel her stiffen under her light touch and was nervously aware of the hostility that emanated from the beautiful redhead. Securing the clasp was a simple matter, certainly not beyond the ordinary capabilities of an adult left hand, but, Marianne conceded, there was nothing of the ordinary about the present situation. She herself could barely conceal the resentment that soured her nature at being thrust like a line of infantry across the path of each new charge by Lady Mauraugh, especially in the face of what she suspected was the active enjoyment of this ridiculous situation by the object of the widow's campaign. Certainly her trustee appeared more relaxed than either of the feminine participants in the exercise, as he blandly described for Lord Andrew's benefit the points of the colt he and Sir Martin had inspected that morning.

Richard had quitted his mother's side to give his aunt a detailed account of his day. She gave him

226

all her attention and he blossomed visibly under its benign influence, showing his pearly teeth in a delighted laugh at his aunt's lively recounting of Nuisance's latest disgraceful behavior.

This left the two younger women disengaged, but so reluctant was each to approach the other that Lady Mauraugh appeared to have her entire attention on the gentlemen's horse discussion while Lady Marianne pretended an equal absorption in the child's conversation with his aunt. Noticing her glance, Richard politely included her in his comments and Marianne had to grip her lower lip with her teeth to prevent a sudden laugh at the absurdity of a four-year-old child being more possessed of good manners than two adults. Subsequently she turned to the countess with an admiring comment on her gown. The other replied with equal politeness but both were relieved to have their uneasy conversation interrupted by Coleman's announcement of dinner.

At this point Richard was reminded of an additional grievance.

"Lady Marianne, you did not bring the drawings you promised to show me. You know, the flower paintings Miss Huntingdon did that you said were prettier than the ones in my book." He impaled his victim with an accusing stare and firmly held his ground when Nurse hastily suggested it was time to say his good-nights to the company. Again Marianne prostrated herself, figuratively speaking, and solemnly promised to bring the paintings to the nursery the following day. Richard was all set to stay and discuss the exact timing of said visit, but Nurse, who had no difficulty in recognizing delaying tactics when they had been put into effect, hastened her charge's exit, and the party proceeded in to dinner.

As usual, Marianne was seated at her host's left hand with Lady Mauraugh on his right. She had braced herself inwardly for an embarrassing ordeal at this first occasion for presenting their pretended courtship to Lady Mauraugh and was consequently all the more surprised to discover that the conversation at table flowed as smoothly as ever. She could detect no change in Justin's attitude toward either Lady Mauraugh or herself, and gradually her tenseness evaporated, giving way to relief that he had abandoned his scheme, at least for the moment. For the first time since witnessing that kiss in the conservatory, she was able to relax and enjoy his company.

The interval before the gentlemen joined the ladies was enlivened by the high spirits of Lady Lunswick. Noting a speculative gleam in the widow's eye as she studied her hostess, Marianne fixed Lady Lunswick with a warning look and hastened to join the conversation before Lady Mauraugh could commence to wonder just what might have occurred to cast their hostess into such transports of joy. As usual, following a session of enforced proximity to the countess, Marianne welcomed the entrance of the gentlemen with a sentiment akin to relief. This was destined to be very short lived, however, for tonight when Lord Andrew requested that she favor them with some music, Lady Mauraugh declined the office smilingly.

"Ah, no, you must be sick to death of listening to my efforts. Lady Marianne enjoys playing the pianoforte I am told. Perhaps tonight *she* will gratify your wish for music."

Marianne felt a distant chill pass down her spine and braved the glittering malice in Lady Mauraugh's green eyes to rush in with a horrified protest.

"Oh, no, I am the merest novice. I would not wish to subject you to an indifferent performance after the high standard set by Lady Lunswick and Lady Mauraugh. Indeed I *could* not, as there is nothing as yet that I have committed to memory."

"If we were to send for your music might you not play that haunting ballad I heard you singing the other day as I passed Lady Lunswick's sitting room?" Sir Martin implored gently with his charming smile. "Shall I confess I lingered outside the door in hopes of hearing another verse after you had finished, it was so delightfully done."

"If you lingered you were more like to hear discords and errors as I worked on my fingering," Marianne returned, but she was deeply grateful to Sir Martin for bolstering her confidence.

"Yes, dear child, do play and sing for us," urged Lady Lunswick. "You are progressing beautifully with your music and we are all of us well-disposed to listen uncritically."

The exquisite absurdity of this remark, at least with respect to Lady Mauraugh, almost overset Marianne's gravity. She averted her eyes from the serene expression on her hostess's lovely face, but in so doing, her gaze met that of the marquess, so filled with conspiratorial appreciation that it drew a spontaneous smile from her, despite her embarrassment and consternation at the situation the widow had so artfully contrived.

Justin smiled warmly at her. "I have been looking forward to the pleasure of hearing you sing," he said with a quiet sincerity that caused her color to rise.

"Yes, Marianne, do not be a pudding heart, throw your heart over the fence." This stout encouragement from Lord Andrew.

Feeling churlish and ungracious in the face of their friendly urgings, Marianne could not persist in her refusal. The marquess volunteered to fetch her music from upstairs. In the interval, Lord Andrew seated Marianne at the pianoforte and opened the instrument for her. He lit the branch of candles on it and, while so doing, spoke for her ears alone. "I say, Marianne, what did Richard mean earlier this evening when he mentioned something about paintings of Sophie's?"

Marianne strove to prevent the triumphant elation she was experiencing at this inquiry from appearing in her voice. "I had promised to bring the paintings Sophia gave me for Christmas up to the nursery to compare with some pictures in one of Richard's books. Why do you ask?"

"Well, I have no recollection of Sophie's giving you anything of the sort. When Richard said that, I remembered that she was used to enjoy sketching in the fields and woods when we were children, but I had no idea she was still inclined in that direction. What are the subjects of the paintings? Or are they sketches?"

"No, they are exceedingly fine watercolors of woodland flowers. There are three of them, all rather small. I think my favorite is of violets nestled amidst their lovely greenery, tucked in and around the roots of an old tree. It's my belief that Sophia's is a rare and delicate talent." She looked at him steadily. "If you were unaware of the gift it is probably because Sophia gave them to me in private. You must know how she dislikes being the center of attention. I do not believe she could bear to have the paintings criticized or dismissed as slight female accomplishments."

"Lord, why should you, or she, suspect I would do any such thing?" Lord Andrew was indignant. "I remember, when we were children, being so frustrated by my own efforts to sketch when the results were compared with Sophie's. May I see them, the ones she gave you?"

"Yes, of course. I'll take them up to the nursery in the afternoon, if you wish to accompany me. I would bring them to the dining room at midday, but Sophie is lunching with us tomorrow, as well as Claire and Aubrey, and I would not embarrass her by producing her work for general comment."

He nodded in comprehension. "I know. Sophie has always been as shy as those forest creatures she delights in. My mother has mentioned bringing her to London with you when you make your come out, but I do not know if it will answer. Even if Justin and I stayed close to lend her support, it's my guess she'd be miserable."

Before Marianne could fully take in these startling words, Andrew had moved aside to make
room for his brother who had returned with her
music, the sight of which had the effect of instantly recalling her thoughts from Sophia's problems
to her own predicament. As her trustee assisted her
in spreading the sheets on the stand, their hands
brushed accidentally. He must have been aware of
the trembling of her fingers because his turned and
captured hers in a brief comforting clasp, while
his eyes held hers with a warm smile in their amber depths.

"Do not be nervous. This isn't a concert hall,
you know."

Although his whispered encouragement was
audible only to Marianne, an involuntary glance
disclosed that from her seat on the blue sofa, Lady
Mauraugh had witnessed the momentary clasping
of hands. If the icy stare she fixed on Marianne
had had the power of its conviction, the latter
would have been frozen on the spot, but strangely
enough it was the shock of this cold enmity rather
than the warm support of her trustee that enabled
Marianne to overcome her momentary panic. The
countess did not sing, and despite her own lack of
training, Marianne knew her clear soprano was
easily adequate to the demands of the simple ballad. Raising her chin a trifle and lowering her
lashes to conceal her expression, she returned the
other woman's stare with a faint smile that brought
forth a corresponding narrowing of green eyes.
Feeling unaccountably braced by her own small

show of spirit, Marianne focused her attention on the instrument.

As the marquess drifted toward a chair that faced the performer, Lady Mauraugh patted the seat beside her and called softly:

"Over here, Justin. That chair is too hard for comfort."

He paused before collapsing his large frame onto the maligned chair and laughed in self-mockery. "Do you know, I must be getting old. I find myself becoming a creature of habit. This is my customary seat for enjoying music and I am loath to change." He smiled gently at the widow, but remained in the cane-backed chair from which he had an unrestricted view of the performer's face. Without turning his head he could also see Aurelie where she sat on the blue sofa, the picture of grace and elegance despite a slightly dissatisfied expression on her face at present.

His thoughtful gaze left the lovely redhead and dwelt in some perplexity on the dreamy-eyed brunette sitting at the pianoforte totally wrapped up in the music she was softly playing and singing. With the exception of her eyes which were the most beautiful he had ever beheld, feature by feature Marianne was quite eclipsed by Aurelie. Although her mouth had a lovely curve it was too large by modern standards, her nose was just a nose, and the arresting, high-cheeked, heart-shaped face appeared uneasily exotic next to Aurelie's classic oval. Both had perfect complexions, but again, the camelia and peach would ex-

233

cite less admiration than the fairer milk and rose. *He* found her abundant black hair quite to his taste, in fact the memory of that satin curtain released from its customary smooth style, rose up before his eyes with increasing regularity, but there was no denying either that Aurelie's luxuriant red-gold tresses contributed greatly to her amazing beauty. The small hands playing competently over the keys, though obviously softer and whiter than when he first encountered them, would always appear more capable than elegant, and suffered greatly in comparison with the slenderfingered grace of the countess. But were decidedly more . . . endearing perhaps?

Now how had that absurd notion risen to the top of his mind? He had been aware of the strength and capability of those hands from the first moment of their acquaintance when she had gripped those ridiculous milk pails almost defensively. And there was another ridiculous notion—that she needed defenses against himself. Had she not shown from the instant of their meeting a complete and unvarying indifference to his reaction to herself? And had she ever exhibited the slightest uneasiness when indulging in frequent actions guaranteed to arouse the ire of any guardian? Though posed in a rhetorical spirit, from his observation the answer must be a decided *no*.

Then *why* was he sitting here in this damnably uncomfortable chair, clumsily repulsing overtures from the most beautiful and desirable woman of his wide acquaintance while indulging in dreams of arousing the romantic interest of a demonstrably indifferent female, possessing no more than tolerable good looks and no accomplishments to speak of, besides coming from a different background and owning an independent nature that totally unfitted her to conform to the typical pattern of behavior expected of a woman who marries into the aristocracy? Did he belong then to that class of men who were only interested in the thrill of the chase and who found no value in the object in possession? Had Marianne's indifference piqued his vanity, while Aurelie's current eagerness cooled his former ardor? His thoughts raced on to the lilting accompaniment of the old song sung just as delightfully as he had once predicted Marianne would sing.

In justice to himself he felt entitled to deny the accuracy of this most exaggerated stating of the case.

With regard to Aurelie, it was certainly true that he had been wildly in love with her once and that she had not changed a jot in the intervening five years. But two other things of surpassing importance were also true. Firstly, that he had never known, therefore never loved, the real Aurelie. She had seemed the physical embodiment of a young man's dreams of the woman he might love, but in his state of bemusement he had credited her also with all the virtues and character a man, perhaps unconsciously, expects to find in the woman who will be his wife. Time had proved Aurelie too selfish and narcissistic to ever wish to conform to any but her own self-estimate. She used her beauty, accomplishments, and undoubted charm entirely to attain her own ends. While he was not prepared to condemn her for choosing to use her attributes thusly, since meeting Marianne he had slowly arrived at the inescapable conclusion that he himself had changed. A young man's dream of the ideal woman was now too shallow and one-dimensional to satisfy him. He could no longer be content with discreet behavior and the appearance of loyalty; he demanded absolute fidelity. No longer would a decorative wife, complete with the admired worldly accomplishments, be the pinnacle of his desires. Now he wished for a woman willing and eager to share every aspect of his existence and remain at his side as his chosen life's companion.

Naturally he was expected to marry and produce an heir, and he had not been unaware that his mother eagerly awaited this event, but until Marianne entered his life he had drifted along with no thought to becoming a tenant for life. In fact, after his experience with Aurelie, he had shied away from forming any but the most casual attachments with any eligible young lady. His title and wealth assured that all he had to do was cast the handkerchief and, practically without exception, any unmarried female of his acquaintance would accept his offer, regardless of her personal feelings about him. It was not particularly gratifying to know that were he doddering with age, of limited mentality, physically repulsive, or morally corrupt, the result would be the same. His worldly possessions would serve to annul almost all defects of person or character.

Right from their initial confrontation Marianne had struck him as different from the commonality of women, but at the beginning of their acquaintance he had refused to admit the attraction of her honesty and genuineness, preferring to censure her for not conforming to the pattern of her contemporaries, though even then he had dimly recognized his reaction as being partially motivated by bruised vanity. His own behavior had begun to strike him as ambiguous in the extreme. On the one hand, he stood back and made invidious comparisons with other young women of her age, but when Claire Carstairs had attempted to set Marianne at a disadvantage, his instincts were strongly protective of his impossible ward. She, meanwhile, remained cool and aloof in his company, never showing him a glimpse of the warm friendliness she displayed toward his mother. At this point he had made her business affairs an excuse to depart for London where, in the increased activity and social contact, he planned to erase the image of an annoyingly disturbing female. Though convinced of the soundness of this tactical maneuver, he found the results somewhat other than he expected. For one thing, an image of a black-haired, quiet-faced girl popped into his mind and intruded when he was in company with other women. And now the comparisons were not always unfavorable. A certain blonde beauty, whose cool fairness had won her an admiring following, suddenly appeared pallid and uninteresting compared with a combination of rich coloring and jet black hair. Another young woman, known in

237

his circle for her liveliness and wit, was unexpectedly revealed to have a shallow understanding and a mere facility with words. He had never questioned the propriety of young women remaining aloof from the more unpleasant facts of contemporary economic and political life, but now it struck him as the height of unwisdom to raise girls to be merely decorative. A vision of Marianne earnestly discussing the problems of the factory workers with Mr. Huntingdon rose up before his mind's eye, rendering the usual run of debutantes sadly deficient in understanding, no matter how accomplished.

He had come home at last, half eager, half reluctant to pursue his acquaintance with his disturbing ward to find—here his gaze which had been dwelling inward though politely fixed on the performer, sharpened and focused anew on her face. He had entered his house and the first sight to greet him had been a vision of loveliness, superbly gowned in flowing blue velvet. The awkwardness of manner was gone, the gypsy tan had faded to this creamy satin, her former coldness replaced by a glowing warmth and vitality. And he had stood spellbound with the sudden knowledge that he had passed the point of denying the loss of his heart. And for an enchanted moment she had gazed back at him with a welcome that shut out the rest of the world and enclosed the two of them in a private haven. He shifted his feet and his eyes sought the figure on the blue sofa listening to the music with an air of polite boredom. The presence of Martin Archer had caused the enchantment to disperse slightly, but it had taken the shock of finding Aurelie in his mother's saloon to shatter the mood completely. Since then his duties as host had prevented him from pursuing a single-minded courtship, but until the unfortunate scene with Aurelie in the conservatory he had been reasonably content with his progress in gaining friendship with Marianne at least. Occasional quiet interludes spent in private conversation with her had satisfied him while the house was full of guests. Until this afternoon.

With the aggressive encounter in the armory their relationship had taken a new turn. He had seized on Andrew's suggestion of a mock courtship as a lifeline by which he might regain the ground he had lost and even begin to push his pursuit of her in earnest. Naturally he had not let her guess that this was a reason, indeed, the sole reason behind their uneasy alliance since he had no need of subterfuge in dealing with Aurelie. In her innocence Marianne had accepted the necessity for the pretense, and it was now up to him to win her confidence and love. Since this afternoon he had already been of a dozen contradictory minds about his chances for achieving his goal in the light of recent developments. But one thing was certain. Sitting back and regretting what had happened would not serve to advance his cause one inch. He was now committed to action.

As Marianne finished the rollicking country song with which she had met the urging of Sir Martin and Lady Lunswick for more music, she determinedly arose from the pianoforte and crossed the room to join her hostess on a small settee. Although she did not suffer from shyness in the ordinary way, her color was slightly higher than usual for she was a modest girl and found it slightly embarrassing to be the center of attention. This did her no disservice in the eyes of the gentlemen present, all of whom hastened to compliment her warmly on her performance.

"Yes, indeed," Lady Mauraugh added her compliments to the others, "that was quite a charming performance. If you had had the benefit of good masters when you were young I am persuaded you would have caused quite a sensation with your music amongst the salons of London."

"I shall be quite satisfied to play occasionally for my own amusement," Marianne replied, while Lady Lunswick declared sweetly that she had formed the firm intention of requesting Marianne to sing at all her musical evenings in the future.

"For you gave us all great pleasure, dear child."

The conversation turned to other matters and remained of a general nature until the tea tray arrived. Justin was prevented from having more than a word or two with his ward by the determined proximity to Marianne of Sir Martin Archer. It had not escaped his notice that his old friend had been displaying a deepening penchant for her society, or that Marianne seemed quite content in his company. She spent a good deal of time with Andrew too, but despite that affectionate gesture in the armory, he would be greatly astonished to discover that her feelings for his brother were other than sisterly. Marianne possessed no coquettish tricks, she reacted to people the way she felt about them, within the bounds of good manners. She was obviously deeply attached to his mother and extremely fond of all the Huntingdons. His close observation of the last fortnight had yielded the strong theory that she accepted the continuous presence of both her cousins with good-natured tolerance but little warmth. And it was with relief that he could hazard a guess that in Aubrey's case at least, tolerance and civility were beginning to wear a bit thin. Marianne's former lifestyle had not taught her any socially acceptable tricks to ward off bores. Nor had it equipped her to repulse the unwanted advances of would-be suitors. He hoped it would be his good fortune to be present (though invisible) when Aubrey finally pushed her good manners too far. The enjoyment produced by this possibility faded quickly enough as he bent a lambent gaze on Sir Martin while he engaged Marianne in what appeared to be a mutually absorbing conversation. Undoubtedly his ward had formed an immediate liking for his amiable friend, and admittedly he had no idea whether her feelings for Sir Martin went deeper or were likely to go deeper than pleasant friendship. As for Martin himself, unless he was greatly deceived, his friend was tottering on the brink of falling in love. He frowned in frustration and prepared to make another attempt to divert Marianne's attention. Andrew was generously contributing to the situation by light-heartedly monopolizing his aunt's interest. She had resisted his efforts initially, but Andrew could be devastating-

241

ly engaging when he chose, and Aurelie instinctively responded to all masculine attention. Thus bolstered, he made an inane attempt to interrupt the annoying twosome, and the knowledge of his own *gaucherie* was reflected in his wry expression. Despite her seeming absorption in Sir Martin's conversation, Marianne had been well aware that Justin was trying to launch his mock courtship and was finding his good friend to be an uncharted obstacle in his path. She met her trustee's frustrated glance with a sparkling look brimful of mischievous appreciation. He grinned ruefully and subsided for the moment, surprised and rather elated by this instant of perfect communication between himself and his reluctant beloved. Had the real object of the exercise been to convince the countess that his romantic interest lay elsewhere he would have been mildly gratified by the sudden tightening of her lips as her observant green glance witnessed the intimate look exchanged between Marianne and himself. However, in his concentration on Marianne he failed even to note Lady Mauraugh's reaction.

As for the other participant in this little drama, Marianne retired to bed that night convinced in her innocence that Justin had not yet had any opportunity to put his plan into operation beyond the momentary annoyance his fastening of her necklace must have caused the countess.

CHAPTER THIRTEEN

To an unbiased onlooker the next two days would seem to have passed quite pleasantly and uneventfully with the tempo of life going on much as usual at the Hall. At lunch the following day the house party was augmented by the presence of the earl of Melford and his lively sister as well as the Huntingdons, and the family increased its covers to include several persons for dinner on the next evening.

If one of the aforesaid onlookers had questioned Lady Marianne Carstairs about her impression of life at the Hall during this period, however, he would have been vastly astonished at a quite different report. As Marianne confessed to her hostess on the morning following the dinner party:

"On the surface everything is pleasant and very sociable, but I have the most unrestful sensation along my nerves as if everyone is watching me. It is quite horrid." She shivered slightly.

Lady Lunswick laughed softly. "Please do not think me unsympathetic, my dear, if I observe that, given the present titillating situation, it could scarcely be otherwise. Aurelie, of course, is watching you like a hawk. But cheer up. It is my belief that she will soon admit that she is beaten and find a graceful way to bring her visit to an end . . . unless . . ." She stared consideringly at the young girl who looked at her in faint puzzlement.

"Unless what, Ma'am?"

"Well, it will not have escaped Aurelie's attention that Justin is not the only man courting you. Melford is making a positive fool of himself over you, and Sir Martin, too, is becoming most particular in his attentions." Without seeming to, she was closely studying Marianne from under her lashes and noted the faint increase in color brought about by her words, but she continued her line of thought without commenting. "It occurs to me that Aurelie may be waiting to see which way you jump, to put it vulgarly, before she cashes in her chips and shakes the dust of this place from her shoes."

"To remain with the vulgar idiom," murmured Marianne provocatively, and now Lady Lunswick chuckled irrepressibly, though she protested:

"But the *Bible*, Marianne. That must always be acceptable, surely." If the girl had thought to drag a red herring across the trail, she had failed to take into account the tenacity of purpose of her hostess for, undeterred, she pursued her original thought.

"Does Aurelie have any grounds for hoping you will accept either Melford or Sir Martin?"

"Since neither has made me an offer, none at all, Ma'am."

The marchioness took note of the slight dryness in her guest's tones, and she flashed her a smile full of apology and affection. "I know, my child, I am no better than a common busy head, but," she persisted, "*have* you a *tendre* for either?"

Now it was Marianne's turn to fix a considering gaze on her hostess. "What would you say, Ma'am, if I admitted I cherished a deep affection for my cousin?"

"Nothing, but I'd dose you with fever remedies until you came to your senses."

Marianne threw back her head and laughed in delighted appreciation at the look of unrestrained disgust on her companion's lovely countenance.

"You need not send for the doctor, Ma'am. I promise you I shall not encourage any suitor except Justin until Lady Mauraugh leaves." She sobered abruptly. "I still do not like this masquerade, but I shall keep my promise."

With this the marchioness had to be content though she was well aware that her earlier query had been neatly evaded.

"May I ask you a rather impertinent question?" Marianne said tentatively after a comfortable silence while each pursued her own thoughts.

"You could not be impertinent, my dear child. Your company is a great delight to me. You must know I could not care more for a daughter of my own then I do for you."

"Thank you, Ma'am," said Marianne, flushing with gratification. "I *do* know it and though I do not feel I have done anything to merit such great kindness, I am terribly grateful. The subject I wished to speak to you about is rather related to daughters, that is, *daughters-in-law*, I mean *one* daughter-in-law." She floundered, then taking a determined breath, plunged: "Ma'am, do you know whether Andrew's affections are engaged?"

A shade of dismay flashed across Lady Lunswick's countenance before she could bring her expression under control, but her voice was quite even.

"Do you mean me to understand it is *Andrew* you love?"

"Oh, no, Ma'am! Andrew is just like a brother to me, as is Jack Richmond, but I have been wondering if *Sophia* might have a *tendre* for him, and if that is why she is so silent when he is around—because she fears to betray herself. If this were true and if Andrew felt the same, would you dislike the match?" The huge violet eyes anxiously searched the older woman's grave face.

"No, I would not dislike it precisely for I am very fond of Sophia and I do not desire an advantageous match in the worldly sense for either of my sons, but Andrew is such a volatile creature and Sophia is such a quiet little wren. I cannot quite believe they would deal well together. Are you certain that it is a case with them?"

"Sophia has said nothing to me of her feelings, nor has Andrew, but he was most interested in seeing the paintings she gave me, and I have noticed that he is always gentle with her."

"But I think he does not seek her out, Marianne, as Justin does you. He treats her more as one would a young sister, rather protectively."

"Aha!" Marianne ignored the first observation and addressed herself to the second. "He treats *me* like a sister, and there is nothing protective about it. Do you not see how differently he acts with Sophia?"

"He treats you like another *brother*," corrected her ladyship dryly, "but I do not mean to pull caps with you, Marianne, because I just do not feel competent to judge of Andrew's feelings, or Sophie's for that matter. We shall simply have to wait and see. But tell me, did he like the paintings?"

"I believe he greatly admired them, and I was impressed with his knowledge of art. In general, you know, Andrew is such a madcap that one tends not to credit him with serious interests."

Andrew's fond mama nodded in acknowledgment of this judgment. "My son is rather a surprising person altogether, but his interest in art is longstanding and quite serious. He has acquired some lovely paintings and pieces of sculpture for Chestnut Hill. I have often thought that it was a severe disappointment to him that his own early efforts were not worthy of encouragement, but he has never admitted this. When he was younger he wanted to be just like the twins, and *they* never sat still long enough to cultivate any artistic or musical accomplishments, though Harry had a pleasant singing voice and Justin was used to whistle accompaniment for him."

The two women were comfortably ensconced in Lady Lunswick's morning room, the elder industriously engaged in putting the finishing touches to a handsome altar cloth that she had not been able to complete before Christmas because of her increased social schedule since Marianne's arrival. The younger was seated at the large table where she was checking over the household accounts for the marchioness. Watching her covertly, the marchioness concluded that for all her disinclination to talk about Justin, there was a new radiance about her young guest lately that intensified her healthy good looks into a state approaching real beauty. And that was true even when she had the misfortune to be standing within comparison distance of Aurelie St. Clair. Of course this glowing look might not be at all attributable to the attentions being paid her by her trustee; she had not actually denied an interest in some other man. But her trustee's mother had not been narrowly observing the constantly changing relationship between these two lovable but reticent young people for almost the entire length of their stormy acquaintance (and *someday* she meant to hear the true story of their first meeting!) without forming some hopeful theories of her own. Though she had long abided by a vow not to interfere in the lives of her children without a specific invitation to do so, it was becoming increasingly difficult to keep her tongue between her teeth, so consumed was she with the ravenous urge to know just how great a degree of pretending actually existed in this mock courtship.

"Marianne," she began, when a peremptory knock sounded at the door. "Enter!"

Marianne looked up from her figures to see Nurse come quickly into the room, but at the sight of her she laid down her pen and came forward. The calm, unhurried air that was so much a part of Nurse's appearance was gone. She looked worried and upset, and her hands were clasped tightly to-

gether. She sketched a small curtsy to Lady Lunswick and plunged:

"Ma'am, your ladyship, have you seen Richard
this morning?"

"Why, no. Have you, Marianne?"

"No, it is my custom to visit the nursery after
lunch. What is wrong?"

At this news Nurse had started to wring her
hands. "Oh dear, I had hoped he might have come
here to get that dratted dog, begging your pardon,
my lady. I haven't seen him for over an hour."

Lady Lunswick cleared away her embroidery
silks and patted the arm of the settee. "Here, Nurse,
sit down and tell us just what has happened. When
did you last see the boy?"

"Over an hour ago in the nursery." Perched
gingerly on the exact edge of the chair, Nurse
tucked a wispy strand of gray hair behind her ears
and continued in flat tones which didn't quite conceal her anxiety. "He was playing happily with his
soldiers so I decided to mend one of his shirts.
I went into my room to get my work basket, in-
tending to bring it into the nursery. But the light
was very good by my chair and it is more comfortable for my short legs than those in the nursery
so I stayed there to finish the job. The door was
open, though, and I could hear Richard singing
to himself while he played. I did not pay any attention when the singing stopped, nor did I hear
the door open or close, but when I went back in
there, he was gone."

Marianne said soothingly, "Perhaps he is playing

249

a trick on you, Nurse, and is hiding somewhere."

"That's what I thought at first, your ladyship. 'Depend upon it,' I told myself, 'the little scamp is hiding, hoping to jump out at me, and give me a fright.' He's a different lad since we've come here, much more playful like, and right mischievous sometimes. Not that I mind," she added hastily, "I like to see boys active, and he always minds me when I call him, but I've searched everywhere and there's no trace of him upstairs."

"Have you tried the kitchens?" queried Lady Lunswick. "Strangely enough I've discovered that Christophe is not at all adverse to having Richard around."

"Yes, Ma'am. They haven't seen hide nor hair of him today. The dog was there earlier but he's not there anymore either."

"Does his mother know? Perhaps he's with her."

"No, Ma'am, he's not. I checked her rooms first and I've just come from there. He's not been there this morning."

"What does her ladyship say? Is she alarmed?"

"I don't know about *alarmed,* but she's annoyed all right, because I asked to have Selwyn help me search for Richard, and Selwyn was doing my lady's hair at the time."

"Have you checked with Selwyn since then?"

"No, Ma'am, but I've told the maids to keep their eyes open. Between us I think we've looked in almost every room."

Marianne, who had been silently standing near Lady Lunswick listening to the details, now spoke up. "I brought him to the armory once and he was fascinated by the collection of swords and firearms. Let me check there now." She was at the door on the words but paused to ask, "Are any of his outer garments missing, Nurse?"

Nurse jumped up from her chair. "I don't know, Ma'am, I never thought he'd go outside in this damp air, but I'll look right now." She hurried through the door after Lady Marianne.

Both were back within five minutes, slightly breathless, but only Nurse had anything to report. "His blue jacket is missing, my lady, and his gloves."

Lady Lunswick pulled the cord summoning Coleman. "I have been thinking since you mentioned that Nuisance was in the kitchens earlier that it is very likely he and Richard have met and gone off somewhere. Nuisance has not appeared whining at the door today as is his custom."

When the impassive Coleman appeared, she issued orders for the footman and maids to search the grounds for the little boy. "I do hope the rain will hold off. It is such a dreary day. But he can't have wandered far."

Marianne spoke for the first time. "I am going out to look also. Where are the gentlemen today, Coleman?"

"They are all out riding, my lady."

The marchioness said bracingly, "I am persuaded we'll have found the culprits by the time the men return."

While the maids combed the shrubbery and the footmen headed past the gate house toward the road that led to the nearest village, Marianne stood undecided at the main entrance, trying to imagine where a small boy and his dog were most likely to take advantage of unexpected freedom. She frowned in concentration as she buttoned the soft, black woolen pelisse to her throat. A gig coming up the carriage drive caught her attention and she watched as the horse drew closer until she recognized the gray mare from the vicarage with Miss Sophia Huntington handling the reins in capital fashion.

"Sophia! I am so glad to see you. You are come just in time."

"Are you on the point of going somewhere?"

"Oh, no, that is, yes, in search of Richard who has wandered off. Will you come with me?"

"Most willingly. Shall we take the gig?"

Marianne's forehead creased as she pondered this, but he was such a small boy. Surely he could not have gotten far and the gig might be a hindrance in the woods. "I think not. Here is Coleman. He'll take care of stabling Bonnie. Let's go on foot."

The two girls set a brisk pace toward the home wood for, as Marianne reminded Sophia, "Richard has grown very adventurous of late, and trees have fascinated him ever since Andrew took him up behind him one afternoon for a ride through the woods. It seems he has a consuming desire to climb a tree, though most of these would be too high. Still there is the occasional low spreading chestnut or oak."

"Did he take Nuisance with him?"

Marianne stopped abruptly and regarded her

friend with respect. "Now, how did you guess that? At least, the dog is missing too, so we assume they are together."

Miss Huntingdon laughed. "That absurd dog is another of Richard's all-consuming passions, is he not? He seems a delightful child, though I have not had the pleasure of meeting him often."

The girls were out of sight of the Hall now because the terrain was uneven, though basically they had been on a downhill course. They began calling to Richard but with no success. After ten minutes or so, Sophia looked at her friend and said uneasily, "It would be awfully difficult for a small boy to avoid losing his way amongst these paths."

Marianne bit her lip. "I know, and it is quite damp and cold in here too. Perhaps he stayed on the lane or headed for the village after all. Let's go just a little further. There is a large tree by itself at the edge of a field a short distance away. I believe Andrew took him in that direction once."

They continued calling to the boy but were answered only by the muted woodland noises. It seemed almost as silent as an empty cathedral in the pauses between their calling. They could see quite a distance now as the trees thinned and could glimpse a field and a row of hedges ahead. They continued to call at intervals, though always unsuccessfully. They were almost out of the trees entirely when Marianne gripped her friend's arm.

"I thought I heard something!"

"So did I. A dog barking, perhaps?"

Redoubling their efforts, they added Nuisance's name and were rewarded as the barking sounded clearer. It also sounded frantic, and the girls began to run toward the noise.

"Richard! Can you hear me? Answer me, Richard!"

Marianne erupted breathlessly from the edge of the wood and cast her eyes swiftly over the field. As Sophia panted up after her she pointed to an enormous, low-spreading oak overlooking the field.

"Look!"

The furiously barking pup left his post at the foot of the huge tree to come running up to the girls. He circled them, wildly barking a sharp welcome until Marianne forcibly restrained his efforts. "Quiet, Nuisance, quiet, I say! Good dog." She patted his head and gentled him for a moment until he had calmed somewhat.

Meanwhile Sophia had approached the tree where a very small figure perched at least twenty feet above the ground with his arms wrapped tightly about a branch. So far he had not uttered a sound.

"Do you think he was treed by an animal?" she asked doubtfully

Marianne chuckled. "He was treed by overweening ambition. The poor child is paralyzed by fear."

She was unbuttoning her pelisse as she spoke and shortly cast it to the ground. "I shall have to climb up for him. Fortunately this skirt is quite full." As Sophia watched silently and Nuisance whined softly, Marianne bent over and grasped both back and front hems of her red skirt in her hands and drew up its folds between her legs. She unfastened the ribbon sash about her waist, and bringing the skirt hem high, retied the ribbon to bind the fabric tightly at the waist, thus fashioning herself a type of pantaloon to make climbing easier.

"Richard," she called in a conversational tone, "can you climb down from that tree?"

A pause, then a very small voice answered, "No."

"That's all right," came the cheerful reply. "You have done splendidly so far. Shall I come up and get you?"

Without waiting for the faint affirmative that eventually drifted down she was already making her careful way up to his perch. It was a perfect tree for climbing, small wonder Richard had felt the challenge too strong to resist. As she attained the branch below the boy she kept up a calm flow of conversation.

"I am going to help you down, Richard. It is a very easy thing, but you must do exactly as I say. Is that understood?" Again came the faint affirmative, but when Marianne put her hands on his hips and told him to let go of the branch so she might guide his feet downward, his grip tightened, if that were possible. Thoughtfully she noted the tear-stained cheek and trembling lip. "Cousin Andrew will be so pleased to know you are big enough to climb trees like . . . like a soldier, but soldiers have to follow orders, you know. If you can follow orders I'll show you the best way to get down from a tree. *That* is much more difficult than climbing a tree, of course, and then you may tell your cousins and your mama that you know how to go up *and* down a huge tree." Her soothing tones became brisk. "Now, the first order is to take one hand from your branch and put it here." She indicated a slightly lower hold and was relieved to see that Richard was attending at last to her words as well as her voice. Slowly he loosened his clutch and did as she requested. She guided his feet as she cautiously backed down the tree. Sophia had moved into position at the foot of the tree to assist.

They had managed about half the descent when the faint but increasing rumble in her ears resolved itself into hoofbeats. Glancing through the bare branches, Marianne could see three riders coming through the field. The gentlemen from the Hall, of course, returning from their ride. She knew her bright red dress would be highly visible and was glad that Richard would be able to ride home. She could see Lord Andrew out in front. Evidently he had seen her and veered from his course. Suddenly she was seized with a brilliant inspiration. She had both hands on Richard's waist now and, since he was obeying her, she brought him down onto the same branch on which she was located.

"Sophia!" she called urgently, "Can you get Richard? I feel so dizzy."

Instantly the younger girl climbed into the lowest branch and reached up for the next, unmindful of her hampering skirts. Richard had frozen again, but Miss Huntingdon's voice was as soothing as Lady Marianne's had been, and he relaxed once more and obeyed her.

Marianne was watching the horsemen galloping closer, hoping Lord Andrew would stay out in front and wondering if she dared go any higher to give credence to her story. She decided she had best remain where she was and, imitating Richard, locked her arms around the branch and clung, though she turned her head for as good a look as possible at what was happening below.

Lord Andrew arrived at the tree and flung himself off his horse in time to assist Sophia.

"I'll take him now, Sophie; pass him to me." Miss Huntingdon, trying to guide Richard's feet and feel where to put her own with the incumbrance of her skirts, was most relieved to be able to stay put and hand the boy down into his cousin's arms. On Lord Andrew's orders she waited patiently while he set the child on his feet before returning to assist her down from the last two branches.

Lord Andrew was gripping her tightly above the elbows, eyeing her with concern. "Good girl, Sophia, love. What happened?"

Miss Huntingdon went a becoming pink at this form of address, but managed to stammer, "Marianne . . . she . . . she felt dizzy."

Lord Andrew looked up, startled, having completely forgotten the silent girl ten feet above.

"I'll get her."

The marquess and Sir Martin had arrived and the former was already setting his foot on the lowest branch and swinging himself up. "Do not move, Marianne! You are perfectly safe."

Safe! In her consternation Marianne had never felt less safe in her life! She had not looked for this complication when formulating her brilliant

257

scheme to test Lord Andrew's feelings for his childhood friend. Irrelevantly she wondered if she had appeared just so anxious when climbing up after Richard as Justin did now. If so, then it was little wonder the child had not immediately responded to her calm tones. After the one look she averted her face and clung to her branch while her brain hastily proposed and rejected possibilities and explanations. With an interested audience just below she could explain nothing. She would have to brazen it through. She was appalled to realize that a wild desire to succumb to hysterical giggles was fast overcoming her. Fiercely biting her lip, she concentrated on the rough brown-gray bark of the tree three inches from her nose, fighting back the laughter that *would* rise in her throat. At this rate he'd consider her a prime candidate for Bedlam. The thought sobered her momentarily.

"Are you all right, Marianne? Has the dizziness passed?" Justin's voice at her side, slightly below hip level.

"Yes." Slowly she turned her head but avoided looking directly at him. "Yes, I am quite recovered now," she gasped. "I'll be able to get down by myself. Do you go down and I'll follow you." Her voice shook with the effort required to choke back the laughter.

Justin had been taking in the delightful expanse of ankle and leg left exposed by her hastily contrived "breeches." Now he looked up and his voice, though low, was absolutely compelling.

"Look at me, Marianne."

Reluctantly she lowered her gaze from the fascinating tree bark and met his intent look, pressing her lips firmly together. She endured a stare that seemed to last forever, then comprehension began to dawn and he said very softly, "You scheming little witch. You are no more dizzy than I am."

"Please don't give me away," she begged in a frantic whisper, and now all desire to giggle had passed. "Sophia would be so embarrassed and so would Andrew."

"Sophie might, but it would take more than this incident to embarrass my brother," he replied dryly. "However, you may rest easy. Now that you have started this, we shall have to see it through. And that will be your punishment, my little matchmaker, to be thought a weak female, given to vapors." He chuckled at her indignant look. "Well, would you prefer to confess all?"

"Of course not," she hissed, "but I am quite recovered now and can get myself out of this tree."

"Oh no, my dear girl! Since you are given to fits of dizziness in high places, you shall be compelled to accept my assistance."

"Hey, up there! Is everything all right? Do you need help in getting Lady Marianne down?" called Sir Martin.

"Well?" asked the marquess softly. "Do you require additional help?"

"No, no," she conceded, sighing in defeat, "please let us get down from this wretched tree, and I hope lightning may strike me if ever I climb another one."

Justin smiled and called below, "I can manage alone, thanks. Marianne is almost recovered. We'll take the descent slowly."

Marianne cast him one fulminating glance, then turned her shoulder on him and proceeded to pull her skirt hem out of the sash. At least she would make no more of an exhibition of herself than was absolutely required.

All during the excruciatingly slow descent she seethed inwardly as Justin ostentatiously placed her feet for her and kept up a constant stream of encouraging chatter that set her teeth on edge. His warm hands on her ankles roused all sorts of desires in her, the best understood of which was a furious urge to kick him.

Sir Martin was waiting with her pelisse which she thankfully donned. By now her hands were numb with cold and she made no demur when he buttoned her into the garment though she was not unaware of Justin's disapproving mien. However when Sir Martin offered her a ride home her trustee said brusquely:

"Mountain is a far stronger horse. I'll take Lady Marianne. If you, Martin, will carry the boy, Andrew can take Miss Huntingdon up before him. They are all quite chilled."

Sophia was looking at Marianne, a mixture of concern and puzzlement in her warm glance. "Poor Marianne, how horrid for you. And you went up that tree so fearlessly too."

"Yes, well I was fine while I was thinking about Richard. It was only when I looked down that I began to feel dizzy." Her explanation sounded weak in her own ears and she carefully avoided Lord Andrew's eyes. He made no comment and proceeded to assist Miss Huntingdon onto his horse.

The marquess inserted smoothly, "Lady Marianne is learning that there is a price to pay for one's impulsive acts on behalf of others." He lifted Richard up before Sir Martin who said warmly to ease Marianne's obvious chagrin:

"It was a very brave act indeed, especially in view of Lady Marianne's fear of heights."

Naturally enough, this kind effort did little to ease Marianne's discomfort. She smiled weakly at Sir Martin and glared at Justin as he held a hand down to assist her in mounting.

Richard, now that all danger was past, was inclined to view his exploit with some little pride. "I climbed up that big tree all by myself and then down again—almost," he added with some concession to truth. "And Lady Marianne says it is much more difficult to climb *down*."

This brought a shout of laughter from all three gentlemen and even a gentle chuckle from Sophia, while Marianne blushed furiously. She said severely to the little earl who was preening himself on making everyone laugh, "And now, young man, you shall have the task of explaining to your mama and Nurse just why you left the Hall without permission and without telling anyone where you were going."

"Oh ho, so that's the tale, is it? Young Richard has been escaping his gaolers, has he?"

Richard looked fearfully at his hero. "I don't

261

know what is *escaping*, but I did not do it. Me and Nuisance was tired of staying inside. We wanted to go out and climb a tree." Richard was more than willing to allocate an equal share of the responsibility to the dog.

"You know you must always ask Nurse when you wish to go outside, Richard. You might have become lost in the woods. What would you have done then on such a cold day?"

After due consideration the boy slewed around from his position in front of Sir Martin. "Nuisance knew the way home," he stated with simple faith and touching dignity, but the day was not to be his for Lord Andrew had the final word.

"Well, old chap, we are all happy that you came to no harm, but you are in line for a thundering scold from your nurse."

Recognizing the brutal truth of this pronouncement, Richard relapsed into a sulky silence for the remainder of the short ride back to the Hall. He made the trip uncomfortably memorable for his host by his constant twisting to assure himself that the puppy was still among the party. Nuisance, happy to be in his rightful place among the humans, was panting but game to keep pace with the horses.

Indeed it was a rather quiet group that slowly approached the great house a few minutes later.

Sophia, never loquacious at any time, was silently treasuring the enchanted moment when Andrew had addressed an endearment to her and looked at her with deep concern. Though she was too sensible to build on what was probably a slip of the tongue—a throwback perhaps to childhood days—there was no repressing the dreamy contentment that brought an especially sweet expression to her comely face.

Lord Andrew was facing some facts he had hitherto blithely ignored and reassessing his immediate future plans in the light of this new knowledge. Strangely enough no one had been more surprised by his recent actions· than he himself, and he needed time and solitude to think things through. His expression was abstracted as they drew near to the Hall but he held his passenger with great tenderness.

Sir Martin Archer, after a swift study of his friend's face when he had refused to allow him to transport Lady Marianne home, had finally admitted to himself that Lunswick was seriously courting his ward. It was rather a sticky situation and he would have to devote some concentrated thought to his own position.

At the beginning of the ride home Lady Marianne was busily engrossed in resenting her trustee's contribution to the embarrassment she had brought upon herself by her pretense of fear when in that tree, though this was certainly mitigated by the satisfaction of being proved correct in her reading of Sophia's and Andrew's unexpressed feelings for each other. In fact the more she thought about it the more complacent she became with her own role in the affair and the more charitable toward the marquess. After all, it would have needed a saint to resist teasing her about her predicament in the tree, and he had *not* given her away. Once before she had found herself being carried home on Mountain, but this time it was impossible to ignore the nearness of the marquess, for her treacherous body was relaxing against him in pure enjoyment, though she refused to think about those few moments when he had guided her down the tree, handling her as though she belonged to him. The inadmissible thought crept in and she sat up straighter, determined to banish it.

As if reading her mind, Justin tightened his hold on her and gently drew her back against his shoulder once more. "You aren't dripping wet this time," he murmured into her ear and was rewarded by a ghost of a chuckle as she settled more comfortably against him.

As the quiet party approached the Hall, all the individual moods were shattered by the reception awaiting them. Coleman must have been watching for the gentlemen because he had the door opened before they were halfway down the drive. By the time they pulled up in front of the main entrance he had been joined by one footman, two of the maids, Lady Lunswick, Nurse, and Lady Mauraugh. Even Selwyn hovered on the fringes of the group, radiating disapproval.

Lady Mauraugh hastened forward to take her son from Sir Martin.

"Is he hurt?"

"O' course I'm not hurt, Mama," came the indignant reply as the earl struggled in his mother's arms until she stood him on his own sturdy feet. She knelt down beside him, as did Nurse, to check the truth of this claim, then looked up with misty eyes at the marquess who had dismounted and was preparing to lift Lady Marianne down.

"Thank heavens you found him, Justin. How can I ever thank you?"

"You cannot, because I had nothing to do with finding Richard. It was Miss Huntingdon and Lady Marianne who came across him marooned in a tree and rescued him." He set Lady Marianne on her feet and smiled at Lady Mauraugh.

"In a tree? What were you doing in a tree, Richard?" queried Lady Lunswick, while his mother and nurse simply stared.

"I *climbed* up the tree o'course, and I wasn't 'rooned," the earl declared with commendable aplomb, "only I did not quite know how to get down, so I waited until Miss Huntingdon and Lady Marianne came, and Lady Marianne showed me how to climb down, only then she got dizzy and couldn't get down herself and Cousin Justin had to go up and get her."

As she listened to this tale Lady Mauraugh's face took on a set expression, but she wore a glittering smile as she rose and approached the two younger girls. She thanked them graciously for their efforts on behalf of her son, then addressing Lady Marianne, added lightly with a brittle laugh:

"It does not sound like you, Lady Marianne, to suffer from a fear of heights, or indeed to fail in any endeavor for a want of nerve."

Marianne returned a sweet false smile. "It is strange, is it not, Ma'am, that we both came to grief over a tree branch? *You* rode into one and I got stuck on one. Fortunately I sustained no injury of any kind, but if you will please excuse me, I should like to change this crumpled dress. Sophia, will you come with me?" She paused in the huge open doorway, but her friend, after checking the time, declined hastily as she was expected back at the vicarage.

Marianne bid Sophia good-bye and headed for the main staircase. She had her foot on the second stair when Andrew's voice, soft and close behind her, halted her movement.

"Oh, Marianne, be sure to take care on those stairs."

She had been lost in thought and his words failed to penetrate.

"I beg your pardon, Andrew?"

"You'll be perfectly safe as long as you do not look down," he assured her solemnly.

She stared into his dancing eyes for a moment, her own blank, then as his meaning sank in, fled up the stairs in confusion, conscious of his mocking laughter rising after her.

CHAPTER FOURTEEN

Lady Marianne Carstairs glided down the main staircase humming softly to herself. A discerning ear might have identified the tune as the ballad she had sung to the assembled household nine days previously. The refrain had been running through her mind ever since and, being unobserved, she trilled a few bars aloud in a slightly theatrical fashion as she approached the first landing.

The last four days had seen changes in the personnel residing at the Hall. Following Richard's adventure in the tree, Lady Mauraugh had made a decision to bring her visit to an end and had said her farewells the very next day. Her hostess had calmly accepted her sister-in-law's explanation that a less stimulating environment would be more beneficial to a child of his tender years, and had cheerfully set her household to the task of assisting in the somewhat precipitous departure of the countess' entourage for London. Not for a king's ransom would the marchioness have pointed out that Richard's alleged need of a more robust environment and additional masculine contacts had been the ostensible impetus for the visit originally. Remembering the flurry of preparations set in train to enable the countess to make as noteworthy a departure as her arrival had been, Marianne smiled and admitted to herself that life had taken on an aura of contentment subsequent to this happy event. She had expected the departure of the countess to signal the end of the distinguishing attentions being paid her by her trustee and had made a determined effort to convince herself that this was a consummation devoutly to be wished. To her amazement, however, the only change she could detect in Justin's behavior was a relaxation in his bearing and a gentler curve to his mouth when he smiled at her. Not even the most determinedly pessimistic of young ladies could have convinced herself that there was the slightest diminution in the number of smiles directed at her by the marquess.

The only occurrence to cloud her happiness briefly was an offer of marriage made to her by Sir Martin Archer on the day following Lady Mauraugh's leaving. Not being a scalphunter like some of her sex, Marianne was cast into low spirits at being obliged to hurt her friend by refusing his very flattering offer, and was thrown into a futher turmoil of agony at the thought of the awkwardness attendant on unavoidable future meetings with someone whose affections she had not been able to reciprocate. Sir Martin, however, as befitted a gentleman of his nice sensibilities, insured that his presence should not be a living rebuke to her by removing from the immediate vicinity. His departure had followed close on the heels of Lady Mauraugh's, and for the past two days the number of persons residing at the Hall had decreased to just the immediate family and Marianne. The two days had passed in a haze of quiet contentment with no visitors and no social activities scheduled. She had spent most of her waking hours in Justin's company, scarcely registering the interesting fact that Lord Andrew was spending a great deal of time at the vicarage these days. He had not mentioned a morning ride either day, and the fencing lessons had been allowed to lapse by tacit agreement.

She paused at the landing and rubbed her hand over the newel post, absently savoring the satiny smoothness of the polished wood as she stood stock still, acknowledging what she had heretofore refused to admit, that the globe of happiness in which she had dwelt these past few days had been designed by Justin and erected during the joyous hours of companionship they had enjoyed without interruptions by other people. It still seemed incredible that Justin should have preferred her to the beautiful countess, but at last she was beginning to accept that he had indeed singled her out from all the lovely and accomplished women of his acquaintance. She could no longer doubt that he was as quietly happy in her exclusive company as she was in his, but she still refused to look ahead to the future. For now, she was quite content to drift along, treasuring each shining new day to the fullest. And this day was already advanced to very late morning. She had best stop daydreaming on the stairs and go to seek out her hostess whom she had been neglecting shamefully in the last couple of days. Not that Lady Lunswick had appeared even to notice that her young guest was spending less time with her. She was happily engaged in a bustle of housekeeping activities these days, but at this hour was likely to be in her morning room. Marianne ran lightly down the last flight of stairs, her soft house shoes making no sound at all. Indeed she felt weightless and perfectly capable of flying today. Smiling a little at this fanciful notion, she turned and headed past Justin's study toward the morning room. She noticed that the door to the former was not quite shut and stopped abruptly, wondering if Justin might be in there. He had not suggested a ride this morning, probably because the skies had been rather threatening. She hesitated at the door, her hand extended, but was prevented from pushing it open by a sudden attack of shyness. No, she could not quite bring herself to seek him out. Her hand dropped, but before she could turn away Lord Andrew's voice drifted out to her.

"Very well, that's settled then. I say, do I recognize this walking stick?"

Justin's laugh. Justin's voice. "Most likely you would not require three guesses. He was here earlier this morning to ask my permission to pay his addresses to Marianne. I had not noticed that he left it here."

In the act of turning away, the sound of her own name froze Marianne in her tracks. *Who* was seeking permission to address her? Her pulses started hammering and she must have missed Lord Andrew's next question, but Justin's laughing reply reached her clearly.

"You guessed correctly. I sent him on his way with no halfway measures about it. He's not going to repair his excesses with his cousin's fortune."

Cousin! Justin must be referring to Aubrey then. She caught only the latter part of Andrew's next remark.

". . . have them all beating a path to your door once Marianne hits the London scene."

"Do I not know it!" came the rueful reply.

"Of course there is *one* way to prevent all the fuss and bother. You might marry her yourself."

Lord Andew's casual tone once again stopped Marianne as she was turning away. She felt suspended in time as she waited, scarcely breathing, for Justin's answer. When it came there was still an undercurrent of laughter running through his words.

"What an excellent suggestion, brother. I shall give it due consideration."

"Especially since you've thought of nothing else since you met her. I never thought to see you tumble head over ears, Justin, but she's a girl in a thousand and exactly right for you. You will suit wonderfully."

These last remarks of Lord Andrew's, though he was unaware of the fact, were delivered to an audience diminished by one, for Marianne was charging blindly up the great staircase, her only thought to put as much distance as possible between herself and the laughing voice of her trustee. It was another voice calling her name insistently that jerked her momentarily out of the state of numbed despair caused by Justin's careless reference to possible marriage plans. Her headlong flight jerked to a stop and she turned with a hand on the rail.

"I . . . beg your pardon, Ma'am. Did you speak to me?"

"*Speak* to you? I shrieked at you rather," laughed Lady Lunswick from the hall below. "Where are you dashing to so madly?"

"Nowhere . . . that is, I . . . forgot my handkerchief and am going up to my room to get one. Did you wish to speak to me?" She was still half turned from her hostess while she sought to compose her features.

"Not really, my dear, but Coleman has just

brought me the mail and there is a letter for you from Yorkshire. I thought you might like to have it now. I was on my way to the kitchens to confer with Christophe when I saw you, so I took it from the bag and followed you." The marchioness smiled and held out a white envelope.

"Of course, Ma'am, I thank you." Mechanically Marianne descended the stairs and accepted the envelope. She managed a creditable smile. "Do not allow Christophe to bully you," she said to break the tiny silence that ensued.

"No fear of that today," Lady Lunswick replied gaily as she turned in the direction of the kitchens. "I can take on an army these days."

Her nonsense brought a real smile to Marianne's pale face. "Let us hope then that Christophe is not feeling just so full of bravado as you today." She headed back up the stairs at a more sedate pace this time, noting but not really absorbing the fact that the envelope she held was directed in the rector's spidery hand.

Once in the shelter of her bedchamber she leaned wearily against the closed door for a moment, still clutching the letter but making no attempt to read it. Instead she was gazing blankly into her future which had instantly been blighted by some half-joking words from her trustee. What a fool she had been, what a stupid fool to allow herself to hope that Justin had begun to love her as she loved him. For the first time she admitted her folly to herself. Despite the wise counsel of her brain which had recognized danger at the initial moment of meeting, she had allowed Justin's charm of manner and that irresistible smile of his to disarm her defenses. Not quite immediately perhaps, but steadily, insidiously, his charm had eroded the sandstone of her pretense of indifference and left her now as bereft as she had felt in that instant in the barn when his quick glance had dismissed her as an object of interest. Why, when she had heard warning bells right from the beginning, had she chained up her intelligence, and thus encumbered, proceeded to jump into the sea? Well, she admitted wearily, she had now sunk without trace and all the blame was her own. She had ignored the blatant signs that Justin was a man incapable of loving a woman in the only way she would accept: by a mutual and total surrender of oneself to the loved one. It mattered little really whether his incapacity could be laid at Lady Mauraugh's door or not, the end result was the same.

She began a slow pacing of the large room, as aimless as her wandering thoughts. Justin had assured her that she would not be wooed for her fortune and she readily acquitted him of having any designs in that direction. She could even accept that there was something in his nature that sought to win the approval of every attractive female who crossed his path, and therefore acquit him of any deliberate intent to wound those whom he succeeded in captivating by the inevitable withdrawal of his interest when a new face caught his eye. Whatever capacity he might have had for forming a lasting attachment had withered and died in the last five years. She knew he liked her quite well and enjoyed her company. He would undoubtedly be a charming lover. For many women, perhaps the majority of those who had lived through the romantic stage of the very young, this mild regard might be sufficient. But she knew by the depth of her disappointment at hearing his casual half-declared intention to wed her to save himself future inconvenience that it was totally unacceptable to one of her passionate nature. Before meeting Justin she had calmly dismissed marriage as improbable in her circumstances. She had not really understood then that her "circumstances" could be more accurately described as a mental and emotional attitude than physical or financial restrictions. But now that she did know what she demanded, she must strive for acceptance of defeat and stop yearning for the unattainable. There was no question of compromise; not for her a half a loaf. Her lips twisted wryly as she acknowledged to herself that she was quite capable of destroying a pleasant marriage of convenience in her disappointment at not having achieved a true marriage.

So, having faced this unpalatable truth, it remained only to remove herself from Justin's orbit, for she had no taste for daily martyrdom. Her place was in Yorkshire with her grandfather. Her hands which had been twisting something absently as she paced the floor, stilled at the thought of home, and her glance fell on a thoroughly mauled envelope. Heavens, the rector's letter would be all but undecipherable after such treatment! With slow deliberate movements she opened the crushed letter and smoothed out the single sheet covered with crossed writing. She read it with the concentration of a lawyer perusing a contract, keeping her unhappy thoughts at bay for the duration. By the time she had completed a second careful reading she had resolved on a course of action. Her angry insistence on wringing from Justin that promise to allow her to go home in return for her cooperation in the mock courtship was proving to be a farsighted policy. All that was required from her was enough resolution to play her part without giving herself away. At this point no one need know that nothing less than Justin's permanent exile would induce her to set foot in Lunswick Hall again. At the thought of never seeing Lady Lunswick again her step faltered in her pacing and the hot tears stung behind her eyelids. Angrily she dashed them away with the back of her hand and glanced at the mantel clock. This was no time to indulge in a bout of weeping; luncheon would be served almost immediately. There would be ample time for the shedding of tears in the years ahead, she concluded somberly—all the rest of her life. She repressed the shudder that rippled through her frame at the idea and, walking to the pier-glass, adjusted her sash with trembling fingers. She pinched her cheeks violently to restore some color to her ashen countenance and resolutely headed for the stage on which it was essential that she give her finest performance.

The beautifully sprung traveling chaise that the marquess' father had had specially built for his wife some few years before his death was swaying crazily as they struck a particularly bad stretch of road. Marianne bent forward to peer through the window at the familiar Yorkshire scenery glittering in the weak sunshine under a thin coating of ice from last night's storm. Even at the snail's pace demanded by the condition of the road they should be arriving at the farm in full daylight and then it would be over, her bittersweet sojourn amongst the nobility. After today she would revert to her former position of farm manager and sometime companion to two elderly scholars. Unconsciously she sighed aloud, but so deeply immersed was she in her sad reverie that she failed to see the quick sympathetic glance cast her way by Agnes, one of the younger maids at the Hall, who had been detailed to be her traveling companion. Agnes, who had never been farther from her village than Bath, and that rarely, was all eagerness to endure a cold, uncomfortable journey in the dead of winter for the privilege of extending her provincial horizons. From her artless conversation Marianne received the indirect but distinct impression that the young country girl intended to make capital of this excursion to raise her status in the servant's hall. In any event she welcomed her undemanding presence and intermittent chatter as an occasional respite from her own unsatisfactory musings, and a buffer between herself and Justin who had insisted on providing her with his personal escort back to her grandfather despite her heartfelt protests that she would do perfectly well with one of the grooms for protection.

As he had on the journey to Somerset, he avoided traveling inside the chaise unless forced to by the inclemency of the weather. At this point Marianne scarcely knew whether to be relieved or desolated that the dry, cold weather had remained with them until last night, thus reducing their actual contacts to shared meal times where they rivaled each other in tacit dedication to impersonalities and mutual avoidance of any real conversation. In the circumstances she knew she should feel nothing save relief at being spared the constant necessity to keep up the pretense of purely platonic friendship that she had adopted before her departure from Somerset as her principal defense against his importunities that she marry him when Mr. O'-Doyle recovererd from the persistent bronchitis reported by the rector in his timely letter. Her grandfather's condition had provided a natural and legitimate excuse to request an unscheduled return to the farm, although subsequently she had been made to feel thoroughly fraudulent by the sincere sympathy expressed by Lady Lunswick and Lord Andrew when she had brought the letter to the lunch table. She had been too unsure of her acting ability to risk looking at Justin, so she missed his initial reaction to her request.

She had not been able to avoid a private audience with him in his study after the uncomfortable luncheon, although she yearned to be able to escape the inevitable confrontation, and acknowledging this, knew herself for a coward. At the table he had promised to make arrangements for her immediate removal to Yorkshire, and he had opened their final conversation by repeating this assurance before coming directly to the point she had dreaded. And the interview had been every bit as painful as she had feared. Heaven knew it had been difficult enough to refuse an offer of marriage from the man she loved for good and sufficient reason. To be prevented by stiff-necked pride from being able to *state* those reasons, and further, to know herself patently disbelieved in the explanation she *did* give, had made the situation infinitely worse. Her well-feigned surprise, that he should have expected her to know intuitively that what had certainly been described to her as a mock courtship had actually been meant as a real one, was met by a searching stare that had reduced her nerves almost to screaming pitch. However, she had clung desperately to this pose of astonished dismay at being taken seriously, and had evaded his demands that she admit at least to a knowledge of his intentions after Lady Mauraugh's departure with nervous murmurs about his propensity for light flirtations. She must have been convincing at last because Justin had looked so sincerely disappointed that, even knowing what she did about him, she had almost faltered in her resolution. Only the unhappy knowledge that such a marriage as his nature was capable of could never satisfy her had enabled her to continue in her refusal in the face of his declaration that so long as her affections remained unengaged he intended to persist in his attempts to change her friendly feelings to something warmer.

This determination, expressed with such convincing charm and earnestness, had straight away panicked her into betraying a lifetime of integrity. Hands behind her back where their trembling could not indict her as a liar, she had looked him straight in the eye and confessed to undying affection for another man.

In the swaying chaise she closed her eyes against the picture of Justin's bleak expression when she had uttered that bald lie, but memory had seared it into her brain. If only she might have believed it and him! She shook her head, determined not to allow her thoughts to wander unprofitably in the land of "might have been." But she could not repress the compulsive reliving of that scene in his study, and she knew with dismal certainty that it would haunt her dreams for years to come.

In the unlikely event that the one lie had not been sufficient to endanger her soul for all time, she had speedily added another one. He had demanded the identity of her lover and, knowing he would not believe her if she named either her cousin or Sir Martin Archer, she had unhesitatingly mentioned the only other man of her acquaintance, her old friend, Jack Richmond. This last had proved effective in terminating the most painful incident of her life. After one burning look he had accepted her statement with a formal bow, and a promise that he should no longer weary her with unwanted importunities. Thereafter he had treated her with a distant courtesy that had the surprising result of arousing a perverse feminine resentment in her breast. Recognizing this last, she sighed again and wondered despondently if she were in danger of losing her reason. She *must* be grateful to be spared any further emotional scenes. She *was*, of course, but the sooner she said her final farewells to Justin, the better for her peace of mind *and* her sanity.

Glancing outside once more, she was astonished to note that the chaise was almost through the village and just beginning the last ascent before turning off onto the lane leading to the farm.

"We'll be there in fifteen minutes," she said to warn Agnes, who began gathering up the yards of tatting that seemed to be an extension of her person, at least Marianne had not seen her without it during the entire journey. For her part, she closed her book with finality and firmly put it away from her, knowing that if asked she would be unable to recall the title, but it had served its purpose in shielding her from unwanted conversation en route. She retied the ribbons of her smart burgundy velvet bonnet and smoothed on her matching kid gloves, aware in an uncaring fashion that in appearance at least she was much improved from the girl who had reluctantly left the farm less than three short months before. What an age it seemed since she had last entered the familiar lane; she felt years older than that awkward but contented girl. It seemed she had improved in appearance, widened her experience, greatly increased her acquaintance—in short, surged ahead in everything save contentment. But she *would* relearn the secret of contentment once she was back in a familiar routine, she thought in sudden panic. She must regain her former attitude if she were to find any value in a life that did not include Justin.

He passed the carriage as it entered the lane, and was already dismounted as the coachman came to a halt in front of the house. How small it now looked, but how dear! Her eyes misted over with tears she was determined not to shed as she waited impatiently for the steps to be put down. Clara and her grandfather had appeared in the door, the latter looking frailer than ever, swathed as he was in a mammoth knitted shawl. Absently she accepted Justin's assistance in descending, then ran to enfold her grandfather in strong young arms. From the moment she had glimpsed his beloved face, her own misery had been forgotten. He should not be standing outside in the cold. Quickly, she bullied him into the warm house, calling a smiling greeting to the dour Clara over her shoulder and in between loving admonitions to her grandfather.

"You know you ought not to leave your bed, let alone venture outside when you have that dreadful bronchitis," she scolded distractedly, leading him to his study where she gently pushed him into his voluminous chair.

"He won't listen to me," Clara declared, handing her another shawl to place tenderly over the old man's legs.

"I know, Clara, but he'll mind me or I'll know the reason why." Marianne soothed the servant and threatened her grandparent in the same speech, all the while pointedly ignoring the satisfied twinkle in the bright blue eyes.

It was a scene of confusion for a further few minutes before Justin and Agnes had been led into the warm room and assisted to remove their wraps. Agnes followed Clara to the kitchen to help her prepare tea. At the appearance of the tea tray Marianne noted her grandfather's wink at Justin as he indicated a bottle on the side table. Soon the gentlemen were savoring Mr. O'Doyle's finest Madeira while Marianne poured the hot liquid into a delicate cup. Now that the flurry of greeting was over, an awkward silence descended on the small party which Justin ended presently.

"I am sorry to find you in such queer stirrups, Mr. O'Doyle, but trust that Lady Marianne's nursing will soon have you feeling more the thing."

Like Marianne he had seen the look of exhaustion spread over the old man's features following a nasty bout of coughing, and he glanced uneasily at the anxious girl. When he had succeeded in regaining his breath, however, Mr. O'Doyle cheerfully dismissed his condition in a raspy voice.

"It sounds a lot worse than it is, my boy, happens every winter, but it hasn't done for me yet. You will give us the pleasure of your company at dinner, of course." He eyed the marquess in a friendly fashion while sipping his wine with enjoyment. "I would like an opportunity to thank you for what you and your mother have done for Marianne. Her letters were a joy to read and she is lovelier than ever."

Marianne's color rose as the eyes of the two men surveyed her, one lovingly and the other with an inscrutable countenance. Her own gaze dropped, and she interpolated hastily, "Justin, may I pour you some more Madeira?"

"No, I thank you, Marianne." He smiled at the old gentleman. "I quite agree with you, sir, that Lady Marianne is exceedingly lovely. It was our very great pleasure to have her company at Lunswick Hall. My mother desires me to add her entreaties to my own that she honor us with her presence again in the very near future, and she is looking forward to making your acquaintance whenever you should feel well enough to travel." He rose from his chair. "And now, sir, I must beg your forgiveness for declining your kind invitation to dinner. There are some rather urgent business affairs awaiting me in Somerset and I wish to take advantage of the daylight remaining to make a start at least today. I have arranged for the maid to travel back in my chaise tomorrow, so I thank you for your hospitality tonight on her account and must regretfully decline on my own."

Marianne had become very still during this formal speech. The tea cup she had been raising to her lips tilted dangerously and she lowered it to the table with extreme care, her eyes on her shaking fingers. There was a buzzing sound in her ears and she missed most of what her grandfather replied. When at last she raised her glance Justin was struggling into his greatcoat. It was an effort to get to her feet, but from somewhere in the far distance her grandfather's voice was urging her to escort Justin to the door. Mechanically her legs obeyed, but her brain could contain only the one thought and its concomitant agony—this was the end. After this moment she would never see Justin again.

At the door he raised her icy hand to his lips. "Good-bye, Marianne, I wish you every happiness in the future. I . . . you know, it is customary to *look* at the person to whom you are saying farewell."

At this she did look up and the stricken expression in her eyes stopped his heart for an instant. He had seen that look once before, when her grandfather had insisted that she accompany him to Somerset. His hand tightened on hers, a sense of urgency drove him to plunge into further speech:

"Marianne, if things do not work out the way you expect here with Jack Richmond, if you find that you . . ."

These hasty words penetrated her cloud of misery. She drew back slightly and gently freed her hand. Now her face was expressionless and he wondered if he had imagined that tortured look.

"I expect everything here to be exactly as it always has been." Her voice was quiet and final. "Good-bye, Justin. Thank you for everything you have done for me."

He bowed silently and departed.

Her final good-bye was whispered to the closed door. For a long moment she stood there staring blankly at the wooden panels, then she squared her shoulders and walked briskly back into the study, even achieving a reasonable facsimile of a smile for the benefit of her delighted grandfather.

CHAPTER FIFTEEN

It was one of those late winter days that presaged an early spring. Standing at the long window in her morning room, the marchioness assured herself that there was actually some warmth in the sun's rays today, and thank goodness for that. She reflected soberly that this winter had seemed longer and more difficult than usual, at least since Marianne had left Somerset. An endless succession of gray cheerless days had dragged past, giving way occasionally to snow or rain but only rarely to weak sunshine struggling to break through the ever-present cloud layer. Today was different, though. She could smell spring in the air. She left the window a trifle ajar for a moment to enjoy the air, but the fireplace began to issue smoke, so she closed it with a sigh and prepared to take up her embroidery. After setting a few jerky stitches she paused, needle in hand, and eyed the delicate work with distaste. Earlier she had much enjoyed the self-imposed task of working some linens for Sophia that had taken several weeks of her time. In fact, it was the knowledge of Andrew's and Sophia's quiet happiness that had made the winter bearable. It was good to see the dear girl lose some of that paralyzing shyness. She would never be a chatterbox or really gregarious, but it was amazing how she had blossomed in the confidence that comes from being loved by the man of one's choice. There were occasional flashes of quiet wit now that were not reserved for the few people she loved. At the very least she had conquered her dread of social gatherings, though her future mother-in-law suspected at heart Sophia would always prefer rambling in the woods and fields to making conversation in an endless round of society visits. But that would present no real problem because Andrew would soon settle comfortably into the life of a country gentleman. She no longer entertained any doubts about Andrew's future happiness.

Which brought her back to her elder son. She sighed deeply and pushed the inlaid tambour frame a few inches away. It seemed of late that all trains of thought eventually led to Justin. He was restless and unhappy, of this she was dead certain, though he contrived to conceal it well, and smilingly discouraged any tentative attempts to invade his privacy. Obviously Marianne was the cause, but his mother was no nearer to discovering just what had occurred between them at the time of his ward's return to Yorkshire. To be perfectly accurate she did not even know for a certainty if anything *had* happened. Justin had been completely reticent, and when in desperation she had asked Andrew if he knew what had occurred between her elder son and his ward, Andrew denied all knowledge of how matters stood between his brother and Marianne, though he had been aware that Justin had certainly had the intention at one time of offering for his ward. And not being privy to all the facts, she did not know what to think. She had been so certain that Marianne loved Justin and that her son reciprocated the feeling. The scene in the conservatory had been a blow to her hopes, but only temporarily. It was in the days following this incident that she had confidently come to expect that a happy announcement was imminent. Which frustrating conclusion brought her right back to her original question. What had happened between her two young people, and what if anything could she do to resolve the problem, especially at such a distance?

Somehow she could not accept that Marianne did not love Justin, but her letters were so unrevealing. She had had one this morning. Taking it from the pocket of her green- and gold-striped morning dress, she read it for the third time. It remained essentially a description of her grandfather's physical condition which had finally improved after giving her cause for concern for the better part of a month. She mentioned that his old friend had called several times and recounted a few details about changes on the farm. She closed with polite wishes for the continued good health of Lady Lunswick and her family. Nothing at all in or between the lines to provide food for conjecture—in short, a totally unsatisfactory communication. She flung it away from her pettishly and in so doing dragged her finger across the needle stuck carelessly into the work on the frame. While sucking on the injured finger she gave the offending frame a forceful shove with her other hand.

"I am sick to death of embroidery!"

She was unaware that she had uttered the petulant words aloud until they startled her by reverberating in the empty room.

"Then why do you continue to do it?" The subject of her concern had paused in the doorway and was looking at her expectantly.

"Oh, Justin, I did not hear you. Pay no heed to me. I am just indulging in a fit of the dismals."

"On such a beautiful day?"

"And what has the weather to say to anything, pray?"

"Quite a lot sometimes, but let us abandon generalities and descend to particulars. Why are you battling a fit of the dismals?"

Tired at last of pussyfooting around the issue, Lady Lunswick plunged recklessly, "For the same reason that you have been bluedeviled this last month—Marianne!"

"Marianne?"

He had moved into the room now. His voice was quite level but the concern on his face had been replaced by a guarded look. "What has Marianne done to cast you into the dismals?"

"I received a letter from her today."

"I . . . see." He turned slightly away from her intense regard to rearrange the papers on the small table. "Then I expect she has announced her engagement." There was just the hint of a questioning inflection.

"Her engagement? Of course not! What can you mean, Justin?"

She thought his jaw seemed a little less rigid as he answered unemotionally, "Well, if it was not a betrothal announcement, what has Marianne written to upset you so?"

"Nothing!" stated her ladyship flatly. "This letter is just like the other two; it contains little more than a description of her grandfather's health and a wish for ours. It is totally unlike Marianne."

Her son remained silent, watching his mother's sudden frown as the meaning of his earlier words achieved a delayed impact.

"Justin, why were you anticipating a betrothal announcement, and to whom, for heaven's sake?"

"His name is Jack Richmond and she has known him half her life."

"I am aware, but it is utter nonsense to expect an engagement when Marianne considers him in the light of a brother."

"How do you know this?" he shot at her.

"She told me so. Justin, *why* did you imagine . . ."

He cut in ruthlessly, "Just like *that* she told you she thinks of Jack Richmond as a brother?"

"Why no, it came up in some quite legitimate context once and I . . ."

"Tell me in what context. Try to remember exactly what Marianne said."

His eyes were no longer guarded but glittering with anger and some emotion harder to identify. His mother experienced a rush of pity for his suffering and in addition, a slight stirring of something else—a tiny seed of hope, perhaps?

"Marianne had asked me if Andrew's affections were engaged, and I thought for a second she meant she was in love with Andrew. I had just been questioning her about Melford and Sir Martin, you see, and she was evasive, but when I asked her if she loved Andrew she laughed and denied it. She said Andrew and this Jack Richmond were like brothers to her, but she suspected that *Sophia* had a *tendre* for Andrew." She stopped and stared at her son's angry and baffled face. "Why did you imagine she might be planning to marry this young man?"

For a pulsating instant she held her breath, fearful that Justin would retreat from any discussion of the situation between Marianne and himself, but at last he looked at her directly and answered simply:

"When I offered for Marianne she refused me with great finality." He pushed his hands into his pockets then removed one to run it through his hair. "I do not mean to sound like a conceited lout, but we had become so—intimate, if you will, that I could not accept that she did not return my feelings." He looked at his mother inquiringly, but she had merely drawn a sudden breath. She shook her head negatively and he continued evenly:

"She claimed she had always thought our mock courtship just that. You knew about that?" At her nod he went on, "I did not believe her at first, but she insisted she had no idea even after Aurelie left, that I meant anything other than a flirtation. She insisted further that *her* feelings were strictly platonic. It was when I told her I'd keep trying to win her affection, after Mr. O'Doyle recovered, you understand, that she dragged in Jack Richmond. She told me flatly that she loved him."

"And you believed her?"

"Well, it came as a shock, but it was the only thing that made sense and . . . well, yes, I did believe her *then*."

"But not now?"

"Now I don't know what to believe." He ran his hand nervously over his hair again, disarranging it even more, as he stared intently at his mother. "Just what was in that letter?"

Silently she handed it to him and he read it frowningly, then looked up. "You are quite correct. She says absolutely nothing. Were the others like this?"

"More or less." His mother had been thinking deeply during his perusal of the letter. "Justin, do you imagine Marianne may have some nonsensical idea that she must remain unmarried while her grandfather lives?"

"She did convey that impression when we first met, but I thought she soon realized it was not an insurmountable obstacle. It could not matter less to Mr. O'Doyle where he lives so long as he has his library, and I am perfectly willing to house his old friend when he retires, if that is a concern."

"It is the only thing I can think of that might cause her to lie about her feelings, but would it?" His mother looked troubled. "If perhaps she feared you would try to overrule her?"

"Mama, were you funning or serious just now when you declared you were sick of embroidery?"

The marchioness eyed her son closely, and presently a reflection of his reckless expression glowed in the china-blue eyes.

"Definitely serious," was the smiling response.

"Do you think a short journey to Yorkshire might affect a cure for this malady?"

"It's worth a try," she assured him solemnly, and went upstairs to check her wardrobe, knowing their departure was likely to be even more precipitous, though much less impressive, than that of her sister-in-law.

Four days later, the marchioness sat staring morosely at the unfamiliar Yorkshire countryside, wondering what sort of madness had come over her that had succeeded in temporarily erasing from her memory myriad unpleasant recollections of past journeys. How, for example, had she come to forget that the swaying of even the most comfortably sprung chaise invariably reduced her to a state bordering on permanent nausea? Unless one could accept that she had been carried along on a wave of determination and optimism generated by a much loved son, the answer to this puzzle was destined to remain obscure. Of a certainty, though her brain had conveniently forgotten this uncomfortable phenomenon, it had not taken above two hours of traveling over indifferent roads at a fast pace to recall it forcibly to the notice of her stomach. For Justin's sake she had tried to muster enough resolution to endure the situation. But one look at her greenish complexion when at last they had stopped for refreshment at a good posting inn, had been sufficient to appraise him of her general condition, and he had promptly ordered a sharp reduction in the speed at which they traveled from then on.

If they traveled slowly and stopped frequently, and if she managed to get a good night's rest, she was able to endure the slightly queasy sensation that was her constant traveling companion. As long as this misery was not all in vain! In addition to having a surfeit of time in which to ponder the basic situation between Justin and Marianne, her uneasy physical condition contributed to a lowness of spirits that *would* prevail despite her valiant attempts to think positively.

In this praiseworthy endeavor she was hindered further by the gloomy presence of Norris, her abigail of many years' standing, a dear, willing creature, but overly fond of predicting disaster. There was not a minor calamity of the past twenty-five years that Norris had not foreseen, which was indeed a remarkable achievement unless one remembered the innumerable predictions of trouble that had *not* come to pass. Since these unfulfilled predictions of disaster tended to slip from memory over the years, Norris's reputation as a seer of ill fortune was in no danger of fading.

She sighed unconsciously and rubbed her temple with two fingers in an attempt to ease the throbbing. Instantly she regretted the gesture; she should have known that nothing she did escaped the sharp eyes of her faithful dresser. How stupid of her to give Norris an opening for another one of her scolds. She closed her eyes, feigning sleep in a belated attempt to forestall the dresser, but Norris was well away on her favorite theme:

"I told you how it would be, my lady, but you never would listen to me. It was ever thus with you

293

charging off with your head in the clouds and never heeding those who have your best interests at heart. This kind of adventure may have been all right when you were a bride, but at your time of life you ought—"

"At my time of life I ought to be confined to a rocking chair by the fire. Is that what you mean, Norris?"

"No, it is not, my lady," the maid replied stiffly. "I hope I know my place better than to make such suggestions, but to be haring off to outlandish places in the middle of winter when you know—"

"It's almost spring," her ladyship rebutted mildly.

"Be that as it may," retorted Norris, determinedly taking the blackest view, "this carriage is cold and drafty, and if you do not end up with a feverish cold or worse, it is more than I dare to hope for."

"Well, cheer up, Norris, though I have no symptoms at present, who knows, I may yet succumb to this feverish cold, then you'll be able to say 'I told you so' and I'll be well served for not heeding your advice."

This provocative remark, uttered with careless good humor, mortally offended the dresser and she lapsed into a huffy silence. Lady Lunswick was well aware that Norris would now be on her dignity with her until she apologized, but at least it insured that she would be spared any more lectures for the remainder of the drive. Surely her ordeal could not last much longer. At the last stop Justin had estimated that they would arrive at their destination in approximately two hours. Though he rarely traveled within the carriage she knew he welcomed her company at meals, even though her stupid stomach compelled a regrettably slow pace on a journey that meant everything to him. His own thoughts had been poor company for too long. At the very least she would discover the true nature of her feelings from Marianne's own lips. There had been enough of misunderstanding and confusion.

The chaise was slowing down now to turn onto a narrow lane. Lady Lunswick, peering through the glass, saw Justin ride past the vehicle. They must be almost at their destination, thank heavens. She leaned forward trying to catch a glimpse of the farm house, and was astonished, as was her son on his first visit, to discover a charming small villa of perfect proportions.

Eagerly she accepted Justin's assistance in descending from the chaise, relieved to have her feet planted more or less firmly on the ground once more, though after hours of swaying, she was equally grateful to have the support of her son's arm as they climbed the short flight of steps to the front entrance.

As footsteps sounded within the house it suddenly occurred to Justin that he had forgotten to warn his mother about Clara. He glanced quickly at her smiling but pale countenance and his lips parted, but it was too late. The door was opened by the stolid Clara who betrayed neither surprise nor pleasure at the unexpected appearance of two peers of the realm. She flicked one impassive glance at Lady Lunswick before addressing herself to the marquess.

"So it's you again."

He waited for an instant, but the grunted comment evidently constituted the servant's entire greeting.

"Good afternoon, Clara, how charming to see you again," he said suavely, not daring to look at his parent. "My mother and I have come to see Lady Marianne. Is she at home?"

"Miss be down at t'barn."

"I see, and Mr. O'Doyle?"

"T'master's asleep in his study."

"And of course you have your instructions not to waken him." Ignoring his mother's astonished glance, Justin prudently inserted his foot in the door to prevent a complete repetition of the events of his first visit. Already a sense of unreality was beginning to creep over him.

"If my mother might come in to await Lady Marianne?" he suggested. "The journey has left her somewhat fatigued."

After a swift but searching look at the silent marchioness, Clara stepped back readily.

"Ah'll fetch 'un some tea."

Lady Lunswick smiled tremulously. "Thank you, Clara, that sounds wonderful."

To the unqualified amazement of the marquess, the dour servant actually stretched her lips in a grimace intended as a smile and led the way into the cozy parlor he remembered, where she left them abruptly, presumably to get the aforementioned tea. There was a small fire in the fireplace which his mother approached with a thankful cry. After a moment or two of relishing the fire's warmth on her ungloved fingers, she stepped back slightly and raised understanding eyes to her son's rigid features.

"Do not just prowl about this room like a caged tiger, dearest. Go out and find the girl! I shall be quite content to sit by this lovely fire and drink as much tea as that fierce old woman cares to provide."

He grinned boyishly in a sudden release of tension and swooped down to plant a teasing kiss on her nose. "You are honored indeed, Mama. Clara has taken to you. Someday I'll tell you about *my* initial reception at her hands."

His mother smiled complacently. "Yes, you shall, dearest, and also about your initial reception at *Marianne's* hands. That is my price for enduring one of the more wretched experiences of my life on your behalf, and in company with Norris for additional punishment. Now, *go!*"

The walk past the hen house and dairy to the barn was much the same as before, contributing to his feeling of unreality, though he noted there was no lantern light flickering over the door this time. Either the days were growing longer or he had arrived at an earlier hour. However, there was the black clad figure just as he remembered her. He watched her quietly while she finished the milking, and remained in the doorway when she lifted the brimming pails and prepared to leave. The light was behind him so she could not have identified the shadowy figure blocking the doorway, but she gasped and jerked to a halt, unmindful of the stream of spilled milk this movement caused.

"Oh no!" she almost moaned, terrified that a month of seeing images of Justin in her mind, and being tortured by regrets that she had not accepted what he could offer instead of demanding the impossible, had culminated in delusions of his presence.

"You don't seem overjoyed to see me."

His harsh words shattered the spell of terror conjured up by her imagination. She strove for outward control.

"Justin! It really is you. Why have you come?"

"To resume our final conversation." He took a step closer and Marianne steeled herself to stand her ground, though her glance hovered no higher than his chin.

"There is nothing more to be said on that subject." She heard her own words with dismay, knowing there was nothing she wished more than to reopen that conversation, and wondered if she had taken leave of her senses.

"I beg to differ with you. It is because my mother has shed some additional light on the matter that we have come to Yorkshire, so that I might reopen the subject. Surely you will agree that such measures—"

"Lady Lunswick is with you?" interrupted Marianne breathlessly. "Oh, I must instantly go and welcome her. We can talk later." She moved forward impetuously, but came up against six feet of immovable masculine object.

"We'll talk now," he grated, removing both pails from her grasp.

Without warning the rigid control, imposed it seemed for an eternity, fell from him and his tensile fingers gripped her soft arms with numbing strength. Marianne was absolutely still in her surprise, staring at his suddenly pale countenance, enlivened only by a flame deep in the amber eyes. There was a white line around his compressed lips and a muscle twitched in his cheek.

"God, Marianne!" he groaned hoarsely. "If you had the slightest conception of how long and how desperately I've wanted you, you would not, could not . . ." He clamped his teeth on whatever he had started to say, bent his head, and fastened his mouth to hers, ruthlessly ignoring her startled protests. Then all awareness of time and place, even daylight, was blotted out by the surcharge of intense sensation that union of lips created. If any other man of her acquaintance had kissed her with such consuming passion, the action would have induced a state of panic in such a green girl that would have sparked a mad struggle for escape. But this was Justin whose lips were draining all the resistance from her body, Justin, whom her heart had recognized in that instant of meeting, and for whom it had beat ever since, disregarding all contrary advice from her intelligence. Thoughts of flight never entered her head. She was drowning in a painful ecstasy and it was not cognition, but pure instinct

299

that caused her to melt within those steel bands, allowing them to enfold her in an even closer embrace.

When at last he raised his head a few inches to stare down into her bemused face, she was intensely grateful that he had released only her mouth because her trembling limbs would not have borne her weight unaided. His eyes alight with tender triumph, he said softly, "After that response, never try to deny that you love me, for you would only brand yourself a liar, my darling. I don't believe I can call to mind any action of my entire life that was so singularly satisfying. Do you not think it demands repetition?"

Her color had risen while her eyes fell before the ardent light in his, but at this she unselfconsciously raised her face, no thought of coy denials in her head.

He kissed her thankfully, tenderly, then as her hands slowly crept up and fastened behind his neck, exuberantly, before sobering suddenly. He kept his arms close about her but raised his head and studied her face, a shadow of remembered agony still darkening his eyes.

"Marianne, *why* did you refuse me?"

Now her eyes briefly reflected the memory of pain. "Because I overheard you agree with Andrew that it might be a good idea to marry me to save yourself the trouble of turning away fortune hunters."

"What nonsense is this? When did you hear such a thing?"

"The day before I left Lunswick Hall. You had

just refused Aubrey's request to pay his addresses to me. You and Andrew were in your study, joking about suitors beating a path to your door when I made my come out."

"Now I remember. But, my darling, if you heard so much you must also have heard us agree that I had thought of nothing but marrying you almost from the moment we met."

"No! I was so upset to hear you speak so casually about wedding me that I simply ran away."

"If you had stayed a little longer we'd both have avoided a lot of misery." His eyes searched her face intently and he questioned softly, "Has this past month been as terrible for you as it has for me?"

Tears misted her vision and she could only nod silently.

"Marianne, there is nothing at all casual about the way I care for you. You must believe me! I love you completely. Will you marry me?"

Again she merely nodded, but those magnificent violet eyes glowed with happiness. His eyes devoured her face, exulting in the knowledge that he was responsible for the radiance therein. He was shaken by such incredible beauty, and filled with a gnawing impatience to possess her entirely, mind, body, and spirit.

"Don't make me wait, my darling. Say you'll marry me soon. I do not think I can survive another month like this last one."

An infinitely tender smile curved her lips. "There will never be another month like the last one, my dearest, because we are sure of each other now, though it is going to take a little time for me to get used to the idea that you really do love me the way I love you." She bit her lip and confessed, "I did not want to love you, Justin. I tried not to because I was so afraid you did not want a real marriage."

"Little coward," he taunted lovingly, giving her a gentle shake. "You do not yet know your own power. I can see you will take a deal of convincing over the next fifty years or so, and as far as I am concerned, the sooner I am allowed to begin the task, the better." He gathered her closer and murmured, "You might begin to convince me of your sincerity also, my love, before we tell your grandfather and my anxious mama our good news."

Blushing rosily, but shyly eager to oblige, Marianne caressed his cheeks with light fingertips and invited his lips with hers. After a mutually convincing and satisfying interval, the arrogant marquess and his impossible ward wandered with arms entwined back along the path toward the house, leaving behind two nearly full, but totally forgotten, pails of fresh milk.

No spirit was wilder,
No passion greater
In vengeance or
in love

Tarifa

by Elizabeth Tebbets Taylor

She was a beguiling child, a bewitching temptress.
Many men worshipped her many loved her,
some even tried to tame her But only one man
could possess her Bart Kinkaid, a daring sea
captain saw past her dark desires to the burning
within. Like ships in a tempest-tossed sea, their
love soared beyond the boundaries of time itself.

A Dell Book $2.5o

*A tumultuous drama
of misplaced love
and betrayal*

Scarlet Shadows

by Emma Drummond

Sweet, innocent, beautiful Victoria Castledon loved her dashing
and aristocratic husband, Charles Sanford. Or at least she thought
she did, until she met the notorious Captain Esterly. He alone
could awaken Victoria to the flaming desires within her, and she
would not be happy until she yielded to love's sweet torment ...

From London to Constantinople Victoria pursues Captain Esterly
only to find out that this man she so desperately loves is her
husband's brother. Her scandalous desire blazed across continents
—setting brother against brother, husband against husband, lover
against lover ...

A DELL BOOK $2.25